HE DID IT

A. G. HAWKINS

AUTHOR'S NOTE

Dear Readers,

When you read my stories, I hope to write relatable characters. My characters go through situations, sometimes dark. For a longer list of what tropes or types of situations you may see within this story or any of my others, you can visit my website: aghawkins.net.

Thank you,

A. G. Hawkins

PROLOGUE

In her last moments, she fought like hell. She was a mother. A friend. An artist. She dug her nails into the skin of the person who held her neck, determined not to let him win. She wouldn't let him take away any more of her life.

He grabbed the necklace around her throat, tearing it off, and throwing it in the distance before shoving her back. She shuffled on her feet in an attempt to keep from falling onto the dark ground below.

"I knew you loved him more than me!" he screamed, his face right next to hers. She winced. Her mouth opened, and he tightened his grip around her neck so that nothing could come out. She hit his chest, but it did nothing to deter him.

In the end, he was stronger than her. He would win.

A lone tear slid down her cheek as she thought about her son. The one solace she held was knowing he was safe. Her eyes closed, and her breaths shortened. All she could see was her son's face.

Her final thoughts were of him, of the life he would live without her, and that she'd done everything she could to protect him.

PART ONE

Chapter 1

*S*tatistically, women are more likely to be killed by their partner or their ex than anyone else.

Taylor Smith leaned forward and reread over her first paragraph for her upcoming paper. *No,* she thought to herself, *that isn't right.* She used her mouse to delete the entire paragraph on her computer before rewriting it. *Yes, that's better.*

It was the end of Taylor's third semester of college. Had you told five year old Taylor Smith that she'd earn a scholarship and end up at college in Southern Georgia, she wouldn't have believed you. Receiving the full-ride scholarship to college made her father cry. She was the first person in her family, and even in her neighborhood, to go to college.

"Would you mind reading this?" Claire, Taylor's roommate and friend, asked. Claire gave a sheepish smile, making her golden brown eyes sparkle. From the moment the two of them met, Claire took her under her wing. She was a little bit older than Taylor at twenty-one. This was her second sophomore year. What she lacked in academics, she excelled in understanding people. She could read anyone within just two minutes of meeting them.

"Sure!"

Taylor read it through as she did with all of Claire's papers or projects. Claire helped her in so many ways, she didn't mind helping her back. Over the past few months, Claire had become like the sister Taylor never had.

"Not bad." Taylor smiled up at her. "Your writing has really improved!"

"Seriously? You aren't just being kind?" Claire plopped down on the chair next to Taylor. Her dark curls fell over her cheeks, and she brushed them away to get a better look. Even though they'd been roommates for nearly five months now, Claire's beauty still kept Taylor in awe. She had rich brown skin, almond-shaped eyes, and gorgeous, curly raven hair. She always looked perfect, even in just sweats and a t-shirt. Taylor had never seen someone so pretty and put together in her entire life. Claire was so unlike herself, who had badly dyed red hair with dull, dark brown roots, boring, brown eyes, and with skin such a pale white, it wouldn't even tan when it sat in the sun.

"I only see a few errors. May I?" Taylor reached out for her pen. Claire nodded her approval. With a few flicks of her pen, Taylor made some corrections before handing it back to her roommate.

"That's all?"

"That's all. You're improving. Soon, you'll be a writer."

"Well, let's not go that far. But thank you." Claire bounced up from her chair. "I couldn't make it through this semester without you."

"Yes, you could."

Claire headed back to her room to correct her mistakes. They lived in an old apartment building that had been turned into dorms for the local college.

When Claire reached the hallway, she turned back to face Taylor.

"Let's celebrate after finals are over! We've both worked so hard!"

"I don't know. I have to work all weekend." Taylor shrugged it off. Taylor didn't have the luxury of taking time for herself. While Claire could go out and have fun weekends and trips with her friends, Taylor couldn't. Claire was the only friend she'd been able to make and maintain this semester, and that was only because they lived with one another.

"Well, when are you going home for the break?"

"I'm not. I'll work most of the time."

Christmas had never been an exciting time for her growing up. It would be better to stay behind, work, and save up money than go home just to be disappointed.

"What if you came home with me for the holidays?"

"All four weeks?" Taylor asked, incredulous. "I have to work."

"Not for Christmas or the New Year, do you?"

"Well, I do have Christmas off," Taylor said. She pondered Claire's question. Spending time with a loving family for Christmas did sound fun. "I guess I could come up, but would your parents want me there? Christmas is usually for families."

At that, Claire chuckled.

"My parents won't care, at all. There are always many people over."

"You're really sure? How would I get there?" Taylor tried to contain her excitement. A real Christmas.

"I can come back and get you. It's only three hours. Or you could take the bus."

"Alright."

"Good. It's settled. I'll call my mom and let her know to get more presents!" Before Taylor could protest, Claire sprinted down the hallway.

For Christmas, Taylor ended up taking a bus to Claire's town. When she stepped off, she saw Claire waiting for her at the bus stop. She looked terribly out of place with her designer purse over her shoulder and high heels.

"You made it!" Claire said with a bright smile. She wrapped her arms around Taylor's neck before letting go. "Come on, I'm parked across the street."

Claire looked across both ways and then latched her arm around Taylor's. She pulled her across with her to her car. Taylor placed the two bags into the trunk, making sure the smaller one didn't get squished.

"What's in that?" Claire asked curiously.

"Oh, gifts for you and your parents," Taylor answered as her cheeks blushed. "I didn't know who all I should…"

"You didn't have to get gifts for anyone! You are our guest, but what is it?" Claire rose one brow, reaching out to touch the bag's zipper.

"You'll have to wait." Taylor pulled down the trunk, making Claire withdraw. She was actually excited about the gifts and hoped Claire and her parents would like them.

"Oh, fine." Claire went to sit in the front seat, and Taylor followed by sitting in her own. Claire tapped her fingernails against the side of the steering wheel.

"Nervous?"

"What?" Claire asked before her eyes fell to her tapping fingers. She laughed. "Well, I don't like driving in Downtown Atlanta, but I made it here. We'll make it back to the house just fine."

And they did. Claire only cussed out a few people on the ride, most of whom had the right of way, but Taylor wasn't about to say anything about it.

Finally, they pulled up in front of Claire's house. Taylor's breath was taken away. It was huge. Never in her life had Taylor seen a house with so many windows. She began to count how many she could see, losing count when she got past ten. Each window had a lit up wreath, and several had a Christmas tree she could spot through the glass.

"How many Christmas trees do you have?" Taylor asked.

"Um...twelve, I think," Claire said, nonchalantly.

Taylor's eyes widened.

"Twelve?"

Claire parked in the front of the four-car garage. Four. A four-car garage. She hadn't even known those existed.

"Come on," Claire said. She stepped out of the car, leaving the trunk open. Taylor went to grab the bags, but Claire stopped her. "I'll make my brother grab them and take them to my room."

Taylor glanced back into the trunk, not used to leaving her luggage out in the open where anyone could grab it. She did as she was told and followed Claire to the front door of her house.

When they reached the door, Taylor's nerves got the better of her. She had little time to think about it, though, because Claire pushed it open and dragged her inside. Taylor's eyes grew as she saw the ornate black and white staircase at the front of the house.

"This looks like something in the movies."

"Oh, does it? Huh, never thought about it like that. Are you hungry?" Claire paid little attention to Taylor taking in her house. Instead, she continued to walk through it, toward the kitchen. Taylor followed behind. She paused when she saw a large photo of Claire's family taking up the wall. Each of the five siblings were dressed in matching blue button-up shirts, and one held a baby. That would be Simone then, Taylor reasoned. She was the only sibling that had a child. She remembered helping Claire wrap a present for her baby shower.

"Mom insisted," Claire said. "We do one every year."

"Every year?" Taylor tried to think back to the last time she and her dad had a picture taken together.

"Yes. It's the worst, but Mom loves it. It's her Mother's Day present for herself."

"I like it," Taylor said, sincerely.

"You're too kind. Now come to the kitchen, I'm starving."

The kitchen was just as overwhelming as the rest of the house. Taylor realized that the pantry was the same size as the trailer she grew up in.

"Take whatever you want." Claire grabbed a bag of crackers. "There are drinks in the fridge."

Taylor opened the fridge to see one entire shelf filled with bottled water. She took one and undid the top. Claire grabbed herself her own water bottle. She took a long sip before tugging on Taylor's upper arm to bring her upstairs and to her bedroom. Taylor entered the immaculate room with a queen bed in the middle. Everything was white; from the bedspread, the furniture, and the pristine walls. The only pops of color came from the gold hangings on the walls that looked like some kind of ball and the television screen, which was also outlined with a gold border. Taylor stood in the doorway, afraid to disturb the room.

"Oh, come on," Claire said. "I know. It's a lot of white. My mom insisted on changing it up when I began college. She said it was time for me to have a grown-up look. Apparently, that's what this all-white monstrosity is."

"It's just...so..."

"I've already spilled chocolate milk on the bedsheets. Don't worry about making a mess. My mom will deal. She's the one who thought all white was a good idea."

"Okay."

Taylor became suddenly aware of her shoes on her feet. She'd always been good about taking them off when she came inside someone's house. She bent down, unlacing them and setting them by the door.

"I hope you're alright sharing a bed. All of my siblings are home for the holiday and so all the bedrooms are taken. I guess I could always see about getting a cot. Maybe we have one in the attic somewhere."

"No, it's fine. I don't mind."

"Good." Claire bounced on her heels. She grabbed the remote from her bedside table and turned on the television. "I just like the noise." She dropped the remote back down and fell back onto her bed. "Please, do feel comfortable. What's mine is yours."

Tentatively, Taylor sat at the edge of the bed. She worried about wrinkling the fabric. Her hands brushed over her legs, hoping she hadn't picked up anything from the bus.

"Oh, stop it! You're fine," Claire said. "Actually, what we should do is go and get some dirt, and then rub it all over the bedspread. It'll give my mom a heart attack."

Taylor bit down a smile. Over the past half year, she'd learned how Claire enjoyed getting under her mother's skin. As the youngest of five children, Claire found ways to get her parents' attention.

"All of your siblings have their own rooms?"

"Uh-huh."

"So six bedrooms total?" Taylor let out a low sound. She stood, walking over to the window to see the outside. The backyard of Claire's home was just as vast as the inside of the house. There was a pool outside, and Taylor noticed people swimming.

"Oh, did you happen to bring a suit?"

"It's so cold!"

"We have a heater. You can borrow one of mine if you'd like." Claire looked out the window with Taylor, seeing who was swimming. "Ah, that's James." She pointed to the guy standing on the edge of the pool. "And that's my other brother, Marcus."

"I met James once," Taylor recalled.

"Right, he came with my parents to drop me off at college. Marcus couldn't be there. He's a big-shot lawyer like my parents."

"Does he work with them?'

"Yes."

They continued talking about Claire's brothers until a knock came at the door. A stunning woman stood in the doorway with the same beautiful features as Claire. Her face, however, was drawn into a deep frown before her eyes moved to Taylor and moved over her frame. The woman looked back at Claire.

"Mom says dinner is in an hour."

"Oh, okay." Claire hardly paid the woman any attention. Again, the woman looked over Taylor before leaving the room.

"Was that Mila?"

"Oh, I'm sorry! I should have introduced you. Yep, that's my sister, Mila. Don't take her personally. She's sour with everyone, even her husband."

Growing up, Taylor never had any Christmas traditions. Her father was usually passed out or working on those days. And her mother was never around. So it thrilled her to be a part of someone else's.

After Christmas Eve dinner, Claire's family opened up presents. Claire said that 'Santa's' presents were opened in the morning.

"Even though we're grown, Mom insists that we still do Santa. All of the stockings will be filled and under the tree in the morning. But tonight, we do family presents."

Taylor nervously looked at the two wrapped presents she'd prepared for Claire and Claire's parents. They were wrapped in gaudy paper in comparison to the extravagant paper used by Claire's family, sticking out like a sore thumb. She began to second guess what she'd brought them.

"Alright, as tradition goes, youngest to oldest!" Claire's dad, Jack, said. "And Taylor, you are also our guest. Here is a gift for you."

Jack handed her a small gift bag. All eyes in the room were on her, making her pale cheeks turn red. She hated attention. Slowly, she pulled out the paper. Inside was a silver necklace with the letter T.

"Oh, how beautiful. Thank you," she sincerely said. It was the first piece of jewelry she'd ever been gifted.

"I'm glad you like it," Claire's mom, Kim, said with a nod and a smile.

"My turn!" Claire jumped up, grabbing the gift from Taylor. Taylor darted her eyes around the room. She'd just been given this beautiful necklace, and now everyone was going to see the lame gift she had brought them. Taylor reached out to try and stop her, but it was too late. Claire had already torn into the paper. She gasped.

"Where did you get this?" Claire asked. She lifted the canvas in her hands to get a better look.

"I did it."

"You painted this?"

"I did."

"Wow, it's amazing." Claire turned the painting of her favorite hot pink heels for everyone to see it. "I love it."

"I know it's not much…" It wasn't Taylor's best work. She was rusty with her painting. Between school and her job, she hardly had time to focus on her artwork.

"Not much? It's beautiful. How on earth did you do this?"

"I…I don't know…." Taylor stammered. Thankfully, James took his turn to open his gift. The attention was off her for a little while until it was Claire's parents' turn to open a gift, and they chose the present from Taylor to open first.

For their painting, she'd painted their dog. Claire always told her how much her parents spoiled their pup.

"This needs to be hung in our home! You really are talented, Taylor. Is art what you're attending school for?"

"Um, no." Taylor shook her head. "It's just a hobby I do sometimes."

"Such talent." Kim passed the painting around the room. Taylor blushed, again.

"I didn't know you could paint," Claire whispered to her. "Why have you never told me?" Taylor shrugged.

"I just don't have much time to do it, I guess."

"Well, you should do it more!"

Taylor didn't answer. She assumed when one had money, one could have time to make hobbies into potential careers. But she couldn't do that. She had to focus on a job that could support her, give her a home, and bring food to the table.

"Taylor's turn!"

Taylor glanced up, surprised. Again, she was given a gift. By the end of the night, she was shocked to find out she'd been given the same amount of gifts as everyone else. And even more surprised when she had more gifts waiting for her the next morning when Santa came to visit.

Back at their dorm, Claire watched Taylor finish a painting for one of their neighbors. With a wave of her brush, Taylor finished the painting of her neighbor's cat, impressing Claire. She'd never known someone so talented.

After Christmas, Claire had shown everyone her painting, and people asked if Taylor could do some for them. With Claire's help, Taylor had many people asking her for portraits, which brought in enough money to allow her to cut down her work hours at the gas station.

"Lacy's going to love it!" Claire said, interrupting her friend.

"I hope she does."

Claire sighed. Taylor lacked confidence. It didn't matter how much Claire told her how talented she was, Taylor never fully believed her.

"She will." Claire sat down on the edge of Taylor's bed. She rubbed the soft, fuzzy, pink blanket Taylor kept folded there. "Do you enjoy doing art?"

"I do. I love doing these pictures for everyone," Taylor said, her cheeks blushing. Claire grinned.

"Then you should change your major to art. Do you even want to teach?"

Taylor's brows knitted together as put down her paint brush.

"I can't change my major, Claire. My life isn't like yours. I have to have a job that will support me. I don't have parents to help me out if I stumble."

"Right," Claire said, frowning. "Life's not always fair, is it?"

Taylor shook her head. "It's fine."

"It's not," Claire countered. She tapped her heel against the ground, trying to think of a solution to this problem. Then an idea popped into her mind. "What about an art teacher? You could have the best of both worlds."

Claire watched as Taylor pondered this. Slowly, the idea seemed to take shape. Her eyes lit up, and she smiled.

"Maybe." Taylor paused. Her smile grew. "That's actually a great idea. Then I could take art classes."

"Yes," Claire agreed. "See! Won't that be fun? I'll go with you tomorrow to speak with your advisor about changing your path of study."

Taylor beamed.

Chapter 2

After making the changes needed to change her path of study to art, Taylor told Claire goodbye before quickly making her way over to the gas station. On her way, Taylor found she held more pep in her step, excited about her new path for her future. Claire broke the code. Her friend helped her to realize she could have both what she loved and a solid foundation for her future career.

With this discovery, she went into the gas station feeling bright. A few customers were meandering around the store by the time she clocked in and got to the counter. She waited for the customers to come up and pay by bouncing on her feet. All night, Taylor stayed up reading through the new classes she would start taking. She couldn't wait. Art had always filled her with so much joy. She couldn't believe that now it could be a part of her future.

A moment later, a male customer walked up to the counter and placed a piece of candy on the counter.

"A dollar and 18 cents." Taylor lifted the candy to scan it.

"Here." The exact amount was set down in front of her. She took it. He then placed a packet of gum up there. "I think I'll take this too."

Again, Taylor scanned the item. Then again, he placed another piece of candy to buy. That's when Taylor looked up to the customer. He had fair skin with a hint of pink on his cheeks, icy-blue eyes, short, dark brown hair, and a crooked smile. Between his two front teeth was a little gap. While he wasn't the hottest man Taylor had ever seen, there was something about him she liked.

"Finally got you to look at me," he said. Taylor blushed. She tried to calm her breathing, hating how her face could give away her feelings so well.

"Anything else you need?" Taylor asked. The guy opened the packet of gum, pulling one out, and popping it into his mouth.

"Pretty girl like you working here?" He glanced around the dicey gas station.

"It pays well," Taylor said with a shrug. "People have to work."

"You have to work?" He shook his head, putting a second stick of gum into his mouth. "If you were with me, I wouldn't make you work another day in your life."

"Oh yeah?" Taylor played back. "Who says I don't want to work?"

The guy chuckled. "Well, then I guess you could work somewhere other than here."

A woman behind the guy cleared her throat, letting Taylor know she was waiting for her turn. Taylor grinned and pointed to the door.

"I need to help other customers now."

The guy tipped his head before turning and walking out of the gas station. Taylor helped the next customer and the one after that. As they left, she noticed the guy still standing outside, but on his phone. He glanced in and gave her another nod before disappearing.

Back in her hometown, Taylor never had anyone interested in her. Or, if they were, she never noticed. All of her time and attention was spent on her education and getting out of her small town. Now, she wondered if this interaction was what it felt like to be noticed. Did this mysterious guy like her? It seemed ridiculous. She likely never would see him again, and yet—

Taylor shook away her thoughts; she needed to get back to work and not think of such frivolous things. If he did like her, he would be back.

Claire looked up from the table where she was typing away on her laptop. Schoolwork drained her. As she noticed Taylor grab ice cream out of the freezer, Claire quickly closed the laptop.

"Oh, is it ice cream time?"

"Yes, come and join me." Taylor patted the seat beside her on the couch.

Claire went to get a spoon before sitting down next to her friend. She dipped the spoon into the pint and got a large spoonful of the mint chocolate chip ice cream. The two discovered they both liked the same type of ice cream early on. Now, the freezer held several containers of mint chocolate chip at a time. Claire made sure they never ran out. Ice cream time with Taylor was one of her favorite times of the day. She always looked forward to it.

"I think this guy was hitting on me today at work," Taylor said after she took a bite of ice cream. Claire saw the pink rise on her friend's cheeks.

"Oh, really? Was he cute?"

"Kind of," Taylor said with a shrug. Her eyes ducked away from Claire before digging her spoon back into the carton. "He kept putting things down on the counter for me to scan until I looked up at him."

"Oh, he was definitely hitting on you." Claire grinned. "Good, get yourself out there."

"Well, I don't know about that." Taylor brushed it off. "It was nice to be noticed."

"Of course you were noticed, you're gorgeous. I'm surprised you aren't hit on more often." Claire shifted in her seat. Anytime she told Taylor she was pretty, Taylor would always shake her head and shy away. She couldn't figure out why her friend wouldn't take the compliment. Taylor was beautiful; her smile lit up a room whenever she entered. The only thing Claire wished she could do was help her with the awful dye job in her hair. She kept begging Taylor to let her take her to the salon for a new look, but Taylor wouldn't allow it.

"Well, this was the first time it wasn't an absolute creep."

"Ew, yes, well, that's much better. Though, I think my brother, James, is still holding out hope for the both of you," Claire added with a gleam in her eye. Taylor cocked up her eyebrow.

"James?"

"Yes, he's had a crush on you since you visited for Christmas." Her brother asked about Taylor every time she spoke with him. Sometimes, she'd even receive a text from him asking how both she and Taylor were doing, but she knew exactly what he was searching out. He wanted to know about her friend. He'd never messaged her this much before he met her roommate.

"But he's like....what..."

"He's twenty-two and in law school," Claire said. "He's ambitious, like you. Of all my siblings, he's the least annoying."

"None of your siblings are annoying."

"Oh please, they are. You don't have to be kind about them to me."

"They really aren't. I like them all."

"You're too sweet. But James is the best one of the bunch," Claire said.

"It's probably because you're both the youngest," Taylor suggested.

"Probably."

Over the course of the next several days, the guy came back to the gas station. Some days, he showed up multiple times in the day. Every time, he grabbed a candy bar or small item by the counter to purchase. Every time, he told her she should be working somewhere else, and that he should be taking care of her.

When he walked in this time, he didn't grab any items. Instead, he walked up to her and handed her a card. Taylor took the card awkwardly, meeting his eyes. He nodded at the card, silently telling her to read it. She hesitated before turning the card over.

"Dylan Montgomery: J.A.C. Auto Shop for your auto shop needs," she read out loud.

"That's where I work," he told her, pointing at the card. "If you ever have any car needs, that's where you should go."

"I don't have a car," Taylor said, placing the card back onto the counter and pushing it toward him. Taylor no longer enjoyed this *Dylan* coming by to pester her at work. At first, she'd found it endearing. Now, she wanted him to leave her alone.

"You don't have a car? But you can drive, can't you?" Dylan leaned over the counter slightly, resting his hands on the countertop.

"Actually, I can't," she answered with a shrug. She took a step back. "I walk or ride the bus everywhere. Never learned how to drive."

"You're joking, right?" Dylan chuckled in disbelief. He stroked his chin.

"No."

"How old are you?"

"Nineteen. I'll be twenty this summer."

"So you're old enough," Dylan said. He shifted on his feet. "That just means I need to teach you." He slid the card back to Taylor. "My number is on the card. You could call me for a lesson."

"I'm not sure…"

"Here, write down your number." Dylan began to dig inside the deep pockets of his pants, putting random items on the counter as he searched for what he needed. Finally, he pulled out a small writing pad and a pen.

Taylor glanced at it, not sure if she wanted to give him her number. Her stomach clenched from her anxiousness, but something in her told her to just do it. It didn't mean she had to go on a date with him. Before she could talk herself out of it, she wrote her name and her cell number. Dylan took it back, glanced at it, and smiled.

"Beautiful name, Taylor," he told her.

"Thank you," she said.

"I'll give you a call tonight."

"You don't have to—"

"Tonight." He tucked the small writing pad back into his pants pocket before leaving the gas station.

"I thought you said this guy had been giving you bad vibes," Claire said after Taylor told her she gave him her number.

"He did, but…" Taylor sunk onto the edge of Claire's bed. "I don't know. He seems nice enough."

"Nice enough? That's where your standards are?"

"He's very nice," Taylor amended. "I guess I didn't realize he would finally gather the courage to ask me out on a date. Before I just thought he—"

"Was a creep?"

"Yes."

"And now you don't think he is?" Claire narrowed her eyes. Taylor had been complaining to her about this guy for days now. She'd had the right mind to go into the shop and ask him to leave her friend alone.

"No," Taylor answered.

Claire scooted forward so she could be closer to Taylor.

"I mean, if you're happy with it, then go for it. But if he makes you uncomfortable, don't."

Before Taylor could answer, her phone began to ring. She jumped up from the bed, grabbing her phone from her back pocket. Claire watched her check the number and then freeze.

"Is it him?" Claire asked.

"It is."

"Well, are you going to answer it?"

Taylor didn't answer Claire. She left Claire's room. The next thing Claire knew, Taylor's door closed. Claire huffed. She'd like to be able to listen in on this conversation.

Claire tiptoed down the hallway before cupping her hand against the door in an attempt to hear what was being said on the other side. However, she couldn't hear anything but muffled sounds. Was that happiness in Taylor's voice? Did she say yes? Had a time been set?

The door opened, nearly making Claire fall forward. She straightened and steadied herself on the doorway.

"Were you spying on me?"

"No," Claire lied. Taylor's intense stare made Claire uncomfortable. "Fine, I was trying to, but I couldn't hear anything. What did you say? What did he say?"

"He wants to take me out on a date," Taylor said.

"And...?"

"I said sure."

"You said, 'sure'?" Claire hummed.

"Why? Is that bad?"

"It just doesn't sound enthusiastic."

"I was," Taylor said. "I've just never been on a date before. I guess I don't know what to expect."

"Ah well, don't worry about that. I'll help you with all the planning."

A week later, Taylor found herself getting ready for her first date with Dylan. He invited her to a local diner for dinner, saying he would pick her up from her place. Since this was her first date, Taylor had no idea what to wear. She hadn't even gone to her senior prom. It wasn't that she hadn't been invited. But she had to work; she had been trying to make enough money for her bus ticket to come to college.

"Here, let me help you with your makeup," Claire offered. She shook her head at the shirt Taylor held, grabbing another blouse from her closet. "This color suits you more," she explained. Taylor took the green top and threw it on.

"Should I braid my hair?"

"Leave it down," Claire suggested. "Now, sit." Taylor did as Claire said. Her makeup collection was bare bones, never really finding it necessary to wear.

"There," Claire said, pleased with her work. Taylor stood and walked over to her mirror, hardly recognizing herself.

"Wow."

"Why are you so surprised? You're beautiful, Taylor," Claire told her, playfully hitting her bottom. "Anyone would be so lucky." She winked. "Oh, maybe I should take a picture for James!"

"No, don't," Taylor pleaded. Claire laughed.

"I won't," she promised.

A knock came at the door.

"I'll get it." Claire grinned before rushing to the door so she could be the first one to answer. Taylor quickly followed behind, not wanting Claire to say anything to embarrass her.

"Hello," Claire said cheekily as she allowed Dylan to walk into their dorm. He stepped inside, wearing a nice pair of jeans and a button-up shirt.

"Hi." Dylan then noticed Taylor. "Hi," he said again, softer.

"Hi," Taylor said, giving him a small wave.

"Well, I'll leave you two to it. Don't keep her out too late!" Claire disappeared down the hallway.

"Don't listen to her. She's just my roommate."

"And best friend!" Claire called from down the hall.

"And my best friend," Taylor added. "Are you ready?"

"Yes," Dylan replied. He reached out for Taylor. She swallowed hard before taking his hand. His fingers were coarse; she was sure it was from his hard work at the auto shop. He walked her to the car, opening the passenger door for Taylor. She gratefully sat down, never having someone open a door for her. Then he went around to the driver's side.

When they arrived at the restaurant, he came back around to open the door for her. She smiled, grateful. He helped her out. His hand fell to the small of her back, leading her inside.

"Are you in school?" Taylor asked him, taking a sip of her soda.

"No." Dylan shook his head. "Moved here because I got a good job at J. A. C., better pay than where I'm from."

"And where is that?"

"Small town around Macon," he answered. Taylor noticed how he didn't quite say where it was. She decided not to push it if he didn't want to share. Taylor knew a thing or two about being embarrassed about her past. "What about you? What are you studying?"

"I'm an art teacher major," she said.

"Oh really? Are you an artist?"

"Well, I don't know about that," she said, her cheeks turning red. "Some people have been buying my artwork."

"Do you have any pictures?"

Taylor pulled her phone out of her pocket, finding a photo of her most recent artwork. She handed it to Dylan.

"Oh, nice. You drew this?"

"I did." Her cheeks grew redder. She tried to read his facial expressions to be able to tell what he was thinking about it.

"Well, now I have to tell everyone I know that I am dating an artist."

"So, we're dating?"

"What do you call this?"

Taylor didn't answer, not right away. It was nice being on a date and having someone interested in her. But she hadn't expected this to become more than one date. She nervously smiled.

"I guess, it's a date."

"Exactly." He took her hand with his own. His thumb moved over her knuckles. "I really like you, Taylor. I'd like you to be my girlfriend."

Taylor gasped. *Girlfriend?* Everything was moving much quicker than Taylor expected. She'd only met Dylan less than two weeks ago. Titles like girlfriend and boyfriend should be saved for after at least a few dates. She shifted uneasily in her seat, giving him an uneasy smile.

"Yeah," she choked out. "Perhaps, we could do that one day."

Dylan squeezed her fingers, smiling brighter.

"You make me happy, Taylor."

"We've only just met," Taylor said. "But I hope as we get to know one another better, I will."

"You will."

He dropped her back off at her dorm after dinner, which he paid for. Dinner had been nice, simple. Not that Taylor needed anything extravagant. He'd ordered for her, telling her that he knew the best food they had. That had been a bit strange, but she decided he was probably right. He walked her up to her door, cupping her face, making her pull back. Her heart raced.

"Sorry, I thought..." He shook his head. "Maybe another time?"

"Yes. It's just our first date."

"Right," he answered. He tipped his head at her. "I'll let you go. Have a good night, Taylor."

Taylor unlocked her dorm room and walked inside. She closed the door before resting her body against it. She didn't know how she felt about her date tonight. He was kind to her and generous. But something about the way he wanted to rush everything made her feel a bit off.

"So," Claire said, walking into the living room. "How was it?"

"Good," Taylor said. She pushed herself off the door.

"He's cute, enough." Claire fidgeted with a curl. "Fun for some dates, but, if you want my opinion—" She paused for a moment, but not long enough for Taylor to tell her she didn't—"You can do better."

"What do you mean by that?"

"I mean, he's...." Claire shrugged as if it explained everything. Taylor frowned. She hadn't expected Claire to judge Dylan based on his appearance. No, he didn't have the nicest clothes, but Taylor didn't either. While she knew Claire could be a little snobbish, she didn't think she would be about something like this.

"He's what?" Taylor countered.

"Look, I can read people pretty well. There is something about him that I don't like. I can't pinpoint what it is, but trust me. You can do better. You *deserve* better."

Taylor tightened her hands into fists at her side, anger coursing through her.

"Not all of us can afford the best clothing. Not all of us were handed everything since birth."

She quickened her steps past her friend.

"Taylor, that's not what I meant—"

But Taylor didn't give her a chance to attempt to explain.

Claire never had been one to hold back what she thought, and she wasn't about to do that with Taylor either. However, she didn't want the two of them to fight, especially over something as silly as a boy.

She knocked on Taylor's door. No answer.

"I know you're in there. Come on, you can't stay mad at me."

"It's unlocked."

Claire turned the knob and pushed the door open. She saw Taylor over at her mirror, cleaning the makeup off her face. She'd pulled her thick hair into a bun on the top of her head and was already in her pajamas.

"Did you have a good time?"

Taylor turned, incredulous.

"Do you actually care? I thought you didn't like him."

Claire's lips pursed at the accusation. She didn't like this Dylan character, at all. But she'd already said her piece about him. She hadn't come in here to argue with Taylor.

"I just want to know if you had a good time. Did he take you somewhere nice?"

"It was a burger joint."

"Did he pay?"

"Yes."

"Well, there's that, at least."

Taylor shot her a look. Claire lifted her arms in surrender.

"Sorry. I won't say another word about how I feel about him. If you're happy, then that's all that matters."

"I am," Taylor said. She turned back away from Claire.

"Good. Then I am happy for you." Claire forced a smile, but it was futile. Her mouth fell into a frown. "Do be careful."

"Why would I need to be careful?"

"Some guys aren't good."

"He's nice."

"Yes, but nice is different than good. It's something my father has always said. People can act nice, but it doesn't mean they are good."

"He is good. He was really..." Taylor paused, trying not to use the word nice again. "He's sweet."

"Alright. Well, I'll let you finish getting ready for bed. I'll see you in the morning."

Chapter 3

When she entered their dorm room, Taylor was surprised to find Claire's older brother, James. He sat on the stool in their kitchen, munching on takeout from the local wings place. His broad shoulders bent forward toward his food, and she debated skirting past him, hoping not to be noticed.

However, before she could disappear, Claire came out from the hallway.

"Ah, Taylor! You're home!"

James turned then, smiling. Taylor had to catch her breath. It'd been a while since she'd seen him last. He was still as handsome as ever, with his perfectly toned arms, deep, brown skin, and intense stare, making her feel as though she was the only other person in the world. Since she'd learned he had a crush on her, she couldn't stop thinking about it. She'd always thought he was cute, but she never thought about acting on it. He was Claire's brother! And also, she would never have the courage to do anything about it anyway.

"I didn't hear you." He pulled an earbud from his ear, setting it down on his shoulder. There was an ease about James that Taylor coveted. She never felt that easy around anyone, well, except maybe Claire. "Long time, no see."

"Yeah," Taylor said, feeling that familiar blush heat up her cheeks. She brought her shoulders up as if they could cover the redness from his view. "How've you been?"

"Good."

"He's staying here for the night. Tomorrow he has some test he has to take on campus, really early. It's easier for him to stay here than do the drive."

"Of course," Taylor said. She tucked one of her stray hairs behind her ear. "Well, I have to change."

"Why?" Claire asked.

"I have plans with…" She paused a beat, knowing Claire's thoughts on him. "With Dylan."

Claire's smile slipped.

"Oh." She made a face as though she'd just eaten something sour. "Well, can't you cancel? I thought we could all go to the movies."

"No, I can't," Taylor murmured.

Claire remained in the way, keeping Taylor from walking through and to her room to change in preparation for her date.

"Surely, you can cancel. Dylan does allow that, doesn't he?" Claire stared Taylor down, making her shift uncomfortably on her heels.

"Of course, but…"

"Why are you giving her the third degree, Claire? She has plans. What's the big deal?" Taylor felt grateful for James's help in this matter.

Claire lifted her chin. Taylor grew warm from the embarrassment. She knew Claire wasn't fond of Dylan, but she'd never expected such a show from her friend.

"Nothing," Claire finally said, removing her arm from the wall. She stepped out of the way. Before anything else could be said, Taylor rushed back to her room.

Claire clenched her jaw. Dylan. She hated him.

"What was that all about?" James asked. Claire slowly let out a low breath before opening her eyes and looking back at her brother.

"Dylan is bad news," Claire said. "Taylor could do so much better."

"What makes him bad news? What has he done?"

"Well, nothing," Claire began. James shot her a look. "He—I can tell these things, James. He gives off a bad vibe. He makes me feel uncomfortable."

"Like how?"

"He just does."

Claire twisted her fingers over the lock of dark hair which had fallen over her cheek. She could tell her brother believed she was being overdramatic about this whole thing, but he hadn't met Dylan. He didn't see how Dylan sauntered around or how often he called or texted Taylor throughout the day. Taylor didn't allow her to see any of these texts, but from looking over her shoulder a time or two, she'd noticed how they were all a bit too needy. Sometimes, he'd even get angry if Taylor didn't respond quickly enough.

"I don't like him."

"Well, I don't think you get to decide that, sis," James said. He brought his arm around her shoulders.

"You could try to seduce her and steal her away." Claire glanced up toward him, hopefully.

James laughed.

"I think you have to let this go, be the supportive friend."

Claire shrugged her shoulders away from James and stepped forward.

"This is me being supportive. I am saving her from a lifetime of misery with a loser."

"You sound snobbish," James said.

"I'm not snobbish. How does that make me snobbish?"

"Because you don't think he's good enough for her."

"No. Now we should stop discussing this right now. Taylor is just in the other room. I need to run to the store anyway. Do you need anything?"

"No."

"Alright. I'll be back in a bit."

When Taylor finished getting ready, she walked back out front to wait for Dylan's knock on the door. He liked not waiting for her to answer. He told her in the past, he'd broken up with girls that made him wait more than a few minutes. When he'd first told her, she laughed it off, thinking he was joking. But her laughter had petered out when she saw the seriousness in his eyes, and she'd swallowed hard. Something about Dylan made her anxious. She wondered if that's how all relationships were.

Growing up, she hadn't seen any healthy relationships to know. Her mom had run off when she was only three, and her dad never dated anyone else. And they had only been teenagers when she was born.

Thankfully, only James was out front.

"She had to run to the store. You're free of her," he playfully said.

Taylor sat down on the couch beside James, making sure to leave plenty of room between the two of them. They sat in awkward silence for a moment, Taylor not knowing what to say.

"Claire says you've started selling your paintings."

"I have."

"That's cool. I wish I had a talent like that. I can hardly draw a stick person."

"I'm sure you can do more than that," Taylor said. "It just takes some practice."

"I doubt that. You have real talent, Taylor Smith. You should be proud of yourself."

A smile crept up. James had a way of making you think it was true, that you really were special.

There came a knock at the door. Taylor jumped up.

"I'll see you later."

She went to open the door. Dylan stood, holding a lone flower before handing it to her. As he did, his eyes fell to the couch where James sat.

"Thank you," Taylor said, drawing his attention back to her. "Should we go?"

Dylan's eyes lingered back inside for a moment before taking her and drawing her outside. It caught Taylor off guard, making her fumble over her feet. She nearly fell forward, but Dylan quickly grabbed her by the waist to hold her upright.

"Sorry about that," he said.

"It's okay." He moved away from his hold, going straight to his car.

He waited until they were in the car and the doors were closed to ask her about James.

"Who was that?"

"Oh, I forgot to introduce you!" Taylor blushed. "That's James. He's Claire's brother. He is staying for the night."

"At your place?" he asked as he reached out to take her hand. He glimpsed back at the door. "He seemed shifty. He kept looking at you weird."

"Weird?" Taylor laughed. "You sound like Claire. She's always, 'my brother has a crush on you'." Dylan's hand tightened its hold on Taylor, making her yelp, but he didn't let go.

"A crush? Do you like him?" he growled, frightening her.

"I—he doesn't like me. It's just that Claire is always being..." She attempted to get away from him, but he was holding on too tightly. "And no, of course, I don't. I hardly know him. You're hurting me." Her voice rose, panicked.

His eyes shifted to their hands before giving an apologetic look and finally unlatching his fingers around hers. Taylor brought her arm up to her chest and whimpered.

"I'm sorry, sweetheart. I don't know what that was."

Taylor didn't respond. A lump formed in the base of her throat, making her feel sick to her stomach. She stared out the window, unable to look at Dylan. She hadn't expected such a reaction from him about James. Was this her fault? She did find James attractive, but she'd never done anything about it. Could Dylan tell? Tears stung her eyes.

When they pulled into the parking lot of the restaurant, Dylan turned off the car. He brought his fingers to her chin, gently making her face him. He frowned.

"You forgive me, don't you?" he asked. "I honestly didn't mean to do that, Taylor. I didn't even realize your hand was in mine. And I don't know why I reacted so strongly about your roommate's brother. My head is somewhere else today."

She couldn't speak. With a blink, she tried to look away, but Dylan kept his fingers under her jaw. His thumb ran over her cheek.

"You know I love you, Taylor. I'd never do anything to hurt you."

Her eyes shot up then. Love. He told her he loved her.

"Please, don't be mad at me. I don't think I could handle it."

Taylor's lips quirked up. She nodded.

"I'm not mad."

He smiled. He leaned forward, brushing his mouth against hers. She kissed him back, hesitantly. As he attempted to deepen the kiss, she sat back. For her fist kiss, this hadn't been what she expected. Where were the fireworks she always heard about?

When his eyes narrowed in on her, she touched her temple with her fingertips.

"I have a bit of a headache."

"Oh, would you rather go back to my place and watch a movie?"

"I..."

"I'll make sure all the lights are low. We can watch something quiet, anything you like."

Not wanting to make him angry again, she replied, "Alright."

Taylor hadn't known what to expect with Dylan's place, but this wasn't it. It was a small house in the middle of an older neighborhood. He parked his car under the overhang before telling Taylor to step outside.

"I didn't know you had a home," she said.

"Yeah, I'm renting right now," he explained. "There's a job opportunity for me closer to Atlanta coming soon. I'm saving to buy a house then."

"You'll be moving?"

Dylan gave a sly smile.

"Don't worry, sweetheart, we'll still be together." He unlocked the front door, stepping to the side to let her go in first. It was small but quaint. He kept it tidy, but there was a lot of clutter, especially on the couch. Dylan rushed in behind her, grabbing the items and moving them to the chair beside her. "Sorry, I was going through my car collection."

That was when Taylor realized all the items were model cars.

"Not a problem."

"Go on, sit. Would you like something to drink?"

"Just water, please," she said.

As Dylan disappeared into the kitchen, she sat down on the couch. Her eyes looked around the room, seeing what she could learn about Dylan. There were no photos of anyone or any photos at all. The walls remained bare. On the bookshelves, there were only a few books, everything else was little knickknacks; either cars or things to do with cars.

"I like cars," Dylan said. He handed her a glass of water that she gratefully took.

"I see that. Have you always liked cars?"

"Oh, yes. For as long as I can remember, I have. Come on, let me show you my room."

He took her to his room down the hallway. There was another room on the way with a bed in it. Taylor poked her head inside.

"Do you have a roommate?"

"No," he simply answered. "Here."

His room was much like the living room, full of car knickknacks and a bed in the middle.

"What movie would you like to watch?" He pointed to the small stand of DVDs. Taylor shrugged.

"I don't care."

"Oh come on, choose something."

Taylor looked at the movie choices. Most were action-packed movies. There was one romantic comedy that looked like it could be fun. She picked it up. Dylan made a face.

"We could watch another one," Taylor quickly said.

"No, I told you that you could choose. I didn't even realize I still had this movie." He shook his head as though it didn't matter before he turned and placed the DVD into the player.

"Oh, I thought we'd watch this in the living room."

"No, the television in here is much better. Go on, sit on the bed."

Taylor sat at the edge of the bed, feeling less comfortable. Dylan turned off the lights and closed the blinds. He went to lay on the bed before patting beside him.

"Come on sweetheart, lay down with me."

Kicking off her shoes, Taylor scooted back to be in his arms. Over time, she settled more against Dylan, no longer as anxious. His fingertips ran along her back the entire movie. When the credits began to roll, Dylan brought her to him. His lips searched for hers. She kissed him back before trying to pull away.

"Oh, don't rush," Dylan rasped against her skin. He pushed her back against the bed, deepening the kiss. "I love you, Taylor. Doesn't this just feel right?"

"I-I think I need to go." She attempted to slide beneath him, but Dylan's hands were running up the front of her shirt.

"Don't you love me, Taylor?"

Taylor made a sound. His eyes met hers. He grinned.

"Just let it happen," he whispered to her. "Shh."

Covered by a flimsy blanket, she stared at the ceiling for a long time as he snored beside her. She felt numb and confused by what just happened. Her mind ran in circles attempting to make sense of it all. He said he loved her. And if he loved her, that meant what just happened wasn't...She wouldn't allow the word to enter her mind.

Had she led him on? She had to have, or else he never would have made that step, right?

He moved beside her. Quickly, she sat up, searching for her undergarments and clothes. She would need him to drive her home. She wanted to be in her own bed. She wanted to shower.

"Oh, what are you doing?" Dylan reached out, bringing his arm around her middle. He sat up, kissing between her shoulder blades. "You aren't ready to leave me yet, are you?"

"I...um, I need to get to bed soon. I have work in the morning."

"You'll sleep here." It wasn't a question.

"But my clothes..."

"I'll take you back to your place in time to get changed. Now, come back to bed, sweetheart."

She conceded, sliding back into his arms and trying to ignore the pain between her legs. It took a while, but she was finally able to fall into a fitful sleep.

Once Claire woke up the next morning, she went straight to Taylor's room. Several times over the night, she'd attempted to call and text

Taylor to find out where she was. It was unlike Taylor not to come home.

Taylor's room sat empty. Claire saw her bookbag still sitting on the chair, so she knew Taylor hadn't gone to work. She then went to check the living room. No sign of Taylor. James had already left for the day, so she was all alone.

She grabbed her phone, attempting to call Taylor again. The phone rang and rang. When it reached Taylor's voicemail, Claire hung up.

"Where are you?" she asked herself. She walked over to the window, peeking out in hopes of seeing her friend walking outside. Deep down, Claire knew her friend was grown and could do whatever she wanted, but Claire didn't like the thought of Taylor staying overnight with Dylan. Perhaps she should listen to her brother; be the supportive friend even if she didn't like it.

The time on the clock read nine. Taylor would need to be home soon to get ready for her job. Unless she had Dylan drop her off there. Claire leaned against the countertop in the kitchen. For now, she had to wait.

When Dylan dropped her off at her place, Taylor hoped not to see Claire or James. Her plans were thwarted when Claire nearly crashed into her as she turned the corner. Taylor ducked her head, just trying to get past her.

"Oh, sorry!" Claire said. "Hey!" Claire added, touching Taylor's shoulder. "Is everything alright? You look terrible. Your pale cheeks are even paler than normal."

"I'm fine. I just need to hurry and get ready for work," Taylor said. Her voice cracked as she spoke. She sucked in a breath, hoping Claire didn't notice.

"What did that bastard do?" Claire immediately asked. Her eyes bore into Taylor, making Taylor shake her head fiercely. The last thing she wanted to do was tell Claire she'd been right about Dylan.

"What?! Dylan didn't do anything. I just didn't get much sleep, and I need to hurry up and get ready, as I said."

"No, this isn't...something happened. Why won't you tell me? You're my best friend." Claire's hand remained on Taylor's shoulder, not letting up.

"I promise I'm only tired. I didn't feel well, so I slept at his place, and his bed isn't very comfortable. That's all."

Claire looked at Taylor, not believing her.

"You know you can talk with me about anything, right?" Her face softened with her question.

"Yes, of course, I do. Will you please let me by?"

Claire let go of Taylor.

"Thank you."

Taylor headed straight into her bedroom, glad Claire hadn't said anything else. Her head pounded from the little sleep she'd gotten that morning. She turned on her shower. While she waited for the water to warm, she called her boss. Since she never called out for work, her boss believed she was ill and couldn't come to work.

Knowing she could sleep the rest of the day, she hung up the phone and got into the hot shower. Her head fell into her hands. No tears fell from her eyes, but thoughts did continue to run through her head. She could not make sense of any of it. He loved her. This was what couples did.

When the water turned cool, she grabbed a towel, wrapping it around her frame. Her phone dinged. She looked at it, realizing she had many text messages from Dylan. All of them told her how much he loved her and how much he enjoyed the night before. She sent a short text back before quickly changing, climbing into her bed, turning off her phone, and going back to sleep.

"The living room is exploding with flowers," Claire said, waking Taylor up from her nap. Taylor rolled onto her back, rubbing her palm against her forehead. Claire walked further into the room, opening up the curtains.

"What?" Taylor croaked.

"Flowers. The living room is exploding with them."

Taylor sat up then. She undid the messy bun from her hair, allowing her red locks to fall to her shoulders.

"Who sent you flowers?"

"Me? They're for you, and they're from Dylan. So what did he do?" The moment the flowers started to come in, Claire knew Dylan had done something. No man sent that many flowers without being guilty.

"Huh?" Taylor slid off her bed, standing. She went to the living room to see the two big bouquets sitting on the coffee table.

"I mean, they're cheap flowers, but nice," Claire said, having to get her dig in at Dylan. Taylor ignored her, grabbing one of the cards.

You are the love of my life - Dylan. Claire scoffed under her breath.

"So, what did he do?" Claire asked again. Claire couldn't let this go. When Taylor arrived back at their apartment this morning, she had this haunted look about her. Then she skipped work and slept all day long. Something had to happen for Taylor to behave this way.

"What do you mean? He sent me flowers because he cares about me. Isn't that nice? Dylan hasn't done anything bad." Taylor's cheeks still held the distinctive red hue to them, but now the color had blossomed further down to her neck, showing she was lying.

"You looked really upset this morning, and you skipped work. You never miss work."

"I told you I didn't feel well," Taylor said. She grabbed the vase of the first set of flowers. "Where do I put these?"

"I don't know, does the trash sound harsh?"

Taylor shot her a look.

"Alright, alright, you can put one on the kitchen table and maybe one in your room?"

"Okay."

"I do hope he is treating you well, Taylor. You would tell me if he wasn't, wouldn't you?" Claire held a hopeful gaze at her friend. She didn't know how to get her to talk to her.

"Of course, I would." Taylor smiled, but it was weak. She placed the first set of flowers on the kitchen table. Then she grabbed the other to take to her room. As Claire watched her, she noticed her friend seemed to be near tears.

"Please, tell me what's wrong," Claire pleaded. Taylor blinked harshly, shaking her head.

"I have the worst headache. I might go back to bed."

"And that's all?"

"That's all."

CHAPTER 4

After all she'd heard about sex, Taylor wondered what was so wonderful about it. She didn't enjoy it, at all. Dylan always whispered in her ear to relax, but she couldn't. Her body was uneasy. But she pushed through, trying to tell herself that this was what was expected in a loving relationship. They'd already crossed that threshold, she couldn't stop now, could she? Well, not if she wanted. Since his first taste months ago, it seemed Dylan often needed it, giving her excuses about being in pain if he got riled up and needing her for the release.

She always closed her eyes, waiting for him to finish. Once he did, she'd get up and rush to the bathroom, saying she needed to pee. Today she sat on the toilet, not surprised to see the blood when she wiped. When was that supposed to stop?

Her eyes closed. Dylan kept talking about the new potential job hours away. Taylor found she hoped he'd get it, and they would have some time apart. The past few months had been a whirlwind with everything moving so fast. She found it hard to keep up between school, Dylan, and work.

After taking a moment, she stood. Like always, when she walked back out, he was sitting there with a bright smile on his face. He pulled her forward and into his lap. He kissed the crook of her neck.

"Oh, I love you," he murmured against her skin, making her smile.

"I love you," she whispered back as he caused a shiver to run up her spine. She didn't know when she'd started saying it back. It was automatic. She knew he expected it. "I'll miss you while I'm away."

Dylan pulled back, his eyes darkening.

"Away? Where are you going?"

"I told you a while ago. I'm going to Claire's parents' house for a couple of weeks for the summer and over the 4th. I leave on Friday since I have two weeks off between summer classes."

"You didn't tell me that."

"Yes, I did," Taylor said. "I told you when we went out to eat at the Mexican restaurant. Her parents invited me."

"Her parents or James?"

Taylor sat back as she remembered the last time Dylan had gotten jealous.

"Her parents. I don't even know if James will be there." She attempted to sound nonchalant about the whole thing, not wanting him to get angry at her.

"Oh right, you have no idea." Dylan's fingertips tightened on her waist, making her jerk up, away from his grasp.

"I don't! What would it matter, you are my boyfriend."

"And don't forget it, Taylor." Now he stood as well. His finger pressed against her chest, making her yelp. "You are mine, not his. But while you are at their fancy house with their fancy things, you'll forget all about me."

"No, no, of course I won't, Dylan." Dylan's finger still rested on her chest, trapping her against the wall. "Claire is my best friend. They like to have me over for—"

"Your friend, Claire, is a bitch," Dylan snarled. Taylor stepped back, hitting the wall behind her.

"No, she's not." Taylor vehemently shook her head. "She's not!"

"She is. She thinks she's better than you and me. You'll see. But have fun with them. I'm sure they make fun of you behind your back, about how you have nothing, and they have everything."

"Claire would never do that." Taylor strengthened her voice.

"Sure, sweetheart. Tell yourself that. But you'll happily see James, won't you?"

"I don't even know—"

"And if he is there, then what?"

"What?"

"What will you do if he is there? Will you come back here?"

"Why would I come back? I-I don't have feelings for him, and he doesn't have feelings for me."

Dylan moved closer to Taylor, making her press her back more against the wall. His nose nearly touched hers before he slammed his fist into the wall beside her. The sound reverberated in her ears, making her jump.

"You want to have more time with him, don't you?" His lips brushed along her ear; she shuddered.

"No...Dylan, I hardly know him. I'm with you. I am dating you." Her heart pounded in her chest. He frightened her. "Please, you're scaring me."

Dylan's nostrils flared, but he backed away. Taylor maneuvered herself off the wall, moving so her back was toward the open door.

"You have to be careful, Taylor," Dylan said. He reached out to her, but she refused his offer. Her eyes glanced behind her, wondering if she'd be able to make it if she ran right this moment. "Men like James prey after innocent people like you."

Taylor blinked harshly.

"But James..."

"Now you're defending him?" he bellowed. Taylor bent down.

"No, no, of course...I don't understand."

Dylan's eyes softened then, as though there was a switch inside him that had been turned off.

"Oh, sweetheart," he soothed. Taylor inched back, still frightened. "I'm only trying to protect you." He touched her cheek. "It's because I love you. Here, let me get you some water, alright?"

"Alright." Taylor remained at the door, but she moved to the side to let him pass. Her eyes shut harshly, replaying the events that had just happened.

When her eyes opened, Dylan stood before her with a cup of water. She took it, taking a sip.

"I think I'd like to go back to my place now," she said, trying to sound sure of herself and not scared.

"Are you sure? I thought we'd watch a movie."

"I'm sure."

Ever since Taylor came home that one morning, Claire sensed a shift in Taylor's behavior. For one, she became glued to her phone, keeping it by her side at all times. Any time it dinged, she rushed to answer it. It was worse than when she'd just started dating Dylan. Taylor also kept to herself more and stayed in her room. Their ice cream dates every evening hardly happened now. Claire hadn't had to buy a pint in weeks.

Any time Claire attempted to spend time with her friend, Taylor found excuses for why they couldn't hang out. Claire knew it was partly her fault. Her feelings about Dylan were well known, but she hadn't thought it would put such space between the two of them.

"You are coming with me, aren't you?"

Taylor peered up over her laptop screen. She'd pulled her hair into two French braids, which were loose and falling out along the ends.

"Hm?"

"To my house, 4th of July."

"Yes."

"Good. Are you sure you don't want me to drive you back?"

"You're done for the summer," Taylor said with a shrug. "There's no need for you to drive all the way back here. I don't mind the bus."

"Right," Claire said. She took a few steps further into Taylor's room. Her eyes glanced around at the paintings which sat along the floor, against the wall. Since Taylor began seeing Dylan, she painted less and less.

Claire lifted a painting of a dog.

"Whose dog is this?"

"Oh, no ones," Taylor answered. She continued to type away on her computer. "I just saw a dog outside on campus and decided to paint it."

The small Yorkshire's tongue stuck out in the photo, while his head was cocked to one side. Claire touched the corner where a splatter of red was, tearing her attention away from the bright and fun painting.

"Did you spill paint on it?" Claire asked.

Taylor turned. She flashed her eyes toward the painting before turning back around.

"No, it's meant to be like that."

"But why on Earth—"

"I am excited about the party," Taylor said, changing the topic.

"Me too. It'll be fun."

Claire's eyes were drawn back to the small splatter of red paint. What could it mean? Was it just Taylor being creative? Or was there some darker meaning behind it? Was it Taylor trying to cry for help?

"It's just paint," Taylor said. "Stop overanalyzing it."

"Right," Claire said, though she couldn't draw her eyes away from it. *What did it mean?*

When Friday finally hit, Taylor received a wall of messages from Dylan. Every time she tried to put her phone down, it would ding again. Claire glanced over at her phone and rolled her eyes. She didn't say anything, however, and for that, Taylor was glad.

Every message held a reminder that he loved her and would miss her while she was gone for the next two weeks. Taylor sent a heart emoji before putting her phone on silent and slipping her phone into her purse. She rested her head back against the headrest in Claire's car and closed her eyes, excited about the next couple of weeks without any pressures.

"You know," Claire said, making Taylor open her eyes. "There will be tons of people over on the 4th of July. You should just enjoy it."

Taylor narrowed her eyes.

"What does that mean?"

"It means, you are still young. You're almost twenty. Enjoy life. Don't let one person hold you back, not yet."

Taylor clucked her tongue on the roof of her mouth. She turned her head to the window to watch the clouds go by.

"You're telling me to cheat on my boyfriend?"

"No," Claire said defensively. "I'm just saying don't pigeonhole yourself when you're only nineteen. You have big dreams and aspirations. Remember those."

"Those are some big words for you," Taylor said in response. Claire tapped Taylor's shoulder.

"What's that supposed to mean?" She laughed. Taylor began to laugh too. The ease of their friendship taking over the seriousness of the conversation.

"You just sound very mature and astute."

"Do I not normally?"

"Well..." Taylor playfully trailed off. Their laughter continued to fill the air as Claire pulled off the interstate.

Since Christmas, Taylor had been to Claire's house a couple of times so she knew they were getting closer now. She sat up, adjusting her visor to keep the sun out of her eyes.

"He does love me, you know," Taylor said a beat later. "So I need you two to get along. You're my best friend, Claire."

Claire's response didn't come right away. Her brows knitted, and she clutched her hands more firmly against the wheel.

"I do hope that's true, Taylor, that he loves you. I really do. Do you love him?"

The question sat in the air for a moment as Taylor pondered it. She certainly replied to Dylan's 'I love yous' with her own 'I love yous," but she wasn't sure if she meant the words when she said them. She didn't really know what love was.

"I do," she finally said. "At least, I think I do."

Claire's eyes shot over to her then, as she pulled into her neighborhood.

"You don't have to be for sure, not yet." Claire winked. "I don't plan on marrying until I'm at least thirty. Who wants to be held back by men?" Again, they laughed. "Definitely not me."

The car was parked in its spot in the large driveway. Taylor stepped out, now knowing to leave her bags in the car and that they would be grabbed later. She took Claire's hand and headed into the house, excited about the weeks ahead.

"Sexy," Claire said, walking up behind Taylor as she stood in front of the mirror, trying to assess the new, two-piece, black bathing suit Claire had insisted on getting her as an early birthday present. Taylor's face contorted, pulling up the bottoms some more to cover her stomach. "Stop it." Claire brought the bottom back to its intended height. "You look amazing."

"I look like a pale, pasty...whale."

"What?!" Claire gasped. "Absolutely not. You're gorgeous. Whatever made you think you look like a whale? You are the perfect size. God, what I wouldn't give for your boobs and hips. What do they call that? Hourglass shape?" Claire grasped Taylor's hips before meeting her eyes in the mirror. "Gorgeous, absolutely gorgeous."

"I guess." Generally, Taylor wore a one-piece, but it was Claire who insisted she should try this two-piece bathing suit. Taylor ran her hands over her belly. Despite all the walking she did, it still remained pudgy. Claire seized Taylor's wrists, pulling them away from her stomach.

"Stop it. You are sexy. Be confident."

Pink rose on Taylor's cheeks.

"Alright. I'll wear it."

"Good."

Claire slipped off her shirt, not caring that she was now topless. She opened up the top drawer of her dresser and lifted out a flowery top, slipping it on.

"Now, where are the bottoms?" She dug more within the drawer before finding it. Her bottoms were pulled down before she pulled her bathing suit bottoms on. "There. Now we are ready to spend the day by the pool. Don't forget sunscreen. You will be red in ten minutes without it."

Growing up, Taylor rarely went to the pool. When she did, it had been a treat. But because of how little she went, she never learned how to swim. Every time until she could stand in the shallow end, she'd remained on the stairs, playing with a small toy. Looking back, she was lucky she hadn't drowned, knowing no one was watching out for her.

With Claire, it didn't matter that she couldn't swim. Claire enjoyed standing in the water and sipping on her cold hard lemonade or laying out by the pool. She wore a large, hot pink hat on her head to shield the sun off her face, and sparkling sunglasses over her eyes. Next to her, Taylor always felt bland.

"Well, look who the cat dragged in," Claire said. Taylor followed her gaze to see James and Marcus walking toward the pool. Marcus had already been at the house, but this was the first time she'd seen James. Her stomach flipped, and she worried Dylan would somehow know that James was seeing her in a bathing suit.

Neither of the boys spoke. They looked at one another before pulling off their tops and doing cannonballs into the pool. It caused a big wave of water to splash both her and Claire. Claire shrieked, holding her drink up higher.

"You assholes!" she yelled. They cackled loudly. "I'm going to have to go in and get another drink. Taylor, do you want one?"

Taylor shook her head.

"I can grab you a sweet tea."

"I'm alright."

Claire stepped out of the pool, grabbing her towel to wrap over her. She took off her hat and glasses, setting them down to dry in the sun.

"I hope you're not too upset with us," James said, gliding over to Taylor on top of the water. He swam effortlessly. Taylor shook her head.

"I'm not."

Using his hands, James pulled up on the wall and sat at the edge. As the water fell from his body, Taylor saw just how in shape James was. His abs were tight and shoulders wide. She took in a deep breath of air.

"Where did Marcus go?" She suddenly realized the two of them were all alone.

"Probably inside to torture Claire more." He laughed. "It's what siblings do."

"I'll have to take your word on it. I'm an only child."

"Lucky," James teased.

Taylor smiled. She maneuvered herself so she could be closer to James before realizing what she was doing. Even if they were just being friendly, Dylan wouldn't like that.

"I'm not sure about that," she said, keeping back. Her arms moved in the water, allowing it to rush over her to help cool her down.

James popped back into the water, going under before swimming onto the stairs next to Taylor. He grabbed a pool noodle and used it to keep him afloat.

"I'm glad you came with Claire."

"I like visiting. Your house is like a vacation. Where I lived could fit in your kitchen."

"Oh yeah?"

"Yeah. And we definitely didn't have a pool. I don't know how to swim."

"No?" he asked in disbelief.

"Yes, it's true. I am unable to swim. But I can manage a doggie paddle if I'm in dire need."

"Would you like me to teach you?"

"How to swim?"

"Yes. It's fairly simple."

"Maybe another time," Taylor said, her heart beating too harshly in her chest. She looked back to the house, hoping to see Claire coming outside to join them at the pool.

"Sounds good." James seemed to recognize Taylor's uncomfortableness, so he swam away to the deeper end of the pool.

They stayed by the pool every day except for Friday when it decided to rain. Claire set up a movie day instead, preparing their media room with snacks and drinks, as well as a large stack of DVDs for them to choose from.

"We can also order something on demand if none of this appeals to you."

"No, I love all of it," Taylor assured her. She took one of the bags of popcorn, opening it and enjoying the smell. She grabbed a handful, but only took a small bite. It was still warm. "So, James has a girlfriend, right?"

Claire glanced up from the pile of DVDs she was searching for. She grinned.

"Well, he did. Why do you ask?"

"I was only wondering if she was coming to the party, is all."

"Oh, is that all?" Claire playfully said. She lifted a DVD; Taylor nodded. Claire stood, placing the movie into the player. She then took the seat beside Taylor, grabbing her own handful of popcorn. "Well, they broke up. She doesn't like cats."

"Cats?" Taylor laughed. "Do people really break up over things like that?"

"James does, it seems. He has always had a love for cats. He loves dogs, too. Really any animal."

"But why cats?"

"I don't know. I think he's just being picky," Claire said, getting more comfortable on the wide couch. "I mean, I guess it's good to be picky about who you date. But she seemed lovely."

"Well, I'm sure he'll find someone who loves cats."

"Do you love cats?"

In her life, Taylor hadn't had a chance to think about owning a pet. Perhaps, in the future, she might want one, but it hadn't occurred to her until this moment.

"Sure." She shrugged.

"I think even if you didn't, James would make an exception for you."

"Not that again," Taylor said. "He doesn't like me, and I have a boyfriend, Dylan."

"Who has been texting you nonstop since you got here. Does he not trust you?"

"He does. He just misses me." Taylor glanced down at her phone; just in the past hour, there were three more text messages from him. She'd sent him a message to let him know she and Claire were watching movies. Another text came across the screen.

Call me!

The heat rose in her cheeks before she texted back. *The movie just started. I'll call you afterward.*

Three dots filled the screen.

Now.

With a groan, Taylor got up and left the room. She entered the guest bathroom and quickly dialed Dylan's number.

"What's wrong?" she asked when he answered.

"Why are you avoiding me?"

"What? I am not avoiding you. Claire and I have been very busy."

"He's there, isn't he?"

Taylor swallowed hard.

"Yes, but I—"

"Damnit, Taylor! Come back."

"I'm supposed to stay here another week. There are a lot of people at the house, but Claire and I are the ones who mainly hang out together. We hardly see her siblings."

"Uh-huh." Dylan made a low sound. "Do you want to cheat on me, Taylor?"

"What, no! Why are you being like this? Do you not trust me?'

"I honestly don't know. I'd trust you more if you did as I asked and came back."

An uneasy feeling filled Taylor's stomach. Dylan had a way of making her feel that way; always making her unsure of her own footing. If she did as he asked, he wouldn't be angry, but he also would win. This was supposed to be her vacation with her friend. She thought back to what Claire said about her turning twenty soon. She was supposed to be having fun.

"I promise you I am not doing anything bad," she told him.

"Fine, have fun with James, Taylor." The line went dead. Taylor's body began to shake. She was tempted to call him back, but knew deep down she shouldn't.

She walked back out and into the room where Claire sat waiting.

"What was all that?"

"Nothing," Taylor lied. "Now, let's watch the movie."

That evening, Claire tried to find something fun to chat about with Taylor, but she was miles away. After her talk with Dylan on the phone, Taylor disappeared into herself. Claire had been enjoying their time together without him around. For the first time, they'd been like the friends they were before Dylan.

"Look," Claire said, lifting a pint of mint ice cream. In her other hand, she held two spoons. Taylor sat up on the bed and smiled.

"Mint chocolate chip in the white sheets, scandalous."

Claire shrugged. She made her way over to the edge of her bed and sat down. She opened the container, dug her spoon in, and then spread the spoon over the comforter.

"Adds a bit of color in this white abyss."

"Your mother is going to kill you," Taylor said, but she was laughing. She inched closer to Claire and took one of the spoons. "Why do you like to annoy her so much?"

"I don't know, because I'm the youngest and I can." She nudged Taylor playfully with her shoulder. "I don't annoy her all the time. I just hate the way she's designed this room. I'm hoping to convince her to change it up soon."

"I'm sure she will," Taylor said. "Didn't you say she gets bored with the look of things about every couple of years?"

"Yes, I guess you're right."

They both grew quiet for a moment, eating their ice cream. Claire took two bites, her mind swirling with things she wanted to ask Taylor. She feared bringing Dylan up might cause a deeper tear already into their fragile friendship. Dylan did a great job keeping them from being as close as they used to be. She couldn't mess this up.

"Um." She paused, cleared her throat, and then gave a crooked smile when Taylor looked up at her in curiosity. It wasn't often Claire sounded unsure of herself. "Did you and Dylan get into a fight?"

Taylor's eyes fell on the comforter, and she picked at the edge of it.

"Yeah," Taylor whispered. "I don't know why, but no matter what I say or do, he's never happy enough with me."

Claire frowned, even though she wasn't surprised. Dylan seemed like the type to make a woman feel like shit just for the fun of it.

"You're wonderful, Taylor," Claire said strongly. "You're my best friend, you know."

Taylor shyly smiled.

"I know."

"Maybe having some time apart from Dylan will be good for you both. Don't you feel less overwhelmed by him here?"

Taylor nodded. She glanced up and that's when Claire noticed the tears in her eyes.

"Oh, Taylor!"

"I think you're right. I think—I think I can't do this anymore with him. It's *so* hard. I don't think dating is supposed to be hard."

"It's not," Claire said. She wrapped her arm around Taylor, drawing her close. "It's supposed to be fun, especially at our age. We're young and carefree."

"Yeah. That's how it's supposed to be."

"It is."

Dylan didn't speak to Taylor for the next several days. Uneasiness remained at the pit of her stomach. She realized it was fear of what he might do when she got back. She'd seen him angry before, and it scared her. She hadn't told Claire anything about how he'd hold on to her a bit too tightly or hit the wall right beside her head. Just thinking about it made her nauseous. However, she reminded herself she was going to end it with him after her return. Claire even offered to return with her to be there for emotional support.

Deciding to push it back in her mind, she walked down the aisles of the convenience store, searching for some snacks to take with her to the theme park they would be attending. As she walked down the aisle, a pregnancy test caught her eye. She passed it, but then looked back.

"No," she whispered. Her head shook, but a nagging voice reminded her how her period was nearly a week late. A pregnancy would change everything; her world would crumble. Despite that, she grabbed a test, making sure Claire was still outside.

Moments later, staring back at her were two glaringly pink lines. She was only nineteen; she was going to be a mother.

CHAPTER 5

"I think I need to go back," Taylor said, chewing on a leftover straw from her drink earlier. Claire, who was painting her toes, looked up from the floor.

"What? You're supposed to stay until Sunday. It's only Wednesday."

"I know," Taylor whispered. Claire saw the distinct tears in Taylor's eyes, making her worry.

"I thought we were going to go back together, so you could break up with you know who. Has he messaged you? Made you feel like you should come back? He hasn't manipulated you out of it, has he?" Her eyes darted to the phone, almost as though mentioning him would summon up Dylan.

"No," Taylor said with a shake of her head. "No, he hasn't called or texted me."

"Good. Doesn't it feel nice to be away from Dylan?" Claire dropped her toenail polish. The bright pink flooded over the stark white carpet. Taylor gasped, but Claire didn't even flinch.

"Yes," Taylor admitted.

"See! I think this trip was just what you needed. And I think you should stay longer. You don't have to rush back. We'll go back on Sunday like we planned. You'll end it for good with Dylan and be free of him."

"I can't," Taylor murmured.

"Yes, you can."

"I can't," Taylor repeated.

"And why not?"

"I'm pregnant."

The moment those words left Taylor, the air rushed out of Claire's lungs. Taylor finally met her eyes, tears now spilling over her eyelashes and onto her cheeks.

"What?" Claire breathed. "Please, *please* tell me you had a random one-night stand with someone and that it isn't that asshole's."

Taylor didn't answer, covering her mouth. Claire slipped onto the bed beside her, bringing her arms around Taylor's shoulders. She held her close for a moment, trying to process what her friend just admitted to her.

"When did you find out?"

"Yesterday. I-I took a test at the store." Claire wanted to ask why she hadn't told her then, but that wouldn't help. Deep down she seethed; Dylan won, yet again. But she had to remain calm for Taylor, who was beginning to break down in her arms.

"I'm going to be just like my parents," she cried.

"Shh, no you won't. It'll be alright," she promised. "You have several options. The most important one being you don't have to tell him." She said that last part carefully. Taylor's eyes widened as she got off the bed.

"He's the father," Taylor disagreed. She sat up wiping under her eyes. "Of course I have to tell him."

"But why? Why do you have to tell him? You said being with him is hard, that you're not happy."

"Because he is the father of my baby."

"So?" Claire said with a roll of her eyes. "Just because he is, doesn't mean you have to stay with him. You and I could raise the baby."

Taylor rose her brow at that, a weak chuckle leaving her.

"You and me?"

"Yes, of course. Why not? If you want to keep this baby, let me help you. Just don't give up your dreams, all right?"

"I will have to tell him," Taylor repeated. "And I do want to keep it. It's my baby."

"Yes, you'll be a brilliant mother, Taylor. You just can't let Dylan use this to manipulate you to stay with him. You don't need him to raise your baby. He can be involved as a father if he so chooses, but you don't have to be connected to him in any other way."

"I don't know what to do," Taylor said, her lower lip wobbling. "How do I finish school and raise a baby? Why was I so stupid!?"

"You're not stupid," Claire said. She took Taylor's hands into her own, giving them a loving squeeze. "We will figure this out together. If we need to rent a house, we will. I'll be the fun aunt. Just please don't go back to him. I'm begging you, Taylor. Don't do it."

The drive back to college made Taylor sick to her stomach. She couldn't tell if it was fear of what was to come with potentially ending things with Dylan or if it was the pregnancy. Claire spoke with her the entire ride, speaking about what she thought the next steps for Taylor should be. However, Taylor couldn't talk about any of it. While she was grateful Claire had decided to come back with her, she was overwhelmed by the fact she was going to be a mother. For so long, she'd worked hard to take a different path than her parents and now here she was, just like them.

When they arrived back at their dorm, Taylor made it to the door first. She saw a letter tucked into the doorway. The handwriting was undeniably Dylan's. She pulled it out, not wanting Claire to see it. She unlocked the door and walked into her room as her roommate dragged in her several bags.

Taylor,

I've missed you while you were away. You were all I thought about. I hope you had a lovely time, sweetheart. Call me when you get back home.

I love you, Dylan

She closed the letter before glancing out her bedroom door. Thankfully, Claire was still busy with her luggage. Again, she read over the letter. Her eyes stung with fresh tears. Dylan loved her. She wanted her baby to have both of them in its life. She wanted better for her baby than she had growing up.

After making sure Claire was nowhere nearby, she lifted her phone to call Dylan. It would be best not to tell Claire what she was doing before she did it.

"Hello?" Dylan answered before the phone even had a full ring. "Oh, Taylor! I've missed you!"

Taylor had to admit she liked to hear how much she'd been missed. He sounded happy and not angry at her. Perhaps while she was away, she'd built him up as this scary man he wasn't.

"Hi," she quietly said, closing her bedroom door. She sat down on the edge of the bed, anxiously kicking her foot against the side of it. "We should talk."

"Oh, don't worry about before," Dylan shrugged off. "Everyone argues now and then. I'm just glad you're home."

Taylor tugged at the edge of her hair, feeling a bit lighter now. She touched her stomach, thinking about the bean growing inside of her. How might he react when he knew about that?

"Really?"

"Of course, sweetheart! I love you."

"I..." She paused, heaviness surrounded her again. "We need to talk."

"Alright. Should I come over and pick you up?"

"Um, yes. That would be good," she said. "I'll wait outside for you."

Claire removed her shoes from her feet, placing them down in their spot in her closet. The front door opened, and her head turned toward the sound.

"Taylor?"

When she didn't get a response, Claire walked toward the door and opened it. Taylor sat on the lone chair on their small front porch.

"What are you doing?"

"I'm going to go and speak with Dylan about the baby," Taylor answered. She wouldn't look at her.

"Why didn't you tell me? I can go get my shoes and come with you."

"No," Taylor said, now twisting her head up to her. "I need to do this by myself."

An overwhelming ache grew in the pit of Claire's stomach.

"You're going to stay with him," she said, just above a whisper. Her hand clutched over her heart. "Taylor, he will only bring you unhappiness."

"How do you know that? He loves me, Claire," Taylor said, growing angry. "I am having his baby. Don't I owe this baby a chance to have his father in his life?"

"You said he makes you unhappy. He's controlling. He makes you feel like shit."

"No, he doesn't. I-I was wrong. It was you getting in my head."

Claire tightened her lips to keep from saying anything else she might regret. She didn't want to begin a bigger argument with her friend. Clearly, she wasn't going to listen to her. Now, she had to decide what that meant. But she refused to make this the end of their friendship.

"You'll think about it, right?" Claire said, finally. "You won't jump into any other permanent decisions without really thinking about it, will you?"

"Like what?"

"Marriage."

Taylor scoffed. She tucked a stray hair back behind her ear. She didn't say anything for a moment, keeping her eyes on the parking lot. Claire glanced up too, wondering when Dylan's car might pull up.

"Don't do it, Taylor," Claire pleaded. "You aren't even twenty yet."

"I'm aware. You should stay out of it," Taylor said. She brought her arms over her chest. It felt like a punch in the gut.

"Fine." Claire swallowed hard. "Fine, do what you want. You're an adult." She said nothing else after that. Instead of remaining outside and having to face Dylan, she went back into the apartment. There was nothing else she could do.

He held her tightly for what felt like forever.

"Oh, Taylor!" he said happily into her ear. Taylor pushed lightly against him.

"You're not angry?"

"Angry? You're having my baby!" He pulled her down to sit next to him. "And this really is the best time. I got that job I've been talking about."

"But..." Taylor paused. "I have school."

Dylan's eyes darkened for a split second, forcing the air to catch in her throat. She blinked harshly, but before she could get too concerned his face had already softened.

"Marry me."

"What?"

Before she knew what was happening, Dylan was down on one knee, holding a ring. Her eyes widened.

"What?" She breathed again. *No*, she thought to herself. *This can't be happening.*

"Please, Taylor. I wanted to ask you next week for your birthday, but since I know you're carrying my baby, I want you to marry me now."

Even though she hadn't answered, he slipped the ring over her finger. He kissed the ring then he kissed her. Taylor sat in shock. Her thumb ran over the cold metal.

"You'll marry me, right? You won't want for anything."

"But what about school? I have a scholarship here. I worked hard for my scholarship."

"You did," Dylan said. "I have to move away. You don't want to keep me away from my child, do you? You'd rather stay here and go to school than be with me?"

"It's not that. I just—school is important to me." Again, tears threatened to escape her. Everything was changing so fast. Dylan's thumb wiped below her eye.

"I know, but there's a school nearby. You can continue classes up there. We can manage. It might take you longer since we'll have to pay out of pocket and the baby, but we'll make it work."

Taylor met his eyes, searching his face to see if it was true. Would he help her continue with her schooling? And her art?

"You'll do all of that for me?"

"I'll do anything for you, Taylor," he promised. "I love you."

He tugged on her shirt, and she knew immediately what he wanted. She sat back, shaking her head.

"I haven't been feeling well," she told him. He kissed the top of her crown, giving her a soft smile.

"Well, you are growing a human." He smiled. "Why don't you rest? I'll get you some water."

He stood, leaving her alone on the couch. Taylor began to spin the ring around her finger, suddenly dazed. A baby. Marriage. A move. She slid further back to lie down. Could she marry someone she wasn't even sure she loved?

Subconsciously, her hand lingered over her stomach. She thought of growing up without a mother and with a father who tried, but never was the same after her mother left. This little bean inside of her needed both of their parents. It was up to her and Dylan to be everything for the baby. It didn't matter that she was only nearly twenty. She had to grow up and do what was best for her child, not herself.

Sickness bubbled up in her throat. She quickly stood, rushing to the bathroom. As she threw up in the toilet, her hair was pulled up and out of her face. Dylan rubbed large circles on her back.

"Shh," he murmured.

He did love her, she told herself. She would have to move away with him. It was what had to be done.

CHAPTER 6

Claire prided herself on being able to compartmentalize her emotions, but when she heard the news that Taylor said yes to his marriage proposal and would be moving away, she burst into tears. Thankfully, she'd been told over a text message so Taylor didn't see her reaction.

She didn't respond to the text message. If she did, she knew her response would only delay Taylor returning to their apartment that evening. There were so many questions Claire wanted to ask her. When would she move? When would she marry him? And most importantly, why?

The best part about getting the news via text was it gave Claire time to decide how she'd respond when she saw Taylor in person. If Claire was right about Dylan (and she was sure she was), her friend would need someone to be there when things inevitably went south. That meant Claire had to handle her reaction to Taylor with care. It was the only way she could be there when Taylor needed her.

Around seven in the evening, Taylor showed up. She came in quietly, but Claire sat on the couch waiting for her. Taylor sheepishly smiled.

"Hi."

"Hey," Claire said. She gritted her teeth and reminded herself not to say anything too outlandish. "So..."

"So..."

"Come on, sit down. Tell me all about it."

There was hesitancy on Taylor's face, but she did as Claire asked. Claire forced herself to smile, to make her friend more comfortable.

"Go on."

"He just—well, Dylan said he planned on asking me on my birthday, but now that I'm pregnant he wanted to go ahead and do it." Taylor lifted her hand to show the ring on her finger. Claire's smile slipped. She took Taylor's hand to get a better view of the ring. It was a simple, gold band with a small stone on top.

"Lovely," Claire lied. Maybe her brother was right, she was a snob. "When's the move? When will you be getting married?"

"I'm not sure. We'll move by the end of the summer. I'll be able to finish my final summer semester. We haven't set a date for the wedding, or made any plans, yet."

"Oh." There was a hopefulness in Claire's voice. There was still time to stop this from happening. "Well, I'll help you plan."

"We can't afford anything fancy. I'm sure we'll just go to the courthouse or something."

"And this is what you want?" Claire searched her friend's face.

"I think..." She shook her head. "Yes, it's what I want."

"Good." Claire's voice was strained. "As long as you're happy, Taylor. I know this has all been so much. Are you sure you're alright?"

"I'm fine."

She lied to Claire. She'd never thought of herself as a liar, especially to her best friend, but she did. She told her she was fine, that this was what she wanted. It wasn't. Once she put herself to bed that evening, Taylor cried herself to sleep.

Never had she felt so out of control of her future. The hot tears stung her eyes when she awoke in the middle of the night.

She could feel her breaths sharpening with every intake of air. Everything closed around her.

The light in her room flicked on.

"Taylor?"

Taylor couldn't process what was going on. She couldn't breathe.

"Taylor!"

Before she knew it, Claire sat in front of her, holding her shoulders. Claire's brown eyes stared straight into her.

"It's alright." Her voice was calm. "You're alright. You're having a panic attack."

She didn't feel alright. It was like she could die right here and right now. Claire coached her through the attack to bring her back to normal. Slowly, her heart rate returned to normal, and she could feel the air filling her lungs again.

"How did you know?" Taylor asked between sharp breaths.

"My sister, Simone, used to have them all the time. She's a perfectionist and any grade lower than perfect would cause her to break-down."

"No...I meant, how did you know I was having one?"

"I heard you crying. When I knocked on the door and you didn't answer, I got worried."

"Oh." Taylor sniffled. "I feel better now. You can go back to sleep."

"Don't you want to talk about it?"

"No," Taylor said, quickly. "I must have had a bad dream or something. I'm fine."

She ran her fingers through her hair, trying to keep it from staying in her face. Claire just stared back at her, not moving an inch.

"It's okay if you're upset. You've just had a lot of life-changing events happen."

"I'm fine."

"You're going to work yourself up into another panic attack if you keep denying how you feel," Claire said, pointedly. "Now, come on." Claire stood, reaching out for Taylor and then lifting her to her feet.

Taylor didn't know what Claire was up to, but they ended up in the living room where Claire told her to sit down at the kitchen table. Taylor then watched Claire grab an ice cream from the fridge and two spoons.

"Here." Claire slid the ice cream pint in front of Taylor. "It's good for the nerves."

"I want this baby," Taylor said a moment later. She hadn't touched the ice cream. Her stomach continually flipped, unable to make anything sound appealing. "And I want to make it work with Dylan. I'm just scared."

"Scared you're making the wrong choice to be with him?"

"No," Taylor replied, though she wasn't sure she was telling the truth. "Just scared of everything changing. I like it here. I like being your roommate. I had dreams."

"I know," Claire whispered. "You don't have to decide right now, you know. Maybe you could tell Dylan you'd like to wait a while longer?"

Taylor knew she couldn't. He'd never allow that.

"I want to do this. It's just a lot."

"Of course, it is," Claire said.

After that, they just sat there for a while, neither one speaking. Taylor realized it would be one of the last times they had like this, with just the two of them. In a few months, she'd be living in a new town, in a new place, with Dylan. She wouldn't have Claire to talk through her thoughts anymore. That realization crushed her.

Taylor's bedroom felt empty with everything boxed up, even though she never really had much in the room anyway. Taylor stared at the blank walls and empty bed. The room no longer belonged to her. Soon, someone else would fill that space. Would that girl become Claire's new best friend?

After one final look, she walked out of the room with her final box. Claire stood in the kitchen, her eyes on the window. In the past few weeks, Claire subtly tried to convince Taylor not to leave. However, she'd not said it outright. She was less vocal about her opinions about Dylan since Taylor had agreed to marry him.

Taylor sat the box down on the coffee table before going to stand by her friend. She couldn't believe today was the day they would say goodbye. It took willpower not to burst into tears.

Her stomach had already begun to round out. Soon, her pregnancy would no longer be able to be hidden with clothing.

"I'm going to miss you," she told her friend. Claire lifted her cup, taking a long sip. "I'll come and visit. It's only about a three hour bus ride."

Claire stood there for a moment, taking another long sip of her drink. Finally, she spoke.

"If he gets violent, you have to call me," Claire said. Taylor hadn't expected that. She grew defensive.

"What? He won't..."

"He has before, hasn't he?" Claire asked, her eyes never leaving Taylor.

Taylor's cheeks reddened. She'd never told Claire about any of Dylan's random outbursts. She never told anyone. Since she'd told him she was pregnant, he had been nothing but gentle and kind. Sometimes, it was like the scary version of Dylan had disappeared the moment he knew he was going to be a father. Being a father might be just what he needed to become a better man.

"No," Taylor lied.

Claire's fingers tapped against the side of the cup in her hands.

"I hope I'm wrong about him, but I don't see how I can be. He has you leaving your dreams, moving somewhere new, and not even..." Claire's eyes drifted down to the box on the table. "Sorry. I told myself I wouldn't say anything else about it. I only wanted you to know that you can call me if you need me, day or night. I will come right away if you're in trouble."

"I appreciate that, but things are going to be great. I signed up at the local college to take two classes. It's all going to work out."

"Right," Claire said. "I don't want to see you hurt."

"You won't."

Claire's face fell, her eyes solemn.

"I do hope that's true, Taylor. I really do."

CHAPTER 7

Taylor and Dylan had a quick wedding at the courthouse, nothing fancy or overdone. Taylor preferred it that way. She never dreamed of bells and whistles when it came to her wedding day. She'd never really dreamed of it at all.

Weddings never seemed important before now. She'd always assumed one day she would meet someone and marry them, but it had never been a part of her life plan. No, her plans now had to be put on hold for a little while.

"To my bride," Dylan said, drawing her close and kissing her cheek. Taylor leaned in closer to him. He touched the small of her back.

"Now what?" Taylor asked.

"We move into our new home; we start our life, just us."

"Right." A lump grew in her throat. She missed college. She missed Claire. She missed painting. And she'd only been away from it all for a week.

Her fingers ran over her phone in her purse, thinking of Claire and what she might be up to right now. It was a random Wednesday afternoon. Claire probably sat in class. Sadness swept over Taylor.

"Sweetheart, are you all right?" Dylan's fingers cupped her cheek, turning her to face him.

"Yes, of course I am."

"I thought we might go out for a nice dinner to celebrate."

"That sounds great."

"You're already married?" Claire asked Taylor through the phone. She sat back against her pillow on her bed, shocked. "I thought perhaps you might wait until—"

"I know," Taylor said. "I'm sorry. Dylan insisted and here we are."

"Well, how exciting," Claire lied. "Now you are Taylor Montgomery, or are you planning on keeping your last name? You could do that, you know, it would be very progressive of you."

Taylor weakly laughed on the other end.

"No. I took his last name. I want to have the same last name as the baby."

"Oh, yes, of course. How are you feeling?"

"Fine."

"Has the baby started kicking?"

"Not yet. From what I've read, it could start any day now."

"Wild." Claire placed her hand on her stomach and tried to imagine what it might feel like to have a baby growing inside of her. Immediately, her hand left her skin. The idea creeped her out. It would be a long while before she was ready for that, if she ever was. "I'm going to send you some baby things."

"You don't have to do that."

"I do. I'm your child's godmother."

"You're not even Catholic. I'm not either," Taylor said with a chuckle. Even though no one could see her, Claire rolled her eyes.

"It's just the principle. I'll be Aunt Claire."

"The only one. I don't have any siblings and as far as I know, Dylan doesn't either."

Claire wanted to question how Taylor knew so little about her husband.

"Well, I will be the favorite, no matter what," she said instead. "Make a wish list, and I'll send you some things from it. I need to get back to my school work. Congratulations on the wedding. I wish you nothing but happiness."

She hung up the phone before Taylor could answer. It was done now. Taylor had married him. She had to pray she had been wrong and her friend would be happy.

As Taylor's stomach grew, Dylan became more and more protective of her, giving her loving foot massages and bringing her home any cravings she had. For a while, she couldn't believe how incredibly lucky everything seemed to be. Dylan didn't even request intimacy as often. The bigger her stomach got, the less he asked.

But he did convince her to drop out of her classes. His reasoning was sound. She'd been terribly ill during her pregnancy, and she needed her rest.

Most of the time, things ran smoothly. He did expect a tidy home and a meal, hot on the table, the moment he came home. Even if she'd been sick all day, he'd comment how he did everything for her and all he asked for was a nice meal and a clean home.

Weekly, packages arrived from Claire with things she'd found for the baby. Once they learned the baby was a boy, Claire enjoyed sending outfits for him. Today when Taylor opened the front door, she found a large package. She checked the tag, making sure it was for her. It was. Then she tried to lift it, but it was too large. That's when she noticed it was a car seat and stroller combo.

Did you send the car seat and stroller? Taylor texted Claire. Immediately, Claire responded.

Yes. That's the one you wanted, right?

I only put it on the registry for the discount.

Well, now you have it. Enjoy! It's from the whole family. Mom and Dad wanted to get you something nice. It's technically from them.

Thank them for me. That was too sweet.

Taylor made a mental note to write Mr. and Mrs. Donahue a thank you letter for such a sweet gift. Since Taylor didn't know anyone nor had any family nearby, there wouldn't be any type of baby shower, and she hadn't been expecting any big gifts.

Since she was unable to lift it, Taylor left it on the front porch for Dylan to bring inside when he got home. She went back to finishing up dinner for Dylan.

The front door opened. She jumped, not expecting him home for another fifteen minutes.

"Dinner is almost ready," she said. She didn't know why Dylan coming home early made her anxious. Looking up, she gave him a small smile.

"Did you buy a stroller?" Dylan asked. Taylor couldn't tell his reaction to it. He stood back, still standing in the doorway.

"No," she squeaked. "Mr. and Mrs. Donahue sent it as a gift for us."

"Donahue? Who are the Donahues?"

"Claire's parents."

"Hum," Dylan said. He flicked his fingers against the package. "Did you tell them we don't need their charity?"

"It's not charity. It's just a gift." The timer went off. Taylor used the distraction to pull out the rolls from the oven. She sat the pan down on the pot holders. "Everything is ready to eat."

"We'll keep the stroller and car seat, but tell your friend to stop sending us stuff. I can provide for you and our son, got it?"

"Of course you can. I think Claire is just trying to be—"

"That's enough, Taylor! I am your husband, do you understand?" Her entire body froze. It took her a moment to find the energy to nod.

"Y-Yes, I'll tell her."

They sat down to dinner.

"I can't wait for our baby to be here. Then we'll be a proper family, Taylor. Just you, me, and our little baby. Us against the world."

Taylor realized she'd never known true love until she saw Zachary's face. While pregnant with him, that love hadn't quite been there. All of the changes she had faced over a short amount of time made it difficult for her to bond with him in the womb. Before he was born, she was afraid they may never bond, but she had been very wrong. She loved him more than life itself.

Things changed soon after Zachary was born. Expectations from Dylan became more difficult to meet. Life was harder.

"Let me see my godson," Claire said on the video call. Taylor turned her phone around, letting her see Zachary. Her two-week-old son slept soundly in his little swing, wrapped up with the blanket Claire had sent him.

"He's so adorable, Taylor. Absolutely precious. I'll be nearby next week. Can we meet up in the middle of the day?" *When Dylan isn't around*, Taylor knew Claire wanted to add.

Claire had come up when Zachary was born, bearing gifts for both her and Zachary. However, outside of that, she rarely got to see her anymore.

"Sure, that sounds great." The thought of going out to lunch with just Zachary and Claire sounded amazing. It would be good for her to get out of the house for a bit.

The sound of the garage opening made Taylor tense. She checked the time on her phone.

"Oh, crap," she said.

"What? What's wrong?"

"It's just…I didn't realize it was already six."

"Does Zachary need to nurse?"

"Um, yes," Taylor said. "I'll call you again later."

"Yes, talk to you soon."

Taylor hung up the phone. She debated lifting Zachary and getting him to nurse, but she wouldn't use her son as an excuse. She had begun prepping dinner. However, the phone call distracted her.

She put on the oven, hoping the chicken would cook quickly. The door shut, and she nearly flew out of her skin.

"I'm exhausted. What's for dinner?" Dylan asked, walking into their small home.

"Chicken and rice," Taylor answered, keeping busy trying to get the rice started. Dylan continued moving toward her, his eyes glancing down at their son briefly. Since they'd brought Zachary home, Taylor could only count on one hand the number of times he'd interacted with the baby.

"Good, I'm starved. Why don't we eat in front of the television? Bring me my plate, please?" He kissed her cheek.

"Okay. It...It'll be about thirty minutes."

Dylan went silent behind her.

"You know I'm home by 6 every day."

"I do," Taylor quietly said.

"Then why isn't dinner prepared?"

"I..." His breath was against her skin; her heart began to race. Dylan hadn't hurt her since she'd fallen pregnant with Zachary, but his past did make her fear what he could do if he got angry enough.

"I provide you with a home. I let you stay home with our son. All I ask for is a clean home and dinner when I get home. Is that too much to ask for?"

"No," Taylor croaked. "I am still adjusting. My body is still healing. Zachary needs to be fed every few hours. I...."

His fist slammed against the countertop, making the drawers shake and Zachary cry out.

"Stop making excuses," Dylan said, slamming his fist once more. Zachary's cries grew. "I don't ask for much."

"I...I..."

As Zachary continued to cry, her breasts ached to feed him and her motherly instinct wanted to run to pick him up. Dylan grabbed her upper arm, forcing her to turn to him. His nose pressed up against hers.

"You're hurting me," she cried, only making Dylan squeeze her arm tighter. "Zachary needs to eat."

"I need to eat!"

He brought her closer to him before dropping her arm, forcing her to fall back and hit her hip against the counter. She let out a whimper. Dylan turned away from her, making his way to the baby. She panicked.

"Don't touch him!"

Dylan didn't listen, lifting the baby into his arms. He kissed the top of his head.

"Goodness, Taylor, do you really think I'd hurt our baby?"

He brought the baby to her, placing him into her arms.

"Go on, feed him."

With hesitancy, Taylor carefully brought her son to her chest. She rubbed his back with calming circles before walking over to the couch to sit and lift her top for Zachary to latch onto her breast. The little boy instantly settled.

"I'm going out," Dylan then said, grabbing his keys from the bowl on the table beside the front door. "I don't know when you can expect me back."

Taylor didn't care to tell him to stay. She watched him exit the house and then a hot burst of tears escaped her eyes.

Once Zachary finished nursing, Taylor placed him back into his swing to begin packing. She grabbed her bag from the closet, stuffing as much as she could to fit inside. Then she began grabbing diapers, blankets, and onesies for her son. The question, though, was where would she go? And how would she get there?

She reached for her phone, knowing she could call Claire. Hadn't Claire made her promise to call if Dylan ever got violent? But she was several hours away, still at school. Taylor didn't have a car, nor did she know how to drive. If she called a taxi, she wouldn't have the money to pay them. Tears stung her eyes.

Finally, she decided she and Zachary would make the fifteen-minute walk to the bus station. From there, she could figure out what to do next. Maybe she would have her father pick her up. Dylan didn't know where he lived. He'd been asking to see the baby.

She placed Zachary into his car seat, adjusted the bags, and walked to the door. Before she reached it, it opened. Dylan walked in, looking her up and down, a sly grin on his face. She hadn't expected him to come back so soon. She spotted his car parked out front. He must have forgotten something.

"And where do you think you are going?"

"My dad's," Taylor said with much conviction.

Dylan just laughed.

"So you think a drunk is a good place to take a baby? Honestly, Taylor, I question your judgment sometimes."

"My dad may be a drunk, but he never hurt me."

"Oh, never?" Dylan countered. "Didn't you have to go to school with dirty clothes and take care of a drunk father when you were only nine? Now, don't be ridiculous. Put the bags down."

"No."

"I won't let you leave with my son."

"He is mine, too."

"Doesn't matter. I'm sure if I called the cops right now, they would insist you left him with me, especially if I told them you were going to a drunk's house. Didn't you say he never cleaned up and lives like a hoarder?"

Taylor didn't respond. Her body began to shake, feeling trapped.

"Now, put the bags down. You're tired and not thinking correctly."

Reluctantly, Taylor did as he asked. As she put Zachary down, she lifted him out of the car seat.

"There," Dylan said with a smile. He walked up to her; she inhaled sharply, prepared for him to hit her, but he kissed her temple. "I love you, Taylor. I had a bad day at work. You'll forgive me, won't you?"

A tear slipped down her cheek, falling on top of Zachary's head. She nodded.

"Why don't you let me make you something to eat? I know Zachary has kept you up all night. Go on, take a seat."

"Alright."

Taylor did as he asked. She sat down, steadying her breathing. Had she overreacted? He hadn't *really* hurt her. And she had been too busy talking to Claire to start dinner on time. She knew how much he liked dinner right at six.

"Here," Dylan said. He placed a sandwich in front of Taylor. "You're tired. You overreacted. It's all right. I forgive you, and you'll forgive me. It's our first fight. All couples fight sometimes."

"Yeah," Taylor whispered. "They do."

CHAPTER 8

With shaky hands, Taylor picked up the glass from the kitchen floor. The sound of it crashing above her head still rang in her ears. If you asked her what exactly had set her husband off this morning, she wouldn't be able to answer you.

Over time, she'd learned his triggers. She learned how to walk on eggshells when he was home, not doing anything that could set him off. Today, though, she didn't know what she'd done to deserve the screaming and thrown glass.

As she placed the final bit of glass into the trash bin, she did one last clean-up of the floor. Zachary had begun taking steps. She didn't want him cutting his bare feet. Thankfully, he'd slept through the yells and screaming.

A grunt came from behind her. She jumped.

"Don't be so jumpy," Dylan said. He walked past her, throwing some trash into the bin.

"I..."

A knock came at the door. Dylan narrowed his eyes.

"It's only six in the morning. Who could be here?"

"I...I don't know," Taylor said.

He walked past her, looking through the peephole of the door. He turned back to her. The muscle in his jaw twitched, and she could see the veins sticking out in his neck.

"You called the police on me?" he accused. Quickly, Taylor shook her head. "I didn't hurt you! Just because we argued?" he continued.

"I didn't...I didn't call anyone!"

Again there was a knock. After glaring at Taylor, Dylan opened it.

"Good morning officers. Isn't it a bit early for a knock on my door?"

"We got a call from a neighbor saying there was yelling," the cop said, glancing inside the house. "We're doing a welfare check."

"I think you have the wrong house. No yelling here," Dylan easily lied.

"Could we speak to your wife? Any children in the home?"

"Um, sure. Taylor, these cops would like to speak with you. And we have a son, who is sleeping. He's only one."

"Could we come inside?"

Dylan moved to the side, letting the two officers in. Taylor stood stuck in the kitchen. Dylan's eyes didn't leave her, making her hands nervously close and open at her sides and her heart race in her chest.

"Was there any screaming this morning, Mrs. Montgomery?"

"Um... I may have yelled, I didn't mean..."

"She got frightened. I remember now." Dylan chuckled, shaking his head.

Carefully, Taylor turned her head to look at him.

"Right. There was a shadow, but it was only a shadow. I thought someone had broken in. I guess I screamed pretty loudly for our neighbors to hear."

"Uh-huh." The cop didn't sound convinced. He leaned in closer to Taylor. "Are you sure it wasn't something else?"

"You know how women can be, officer," Dylan broke in, moving beside Taylor.

Taylor opened her mouth to say something else. If she told them what Dylan had done this morning, would they take her somewhere safe? But he hadn't hit her. He hadn't even touched her. She swallowed hard, not sure the risk was worth it.

"Well, I'm glad it was only a shadow, Mrs. Montgomery. If you're afraid again, give us a call."

"Thank you."

The officers walked out of the house, but Taylor couldn't calm her racing heart. She should have said more. She should have tried. She should have...Before she could think of anything else, Dylan grabbed her arm and turned her to face him.

"Don't even think about it," he said. "I give you a good home. You just know exactly how to hit my buttons, Taylor. If you were to tell those officers exactly what went on this morning, I assure you, they would see you as the crazy one."

Taylor weakly nodded. He dropped her arm.

"Now, I'm going to be late to work. I expect the kitchen all cleaned up when I get home."

By that evening, Dylan was a completely different person. Sometimes, it felt like she lived with Dr. Jekyll and Mr. Hyde. He pleasantly entered the house, happily smelling dinner. He didn't even inspect the kitchen for cleanliness.

"I got a raise," he told her.

"Oh?"

"Yes, and I thought with it, perhaps you could start back with school."

"What?" Taylor asked, not believing it. "Really?"

"Of course, sweetheart. I know how much you want to go back."

"I really do."

"Good. Get the paperwork, and we'll go over it this weekend. I bet we could get you started in the fall."

"Yes, I'd like that."

He bent forward, capturing her lips with his own. His kisses were always greedy and wanting more. She gently pushed him away.

"I'm starved," she said as an excuse, praying it didn't upset him. However, he seemed in good enough spirits that nothing would.

She began eating, her thoughts going to school. She had no idea where she would start, but she didn't care. She missed the classroom. She missed doing things for herself. She drew and painted sometimes. There was a small loft toward the back of the house that was her studio. However, she was always so busy with a small baby and housework that it had gone by the wayside. Now that Zachary was older, she tried to spend his naptimes working in there.

"I thought I might try to sell some of my paintings," Taylor said then.

"Huh," Dylan pondered. "Well, maybe. Aren't they just doodles?"

Her chest ached with hurt. *Doodles?*

"No, I've sold my artwork before."

"I know you can draw, sweetheart. But I just don't want you getting your hopes up, alright? You're not a teenager anymore. People expect more from adults."

"Right," Taylor whispered. She moved her fork around her plate, not feeling as hungry anymore. Sometimes, it was hard for her to remember that she was only twenty-one.

"Come on," Dylan said, lifting her. "Zachary is already in bed. Let's enjoy the quiet."

"But..." Taylor tried to pull away.

"Sweetheart." He tugged her back to him, kissing her eagerly. "I've dreamed about you all day."

Slowly, Taylor nodded. Over time, she'd learned it was easier to just give in.

A flash of energy went through Taylor as she pushed Zachary through the campus. It was a small, local college, but it was enough for her to work on her teaching degree again. After speaking with one of the advisors, she learned her classes from before would transfer over.

Her phone rang.

"Hello?"

"Oh, Taylor! You'll never believe it. I got a job!" Claire's voice enthusiastically rang through the phone.

"Is it the job you wanted? The party organizer job?"

"Yes! So I'll be moving up there in just a few weeks! We'll only be an hour away from one another. You and I will finally be closer. I feel like I haven't seen you in ages."

"I know," Taylor said. "It will be fun to have you nearer."

"It will! We should try to get together every other week for lunch! I'll come to your town to pick you up, unless you have a car now?"

Taylor shook her head, though she forgot Claire couldn't see her face. There had been talks of teaching Taylor how to drive, but Dylan kept putting it off.

"I don't, not yet. But I have my own news. I'm going to go back to school."

"Seriously?"

"Yes."

"That's amazing. I never thought he'd let you go back." It stung to hear those words from her friend. Not because she said them, but because deep down, Taylor had questioned the same thing. Yet, it still made her defensive.

"What's that supposed to mean?"

The line went silent for a moment.

"Nothing," Claire tried to brush off. "It meant nothing. How exciting for you!"

"Claire." Taylor sighed. "He wants me to be happy."

"Good. I should hope that is what he'd want for his wife. Well, what classes will you be taking?"

"I'm not sure yet. I spoke with an advisor today. He's made me a list of classes I will choose from."

"Well, that sounds exciting. My parents and I are meeting up this weekend to look at possible houses for me. Do you think you and Zachary could meet up with us for lunch? I can pick you up."

"I don't know. That's a lot to ask of you."

Taylor brushed her hair behind her ear.

"I don't mind. I want to see you! I haven't seen Zachary in months. He's going to forget his cool Aunt Claire!"

"I'll see if I can come."

"Okay, I hope you can! Mom and Dad would also love to see you!"

Taylor said her goodbyes and hung up the phone. A frown formed. Dylan likely would not allow it. She would have to wait until he was in really good spirits and ask him then.

"Look," Taylor happily said. She handed Dylan the paperwork from the school, adjusting Zachary in her lap. He held a small toy, happily lifting it up and down.

"Oh," Dylan said. He quickly glanced over it. "About that, Taylor."

Her face fell. She should have known this was too good to be true. Tears filled her eyes.

"What?"

"Zachary is still really small. I didn't think about who we would get to watch him while you were in classes. Maybe we wait a little while longer." He shined a smile at her, trying to act as though this was completely out of his control.

"We could hire someone, or ask a neighbor." Taylor needed to find a way to work this out. She needed to go back to school.

"A neighbor? One of those people who called the cops on us? No. And what, do you think I'm made of money, Taylor? How do you think we'll afford someone?" he scoffed.

"I…I don't know." The tears threatened to escape. She blinked hard and took in a deep breath to keep them at bay.

"Exactly. You will get to go back," he promised. "Now is just not a good time."

There was nothing else Taylor could say to that. She deflated, not even wanting to mention Claire coming up this weekend. Dylan made it very clear what he thought about her, and she didn't want to start an argument.

Taylor often spoke to Claire when Dylan was off at work. It was the highlight of her days. Speaking to Claire reminded her of a world outside of Dylan. She missed Claire, so much. She hated how little she got to see her.

Taylor stood, wrapping her arms around her son. He rested his head on her shoulder while rubbing his eyes.

"I should take him to bed."

When she reached his bedroom, Zachary stretched toward his bed. Taylor knew she was fortunate that her son liked to go to bed at night. She placed him into the crib, patting his back a few times to settle him. He drifted into sleep. She stood there, watching him for a while. A few tears slipped down her cheeks, but she reminded herself that Zachary was her world now. Her dreams meant nothing if Zachary wasn't in them.

One day, maybe, she would go back to school. Until then, she had to be the best mom to her son.

Taylor did call the police this time. When they showed up, she rushed to answer the door. Her eyes darted out to see if Dylan was anywhere around, but his car was gone. She moved back, allowing the two male officers inside.

"He...he isn't here," Taylor said, fidgeting with her wedding band.

"Your husband?"

"Yes," she whispered.

"Could you tell me what, exactly, happened?"

Zachary cried out from his bedroom, making Taylor tense. He usually slept all through the night. The commotion must have woken him up.

"Will you give me a minute?" she asked.

They both nodded. Taylor rushed to her son's room. He was standing in his crib, holding out his pacifier. She lifted him. She could tell he was still exhausted as his head fell to her shoulder.

By the time she walked back out into the living room, Dylan was back. He stood, chatting with the officers. All three of them were laughing.

"Oh, sweetheart!" Dylan said. He strode over to her, handing her a candy bar. "I thought you might need some chocolate." He turned his head toward the officers. "You know how women can be during that time of the month."

Again, they laughed.

"That...that's not what this is," Taylor said, trying to find her voice. Her head shook.

"Oh, your husband explained it all. A little spat over dinner happens all the time." The officer shrugged. Taylor looked between all three of the men. Her hand rested on Zachary's back, feeling protective of him and like she could trust none of them.

"He...he..."

"Yes, we know. You both got physical. He said you hit him first?"

Taylor's lower lip began to tremble. It wasn't a lie. She had.

"Yes, but..."

"I think everything appears settled now unless either of you'd like to make a report on the other?"

"Either of us?" Taylor recalled stepping back while Dylan screamed in her face, his hand tightening on her hip. As she tried to get him away, her hand hit his chest. He'd grabbed her wrist before twisting it back behind her and slapping her right across the face. It still stung.

"I think we've got it all settled now," Dylan answered. "Sweetheart, go on and put Zachary back to bed."

She glanced back at the one police officer closer to her one last time, but he was too busy smiling down at Zachary, reaching over to say hello. With a quick step back, Taylor turned. She went into her son's room and sat down on the rocking chair. She started to calm him back to sleep, placing his pacifier back into his mouth.

From Zachary's room, she could hear all three of the men chatting and laughing. The pit of her stomach twisted. She rested her head on top of her son's, needing a moment.

Once the door shut, she continued to rock her son. She needed to remain calm.

Footsteps came down the narrow hallway. The light turned on. Dylan stood there, leaning against the doorframe, his gaze set on her.

"Ah, Billy and Tommy are good guys," he said.

"You...you know them?" she croaked.

"Yeah, they come to the shop sometimes. I give them discounts for being part of the force."

"Oh," Taylor whispered. She stroked her son's back, more in an attempt to settle herself than him.

"You know you're doing a poor job of showing me that you love me," Dylan said. Taylor kept her eyes downcast. "You can't call the cops over some disagreement."

"It wasn't a disagreement," Taylor began, a random flame shooting through her. She looked up. "You screamed at me. You twisted my arm and slapped me!"

"Shh...sweetheart, you'll wake our son."

Taylor took in a shaky breath.

"And I only slapped you because you hit me. Remember?"

She blinked, looking up at the ceiling.

"Now, put him to bed and come to bed yourself."

Taylor ignored him, continuing to rock their son.

"I will leave you," Taylor whispered. Dylan paused, his eyes boring into her.

"No, you won't," he simply said in response before starting to walk back to their bedroom. "And get rid of that pacifier. I've told you he's too old for it."

The next morning when Taylor awoke, she smelled frying bacon. She sat up, rubbing her eyes and checking the time. It was only six, but it was the weekend. Dylan didn't have to go into the shop until 10 on Saturdays.

She got up from the bed, tiptoeing down the hallway to check in on Zachary. She peeked inside to find him still asleep. Then she went into the kitchen. Dylan stood by the stove, munching on a piece of bacon. On his plate, there were some eggs. He turned to face her.

"You're up early," he commented, taking another bite of his bacon.

"I couldn't sleep."

Dylan placed a piece of bacon and some of his eggs onto another plate, handing it to her. She took it.

"Thank you."

"Don't thank me," he said. "Call the police on me again and you'll regret it."

Every bone in her body froze.

"What?"

"You will regret it," Dylan said again, punctuating each word. "That little slap was nothing, Taylor. And don't even think about leaving me."

"I..."

He stepped up then, grasping at her wrist that held onto her plate. She gasped and tried to pull away.

"You have nowhere to go. Nowhere," he growled. "I provide for you, Taylor. I've given you this home. I've allowed you to make our small loft into an art studio. I pay all the bills. You have nothing to your name. And if you leave, I will find you."

Taylor tugged her arm away again. He let go at the same moment, making Taylor stumble back. The plate fell from her grasp, crashing onto the floor. Dylan just stepped over it as Zachary cried out from his room.

"You better clean that up," he said, walking towards the door.

"Where are you going?"

"Don't worry about me, sweetheart. I'll be back by dinner time. I expect a much better meal than last night."

The door slammed behind him. Taylor sunk onto the floor, completely distraught and feeling absolutely hopeless.

CHAPTER 9

For the first time in a long time, Taylor was excited. She'd convinced Dylan to come with her to Claire's parents' house for the 4th of July party they were holding. She'd asked him after a particularly good day when everything aligned just right. The day before, he'd shoved her against the couch, causing a large bruise on her hip. So he'd been extra kind the next day, much like he often was after a big blow-up, trying to soothe things over.

To be honest, she had been afraid of what he might say to her. She worried it would change his mood, but it hadn't. He easily agreed. Taylor already planned a sitter, their neighbor. She was a kind, older woman who sometimes kept Zachary in the middle of the day while she worked on some of her artwork. The lady wasn't fond of Dylan, though. Taylor only knew that because she'd only keep Zachary when Dylan wasn't home. Sometimes, Taylor believed it was the neighbor who called the police from time to time. Though, she'd never be able to ask her.

It would be nice to be somewhere different. Taylor rarely left the house. Once a week, Dylan dropped her and Zachary off at the grocery store with a specific amount of money for her to do the shopping. Other than that, she had to either walk to the bus stop or ask a neighbor for a ride. She and Zachary did walk to the neighborhood park every day when the weather was nice. But they remained in their small bubble. She couldn't even remember the last time Dylan had taken her out on a date. Probably when she was pregnant with their son.

She kept working on her art, hoping that maybe in the future, she could sell some on the side. She had dreams of making enough money to afford her own car. Of course, she'd have to learn how to drive first.

"This is their house?" Dylan asked. He scowled. The excitement left Taylor immediately.

"Yes," she said, unsure. "Why?"

"It's just...big. No wonder your friend doesn't like me. I'm not rich enough for her blood, huh?"

"Don't be silly," Taylor said, trying to play it off. "Claire likes you."

Dylan gave Taylor a look.

"She thinks I am the scum of the earth because we live in a small house."

"No, no she doesn't." Taylor shook her head. "She doesn't care how much money you make. She's never judged me based on where I'm from."

"Right. I'm sure you're just her little project and when you met me, she realized she'd failed."

"Stop it," Taylor said angrily. "That's not who Claire is at all. I thought we were having a nice night out without Zachary. We've driven this far and booked a hotel room. Should we just cancel it all and go back home?"

Dylan sat back, slightly shocked. Over time, she had learned to use her voice. However, she used it sparingly. If Dylan caught wind of her doing it too much, he'd put a stop to it.

"Alright," he said, taking her hand. "Let's have a good night. We don't have to stay too long. We do have that hotel room."

"Yeah." Taylor tried to sound enthusiastic, but thankfully, a knock on her door interrupted their conversation. She turned to see Claire standing by the door, grinning brightly. Taylor opened her door.

"Taylor!" Claire happily screeched. She tugged at Taylor's arms to pull her up and bring her into a tight tug. "I'm so glad you're here!"

"Yes, me too."

The door shut behind her. She turned to see that Dylan was now out of the car. He looked at Claire, his jaw clinched.

"Claire," he tightly greeted.

"Dylan," she tightly greeted in return.

"So," Taylor said, breaking up the tension. "Where's the party?"

"Out back! We have a DJ and an open bar. I know you don't drink, but they have sodas and other nonalcoholic beverages."

"Oh, nice."

"I really didn't think you'd come," Claire said. They stood over in a corner of the backyard where the music wasn't too loud. Dylan disappeared at some point in the night, much to Claire's relief. She preferred her time with Taylor alone.

"Why is that?"

"Taylor," Claire started with a laugh, "I've invited you to many events over the past two years. This is the first one you've shown up to."

"Yeah, well, I have a young son," Taylor said, defending herself. "This is my first time without him overnight."

"And how does it feel to leave him?"

"It's one of the most difficult things I've ever done," Taylor honestly replied. "He's my baby, but I know he's safe where he is. My neighbor watches him sometimes for me during the week."

"Well, that's nice," Claire said. A song came on and they both locked eyes. "Our song!"

Claire sat her drink down on some random table outside. Then they grabbed hands and ran onto the dance floor. Taylor laughed as her friend swung her around, causing her hair to fall out of its bun. Claire brought her fingers up to Taylor's hair, helping to pull the last of it down.

"I've always liked your hair better down. It's so gorgeous!"

"I miss it being red, though," Taylor said.

"The brown looks beautiful, but if you miss it, perhaps we can set a date at the salon soon!" Claire knew it had been a while since Taylor had her hair her preferred color. It seemed she didn't have the time to change it back since having Zachary.

"Perhaps."

They continued to dance, even when their favorite song had ended. For the first time in a long time, Claire saw her old friend, Taylor. She was the Taylor from before Dylan entered her life. She laughed, she danced, and she had a good time.

"This is fun," Taylor said a moment later.

"It really is."

They danced forever, ignoring their aching feet.

After a short break to grab some water, Taylor went back to the dance floor with Claire. She didn't know where Dylan had disappeared to, but she didn't care. They began to dance to the next song.

A harsh tug around her upper arm made her jerk. She turned to find Dylan's eyes on her.

"We need to go," he growled into her ear.

"I..." Taylor stuttered. He dragged her off the dance floor as she tried to protest. "It's not even that late!"

"What's going on?" Claire said, coming up behind them both.

"Stay out of our business," Dylan warned. His grip tightened around Taylor's arm. She whimpered.

"Let go of her," Claire said. She stepped closer to Dylan, warning him.

"Listen, Taylor is my wife. You go back to your little party and leave us be. We need to get going."

"Why?" Taylor asked, despite her arm aching. "Has something happened with Zachary?"

"No."

"Then why are we going? You said..."

"Stop questioning me," he spat into her face.

"Hey! You can't treat her like that."

"She's my wife. I'll treat her however I please."

Dylan tugged Taylor further away from the crowd. Claire quickly followed behind, yelling at him to let Taylor go. Taylor didn't know what to do. In all of their time together, Dylan had never made such a show in front of people. When they rounded the corner, James was there with his arms crossed over his chest. But it wasn't just James; Marcus stood next to him and some other guys Taylor didn't know.

"Let her go," Marcus spoke up first.

Taylor could feel the bruises already forming on her arm. Dylan clenched his fingers tighter for a moment before releasing her. Taylor nearly fell, but Claire grabbed her hips to hold her steady.

"This is bullshit," Dylan said. He looked at everyone around them before walking away. Taylor watched hopelessly, not knowing what to do next.

"Come on," Claire whispered into her ear. She guided her inside the house and had her sit down in the kitchen, handing her a cup of water.

"I don't know what got into him," Taylor said, shaking her head. "That's...that's not like him."

Claire shot her eyes up at Taylor in disbelief.

"Never?"

"Not..." She paused her words, not able to say she meant not in front of others. "He's probably had too much to drink."

"Right." Claire tightened her mouth thoughtfully. "I could send someone to pick up Zachary, or we could go together."

"What?" Taylor asked, shocked.

"Well, it obviously isn't safe for you to go back home with him, Taylor."

"He's just drunk. He wouldn't hurt me, not really."

"Dylan just dragged you harshly across my parents' lawn in front of everybody. Who knows what would have happened if I hadn't been there? Or if Marcus or James hadn't been? He's dangerous, Taylor!"

Taylor didn't respond. A big part of her knew that her friend was right. Her husband did tend to get angry quickly. However, Claire didn't understand Dylan and the stress he was under trying to provide for her and Zachary. She would never have to understand the stressors of wondering if you'd be able to pay your next month's mortgage.

"Um, hi."

Taylor turned at the sound of her husband's voice. He stood right outside the kitchen with a sheepish expression on his face.

"I wanted to apologize for my behavior. I think I..." He trailed off, not being able to find a good enough excuse to cover up for how he'd treated her. Taylor knew he hadn't had the time to make one up. "But we do need to go. If we don't check into our hotel room soon, they'll give our reservation to someone else."

Taylor stood right away, but Claire's hand rested on top of hers. She faced her friend, who gave her a look pleading with her not to go with him.

"I need to go to the restroom first," Taylor said.

"Of course."

Taylor skirted around Dylan and went into the restroom. It had been a lie, she didn't have to go. But she needed a moment to sit and think without both Dylan and Claire looking on at her. What would happen if she stayed here with Claire? If they went to pick up Zachary in the dead of night? Would Dylan even allow her to leave? Did she want to leave him? It wasn't too long ago that she'd threatened to do so.

She turned on the tap, allowing the water to warm up. When it did, she splashed it on her face. That was when she realized she was shaking from the adrenaline from everything. She met her eyes in the mirror.

You have nothing but Dylan and Zachary, a voice within her said. It was right. She'd have to leave with him.

Claire tapped her fingers on the edge of the island. One chair stood between her and Dylan. She kept her eyes away from him, not wanting to look at him.

"I really do love her," Dylan said, breaking the silence. "What happened out there has never happened before. I don't know what came over me."

Claire turned her eyes to him.

"I don't believe you."

Dylan rose his arms in surrender.

"I've never laid a hand on Taylor, ever."

"Liar." Claire took a step closer to him, leaning over. "I have acres and acres of land here."

"Are you threatening me?"

Claire laughed. "No, I'm just letting you know. I don't ever want to hear from Taylor about you putting your hands on her, ever again."

"I'm not just going to stand here and listen to threats from some ....woman," he said with a snarl. "Taylor won't be spending any more time with you."

"Oh, so you do control what she does with her time."

"I don't let her hang out with people like you."

"And what's that supposed to mean?"

They stared one another down. Claire wasn't scared of him, at all. She was about to say something else, but the bathroom door opened. Dylan stepped forward, took Taylor's hand, and didn't even allow her to say goodbye.

When they reached the car and the doors were shut, Dylan grasped Taylor's upper arm. His nose was against her cheek as she let out a squeal.

"Did you enjoy dancing out there like some common whore?"

"Let go of me! You're hurting me!"

"Were you hoping that James would see you, huh?"

"What? No! I was only having fun!"

He dropped her arm then, turning on the car. She briefly wondered if he should even be driving, but he didn't appear as drunk as she'd originally thought.

He drove to the hotel without incident, checking them into the hotel. Then they went inside.

That night was the first time Taylor regretted not listening to Claire and staying at her house; not trying to escape. She woke up sore all over and with her first busted lip. This time, no apologies came for his actions. This time, he told her she better watch herself or it would be worse next time. This time, Taylor knew she may never escape.

CHAPTER 10

"I can come right away," Claire said into her phone. Finally, her friend asked her to come and take her and Zachary away from Dylan. It had been months since the 4th of July party where she witnessed Dylan's abuse firsthand. Since then, she'd hardly spoken to Taylor. Any time she attempted to reach out, she rarely got a response.

"No. Tomorrow. I need time to pack."

"I don't think you should wait, Taylor. That gives him time to try and talk you out of it. I'm coming now," Claire said. She tightened her hold of the phone against her ear. She checked the time on the clock. If she left now, she could be at Taylor's in a little over an hour.

"I haven't packed."

"So? You just need to get out of there. I'll leave right now."

"No," Taylor disagreed. "Please come tomorrow. Can you come tomorrow?"

Claire closed her eyes while taking in a deep breath. She wanted to scream.

"Of course I can come tomorrow, Taylor," Claire said a beat later. "I'll be there first thing in the morning."

"No! Don't! You have to wait until he's left for work. If he finds out, he...he won't let me leave." Claire's heart clenched at the panic in her friend's voice.

"Alright. What time should I come?"

"After lunch. I'll need to grab our things while he naps."

Claire didn't like this. The longer Taylor was there, the more likely it was she would stay. But Claire held her tongue.

"I'll be there at 1."

"Thank you."

Zachary cried out for his mother's attention, so their conversation had to end. Claire sat down at her desk to grab a paper to make notes for one of her co-workers tomorrow. They'd have to figure out the details with their clients.

When Claire looked up, she saw her newest co-worker, Lucas Mack, standing in her doorway. He leaned against the side of the door. He was tall and handsome with round hazel eyes, warm beige skin, and chestnut hair that was long in the front, falling past his eyebrows and nearly covering his eyes. Every time she saw him, she wanted to walk over to him to push his hair off his face or take a pair of scissors to it.

"What do you need?" she asked with a huff. Her mind was still with Taylor. Now that she'd finally gotten the call, Claire was antsy. She needed to get Taylor and Zachary out of that house. She knew she wouldn't settle until she knew they were safe.

Lucas walked into her office, holding out his work phone. He gave her a sheepish look.

"I can't work this."

"You're helpless," Claire said. "How will you survive tomorrow without me?"

"You won't be here tomorrow?" He ran his fingers through his hair, making the hair fall back over his brows. Then he handed her the phone. Claire took it, pressing a few buttons to get him to the home screen. It was the second time this week he'd asked for help with his work phone. She was pretty sure he was just using it as an excuse to come and talk to her.

"No," Claire answered as she gave him back his phone. "Will you be able to survive?" she teased. He grinned.

"I'll try my best."

It was a quarter past noon. There was plenty of time before Dylan would step back through the front door, and yet, Taylor moved as quickly as possible. Her two-year-old son was taking his nap while she packed all the belongings she could fit into two small bags. Within the hour, Claire would be there to pick up her and Zachary.

Just the day before, Taylor found the texts confirming what she already knew: Dylan was cheating on her. It shouldn't have surprised her. There were days when he wouldn't come home until after midnight, and others when he'd never come home. He always used his work as an excuse, but Taylor knew they closed at six. Even a late night wouldn't go that late.

The cheating added just another notch on the belt of how he'd hurt her over the past few years. The moment she'd told Claire she was finally leaving him, she could have sworn she'd heard her friend let out a cry of relief.

Her phone rang. She froze. When she saw it was Claire, she quickly answered.

"I'm stuck in traffic, but I am on my way," Claire said. "It's lunchtime traffic. I should have gone the back way."

"It's fine," Taylor said. "He won't be home until later."

She told her friend goodbye and hung up the phone. She had zero plans after Claire picked her up. What would she do? She had no skills. No job prospects. No one to care for her son.

With a shake of her head, Taylor reminded herself that all she needed to focus on now was leaving. All those things could be settled later. She zipped up her bag and lifted it. Then she walked down the hallway to place it by the door.

As she walked back to finish filling the other bag, she looked up the stairway to her art studio. There were so many pieces in there that she'd likely have to leave behind. Tears began to form behind her eyes, but sacrifices had to be made.

She tiptoed into Zachary's room to grab a package of diapers and a small stack of clothing. Her eyes peeked into the crib to find him still in a deep sleep with his favorite stuffed bear in his arms. She bent over, brushing his wet hair off his cheek.

"We'll be safe," she promised.

She quietly went back out into the main living area. There, standing in the doorway, stood Dylan. His eyes were on the suitcase by the door. Her heart skipped a beat.

"You're leaving me?" he asked.

"Why are you here?" Her voice shook. She widened her stance and lifted her chin. She couldn't let him scare her. Claire would be here soon.

"So, that's what this is? You deflect?" Dylan took a step forward. Instinctively, Taylor brought her arms up to protect herself. "I came home to be here for you because I heard your mother died."

"What?" Taylor dropped her arms before shaking her head. "How would you know that? I...I haven't spoken to my mother since I was a child. This is some attempt to...get me to stay or something. I'm not. I do know you've been cheating on me. I...I'm done. Claire is coming to pick up Zachary and me. You should just go back to work. Let us go."

Dylan's eyes flashed with anger, making Taylor tense in preparation of being hit. However, his face softened, and he reached out to touch her shoulder. She stepped back.

"Your father told me," Dylan said. "He called me at the shop."

"You're lying. Why would he call you?" Dylan and her father had only met a handful of times. She was surprised he even knew Dylan's work number.

"He said he tried to call you and you didn't answer. Call him yourself to see."

"No," Taylor said. "This is a distraction. You've been cheating on me! I'm leaving."

Taylor took a determined step forward right as Dylan grabbed her upper arm.

"Let go of me!"

"You can't just leave this life we've made, Taylor! I love you. I love our son! Do you really want him to grow up like you did?"

That made Taylor whimper. Dylan let go of her arm and turned around. He ran his fingers through his hair before turning back to face her with tears in his eyes.

"I didn't cheat, not how it counts," he said. "I never would do that, sweetheart. I love you. I *want* you. But we'll do therapy. We'll start over. You need to stay with me."

"No, I don't," Taylor said. She could feel her resolve fading.

"You just lost your mother."

"I don't believe you."

"Call your dad."

Taylor nervously curled her hand beside her. Her eyes met his. They were still full of tears.

"Sweetheart, your mother is dead."

She didn't respond. Taylor walked away and upstairs into her sanctuary of the house to call her father.

"Oh, Taylor," Larry Smith gruffly said. "Hello. I'm guessing Dylan told you?"

"It's true?" She let out a breath. Slowly, she sank onto the stool that sat by her easel. The painting before her wasn't finished yet. She'd tried to do a painting of Zachary laughing. She still couldn't quite get his eyes right.

"Yes."

"How?"

"Overdose."

A harsh whimper left her. Dead. Her mother was dead. Though she hadn't had a relationship with her since she'd left her and her father all those years ago, Taylor found it to hurt more than she ever could have expected. She leaned forward, pressing her face into her hand. There never could be a future with her mother in it. Her mother would never meet Zachary. This was the end of her story.

"I'm sorry," Larry said. "The funeral will be next week. I'd love for you three to come down. Do you think you could do that?"

"I...probably." Taylor sniffled. "I think we can."

"Good. I'll send you the information. You'll probably want a hotel."

"Yeah. I...I should go. Love you, Dad."

"Love you too."

Taylor set her phone on the table beside her stool. She leaned forward and silently cried. Fingers ran down her back, and she looked up to find Dylan on one knee in front of her. He gave her a solemn smile.

"I'm so sorry," he murmured. "Why don't I take some time off work, and we go down and visit your dad?"

Taylor rubbed under her eyes.

"We'll start over. You and me. My job is stressful. Perhaps a week away is just what we need."

"How do I know that you'll change?" Taylor asked. "You haven't in the past."

Dylan stood before bringing her up with him. He rubbed his hands up and down her back.

"Because I don't want to lose you, Taylor. I love you."

"Do you *really*? Because it doesn't always feel like it."

His hands moved to her sides and then up to her cheeks. He held her tenderly. She couldn't recall the last time he'd touched her so lovingly.

"I'm sorry. You'll never question me again. We'll start over. We'll let go of all the negative people around us. I'll delete her number, and maybe you shouldn't speak to Claire as often."

"She's...she's my best friend, Dylan."

"I know, but she doesn't like me. Do you really think that's a good idea to keep her as a friend when she's got that bug in your ear? How can we do better?"

"I..."

"You don't have to decide today," Dylan said quickly. "We can discuss all of that later. Let's focus on getting ready to go down to see your dad, all right?"

Taylor kept her gaze on him. Tears flooded her eyes.

"Alright."

There came a knock on the door.

"That's Claire. I should..."

"I'll get it."

"I..." Before Taylor could protest, Dylan was already down the stairs and heading to the front door. She walked to the window to look down where Claire stood. She couldn't hear the conversation very well. It was too muddled, but she could see the way Claire looked around him in distress. Suddenly, she looked up and saw Taylor standing at the window. Taylor lifted her hand, giving a wave that said please forgive me. Claire stepped back, her eyes not leaving Taylor.

What is going on? Claire mouthed.

"I'm sorry," Taylor just said back before closing the curtains and turning away.

Claire remained outside Taylor's house for a while. Her eyes kept staring at the window in hopes of seeing her friend's face peek back through the curtains. They never did. Dylan had been smug when he opened the door, telling Claire to leave and that Taylor didn't want to see her anymore.

"Are you her friend?" Claire turned to find an older woman standing at her front door.

"Hm?"

"Are you Taylor's friend?"

"Yes, I'm her friend, Claire."

"I thought you might be. When I saw you pull up, I thought maybe she was finally leaving him." The woman's eyes peered back at the house before bringing them back to Claire. "I hear so many screams in that house. I've tried calling the cops."

"You have?"

"All the time. They stopped coming, though. I think Dylan knows some of them. It's a shame. Taylor and that little boy deserve much better." The woman held onto her robe to keep it closed in the middle.

"They do."

Claire dug inside her purse and pulled out her business card. She walked over to the neighbor's house, holding it outstretched.

"Here's my number. Will you please call me at any time you think Taylor needs help?"

"Mary," she said. The older lady took the card, reading over it. "Nice to meet you, Claire."

"Nice to meet you, too."

Taylor received texts and calls from Claire all night and all the next day. Eventually, Taylor texted her back telling her she'd made a mistake and that she and Dylan were trying over again.

I don't understand. Why won't you leave him, Taylor? Why?

I can't.

Taylor put her phone on silent after that and muted Claire's texts. She didn't tell Dylan about the texts, but she was sure he knew. He kept looking over her shoulder whenever she was on her phone.

"It's why you need to take a break from speaking with her," he said gently. He took it and put it in the middle console. "She doesn't understand us, Taylor."

They were driving down to see Taylor's dad and go to the funeral. She hadn't been to her hometown in a while. A large part of her never wanted to return. She much preferred her dad coming up to visit her, though that was rare. He didn't like leaving his little, safe oasis. Everyone knew him in their small town. They made excuses for his drinking. No one held high expectations for him.

"I hope the hotel we booked is nice," Dylan said. As promised, he'd been gentle and kind since she agreed to stay. Taylor allowed herself to believe he might actually change this time.

"It's a new one, so it should be."

"Good."

"But I do worry about how Zachary will sleep."

"Ah, my boy is a good kid. He'll sleep just fine."

"I hope so."

Her father reeked of alcohol when they met him the next day for lunch. Taylor pulled Zachary away from him and held him in her lap. He seemed more drunk than usual. While he had the same pale white skin as Taylor, it had been weathered overtime from lack of sunscreen while working outside. As much as she begged him to see a dermatologist, he never would go.

Despite the fact her mother had disappeared years ago, she had always been her father's first and only love.

"I miss her so much," her father murmured, looking over at Zachary with a crooked grin. "He looks so much like her."

"Does he?" Taylor assessed Zachary in her arms. To her, Zachary looked like his own little person. Sometimes she might see flashes of her or Dylan in him, but not all the time. Taylor loved that too; she loved that he was just Zachary and not the mirror of either of them.

"We should probably go soon," Dylan whispered in her ear before sitting back in his chair. Throughout their entire lunch, Dylan had said maybe one or two words to her father. He got up a moment later and grabbed his phone, stepping away and saying he had a work call.

"So, um, what are the plans for the funeral?" Taylor asked. Her dad's eyes moved past her to follow Dylan. He smiled.

"I'm just so happy to see you with your own family, Taylor. So happy."

Taylor sighed, but nodded. "Yeah, me too."

That night had been long. Zachary took a long time to settle being in a new place. Unlike he'd promised, Dylan didn't offer any help. He just remained on the bed as Taylor walked Zachary back and forth until he finally fell asleep.

"We have to go back," Dylan said later that night.

"What?"

"I have to get back to work. The boss is angry."

"But the funeral isn't for another couple of days."

"I know. You could stay. I guess I could come back and pick you up," Dylan said. "But we need the money."

Taylor blinked to try to keep the tears from coming. Dylan cupped her cheek, rubbing her skin with his thumb.

"Your father is drinking so much, sweetheart. I can tell you don't like Zachary being around him when he's like that. Maybe we could come back over the holidays?"

"I guess."

Dylan smiled. He leaned forward and kissed her.

"I love you."

"I love you," Taylor said. Zachary cried out in his sleep. She sat up, but he was still asleep. He'd accepted a small stuffed toy they found from the gas station for now.

"Things will be better, Taylor," he promised. "You and I will be stronger than ever."

CHAPTER 11

"Good morning," Lucas said gruffly in Claire's ear. Claire moaned, never being much of a morning person. He brought his arms around her, kissing her shoulder blade.

"Good morning." Claire grinned and turned to face Lucas. She nuzzled her nose against Lucas's cheek before touching his chin with her fingertips. He struggled to grow any hair on his face, but she didn't mind.

The two of them had been dating for several months now. Claire couldn't quite pinpoint when they'd gone from co-workers to friends to dating. Lucas swore their first date was when they went to the Braves' game and had their first kiss. If that's what he thought, then she'd go with it. He was her first official boyfriend. Something she hadn't planned on having for a few more years, but then it just happened.

"No work for me today until after lunch, but don't you have to go in this morning?"

"I do, but not for another couple of hours. We could go out for brunch."

"We could," she agreed. Claire gave him a quick kiss before sliding out of his arms and sitting up. She reached for her phone, checking the screen to see if she had any new messages. Every morning she checked to see if she'd heard anything from Taylor. It had been nearly a year since she'd spoken to her last, and yet, she kept hoping to see any form of communication from her.

For Taylor's birthday, Claire sent a text and an email, too afraid to send anything physical that Dylan could intercept. No response. Nothing came on her own birthday, either. Dylan successfully put a bridge between the two of them.

"Yes," she said, speaking up again. She placed her phone back onto the bedside table, deciding this wouldn't ruin her day. "Let's go for brunch."

There was a kick against her side. Taylor sat back in the rocking chair, pressing her palm against the spot where her baby kicked. Her pregnancy was much different this time than it had been with Zachary. She was less sick and was able to enjoy it more. Though life in this house wasn't perfect, Zachary and this new baby gave her hope for the future. They would be her happiness.

In the past year, things had been better. Dylan still got angry on occasion, but he hadn't laid another finger on her. Only sometimes had she questioned her choice to stay.

But she did miss Claire. She thought of her often, nearly daily, wondering about her life and what she was up to. It was much harder not having her in her life. She needed her best friend. She hoped that maybe after the new baby was born, Dylan would be in a better headspace and let her contact her again.

"Sweetheart?"

Taylor sat up in her rocking chair.

"I'm up here." She hadn't expected him home so early this afternoon, but it didn't surprise her anymore. He'd come home at unexpected hours now, almost as though he was checking in on her. Though it had nearly been a year since she'd tried to leave, he always wanted to make sure she wouldn't leave him again. He played it off as being concerned about her, and proving to her that he was no longer seeing that other woman.

"Why are you up here?" he asked. His eyes scanned the nearly empty room. He'd convinced her to give up her painting, said she needed to focus on the children.

"I like it up here," she said.

His face darkened before sweeping his eyes over the room again, as though he was searching for something hidden. She stood, placing her hand protectively over her belly. He didn't like her being up here, alone. He thought it played into her old hobby of which he no longer approved. He said she needed to get her head out of the clouds, focus on them as a family.

"I don't like you being up here."

"It's just quiet in this loft. I've been feeling tired. Why are you upset? Did something happen at work?" Over time, she'd learned these outbursts could be worse if he had a bad day at work or something similar. When that happened, she'd unluckily get the brunt of his anger.

"No, and why would you ask me such a thing?"

"I...I don't know. I'm just tired," she tried to defuse the situation. She walked past him, hoping to get away before his anger could grow. He grasped her wrist, bringing her around so that she stood with her back to the stairs. She looked back and then took a big step forward. He tightened his grip.

"You're hurting me," she said. "Let me go."

"Why were you up here?" he asked again.

"It's quiet. Zachary is taking a nap." Her voice weakened. She hadn't seen him this angry in months. "I just...I was thinking of how we'd decorate it into a playroom for the children."

"Liar," he growled. "You were speaking with your boyfriend, weren't you?"

"Boyfriend? I don't have a boyfriend."

"You come up here so you can speak with James. Don't lie to me, Taylor."

"I...I don't even know his number." She tried to read her husband's eyes. She realized he was drunk. "Why were you drinking at work?"

"Don't turn this on me, Taylor! I know you talk to him. I know you're in love with him." Despite his anger, he let go of her.

"I'm not! I wasn't. My phone isn't even..."

Before she had a chance to say another word, he shoved her belly. Her hands flew to her stomach, but she lost her balance, not realizing how close she had been to the edge of the stairs. She tried to reach out to grasp at the walls, or anything to keep her steady. Dylan just watched, anger apparent on his face as her body fell. Taylor's arms attempted to protect herself and the baby, but with each step she went down, it came harder and harder. Her cheek hit something, she cried out. Something popped in her arm. Then her stomach hit the edge of a stair. Finally, she was at the bottom.

Above her, she heard footsteps rushing down.

"Taylor! Sweetheart! Taylor!" Dylan bent down at her side, trying to help her up.

"Don't touch me!" Taylor yelled back at him. She attempted to pull herself up, but her whole body ached and harsh cramps kept coming over her belly. "The baby!"

"Shh, the baby will be alright. You just fell. It was an accident!" Again, Dylan tried to help her stand. Taylor clutched her belly, then wetness pooled between her legs. "Oh my god!"

Blood seeped into the carpet.

"I'll call an ambulance. It's alright. It's going to be alright."

As Claire organized some information for an upcoming wedding reception, her phone started to ring. She jumped, surprised by the sound.

"Hello?"

"Um, Claire?"

"Yes, this is her. May I ask who I'm speaking to?"

"Mary. We met about a year ago. I'm Taylor's neighbor."

Claire's heart sunk.

"Is—is she alright? What's happened?"

"The ambulance came and left. I saw Taylor being taken away."

"What? How? What happened?" A million thoughts ran through Claire's mind. Had he done it? Had Dylan killed her? Had he gone far enough to hurt her so badly that she needed the ambulance?

"I don't know," Mary said on the other end of the phone. "I just saw Dylan holding Zachary in the doorway as the ambulance drove away."

"Did you hear screaming? What—"

"No, no screaming. I'm just worried about her and the baby."

Tingles ran up Claire's spine.

"Baby? Taylor's pregnant?"

"Oh yes, pretty far along too by now."

Tears formulated on the edge of Claire's eyelashes. She had no idea Taylor was having another baby.

"I..." Claire blinked away the tears. "Do you know what hospital they took her to?"

"Probably Freemont. It's the closest one."

"Thank you."

Claire grabbed her keys, didn't even tell anyone she was leaving work, and headed straight to the hospital.

Mia, her baby, was born sleeping. Taylor held the lifeless baby in her arms, unable to feel anything other than the deep pain within her chest. Her hand cradled her baby's, kissing the fingertips.

Silent tears fell down her cheeks as she murmured sweet nothings to the baby within her arms. Mia had wisps of curls on top of her head, just like Zachary did when he was born. She wondered if they, too, would have fallen out to be replaced with darker straight hair as she got older.

"I'm sorry," she murmured.

Dylan showed up about an hour after she'd arrived at the hospital. He came in disheveled and nearly manic. Thankfully, security stepped in and escorted him out of her room.

"Mrs. Montgomery?"

Taylor glanced up; the nurse stood by the door. She brought Mia closer to her chest, running the back of her finger over the curve of her jaw. She closed her eyes, her head pounding from the way she hit her head against the stair and then the birth right after.

"I want the police called," she said. "He pushed me down the stairs. It's his fault that our daughter is dead."

More tears came. This time she couldn't control them. Sobs escaped, and she clutched her daughter tighter to her chest. Gone. Her daughter was gone.

The nurse rushed forward, kindly sitting behind her and touching Taylor's back.

"The police have already been contacted. Whenever you are ready to give a statement, they can come into the room. Is there someone I can call for you to have by your side?"

She felt alone in this moment. Dylan had made sure to separate her from the world around her, so that she would be helpless without him.

"Claire," she said finally. "My friend, Claire."

Soon after Claire arrived at the hospital, she received a call from a nurse telling her Taylor requested her to come to be with her. Claire had already been at the front desk, asking to be sent to her room. Apparently, because of the seriousness of Taylor's visit, they weren't allowing just any visitors. The nurse told her which floor to come to and where to check in. As soon as she did, she was led to Taylor's room. Taylor lay turned away from her.

"Taylor?" Claire whispered. She took a tentative step forward. "Oh, Taylor." She sat down on the hospital bed, carefully touching Taylor's arm. "I'm here now."

"I never should have stayed," Taylor cried. She slowly turned to face Claire. Claire gasped in shock. The right side of Taylor's face was covered in a large black and blue bruise with a cut along her cheek.

Claire calmed herself before saying every horrid thought about Dylan out loud. Right now was not the time for that. Right now, she had to be here for her friend.

"It's not easy to leave. If it were, women would leave right away," Claire said calmly. "But you are safe now."

"I lost my little girl."

"Oh, Taylor." Claire blinked back the tears. She ran her fingers gently through Taylor's hair. "I'm so sorry."

Dylan was arrested, but only kept in custody for a few days. The days were long enough for Taylor to pack up her bags, get Zachary from the neighbor, and move into the upstairs guest room at Claire's house.

He wasn't charged with the murder of their daughter, only slapped with a small fine and a small charge. The only positive outcome was that he was given a restraining order against her.

PART TWO

CHAPTER 12

A squeal and then shushing were the two sounds that woke Claire. She rolled to her back and let out a loud yawn, checking the clock beside her bed. It was only seven in the morning. Claire rubbed her fingers against her temple. Today was Saturday. Sometimes she missed the late Friday nights with her friends and sleeping in on the weekends.

Bang! Bang!

Claire jerked up to the sound of fists hitting her door. She groaned.

"Shh, no," Taylor whispered in the hallway. Feet began to walk away.

Claire stood and grabbed her robe next to her bed. She wrapped it around herself before stepping out into the hallway.

"Aunt Cware!" Little arms wrapped around her legs. Claire placed her hand on the little boy's head, mussing his hair.

"I'm sorry," Taylor said. She walked up, taking Zachary's arm gently to tug him away from Claire's leg. "He's full of energy this morning."

The pale skin of Taylor's cheek still held purple and green from the healing bruise. Her right arm was held by a sling, which made it more difficult for her to manage Zachary on her own. Not to mention all of the other pains Taylor still dealt with since that bastard pushed her down the stairs.

"It's not a problem." She bent down and gave her godson a smile. "You just wanted to play, didn't you?"

Zachary nodded.

"Then let's play." She reached out her hand for Zachary to take it, trying not to make a face when his sticky fingers entangled with hers. "You, go take a nap."

"I don't need to sleep," Taylor said, though the dark circles beneath her eyes said differently.

"You do. Go on, now. Zachary and I will draw or play with toys."

"Oh, alright," Taylor said with a yawn. She patted the top of her son's head, telling him to behave before disappearing down the hallway to go back to her room.

Claire took her godson downstairs to the living room, where her television was already blaring with one of the obnoxious television shows. She grabbed the remote to turn it down. Over the past few weeks, her life had changed dramatically. No more weekends with Lucas or her friends. She needed to be here to help Taylor.

In her twenties, Claire was nowhere ready to have children. She didn't feel she had a maternal bone in her body. She could, however, manage an hour here or there with Zachary to give Taylor time to heal.

"Wook, my teddy!" Zachary lifted up his small teddy bear.

"Yes, I see," Claire said with a smile. "Have you eaten?" Zachary shook his head, though the syrup on his cheek gave away that he had. "Why don't I get us some cereal?"

"Yes!"

Much like Claire, Zachary had a love for sweets. He jumped up from the couch and followed Claire into the kitchen. She opened her large pantry, picking up Zachary to have a good look at all the cereals she had. His pudgy finger pointed to the colorful one.

"Perfect. I'll have that one, too." Claire placed Zachary back down on the floor before pulling out the cereal box. She grabbed two bowls and filled them up to the rim, making them each their own. "Now sit down."

The two sat together at the table. Zachary kept smiling up at her between each spoonful, melting her heart. Even though she'd worried he wouldn't remember her, he had happily become her best friend.

"More sugar?" Taylor stood in the doorway.

"You're supposed to be sleeping," Claire reminded her friend.

"Couldn't sleep." Taylor stepped inside the kitchen, pressing a kiss at the top of Zachary's head. She then turned and walked to the sink, rinsing the dishes in there to place into the dishwasher.

"I can handle that. You can't overdo it." Claire got up and went over to Taylor, taking the plate. That's when Claire saw Taylor crying. Her dark locks covered her face, but from this angle, Claire could see the fresh tears sliding down her friend's face. She reached up, brushing a tear away.

"I'm fine," Taylor bristled. She shook her head, stepping away from the sink.

"All of this is tough. Why don't you try to at least rest? You don't have to sleep, but you do need to rest. You've been through a lot."

Taylor's eyes moved over toward Zachary, who was innocent to all that was happening around him.

"He called me last night," Taylor said.

"What?" Claire breathed. "I thought...you didn't answer did you?"

Taylor shook her head. "No, but then he texted me. He says he wants to see Zachary."

"Well, I hope you told him no."

"It's not that simple." Taylor brought her left hand up to massage against her right shoulder, her face wincing at the feeling.

"Sure it is. You say no."

"He is his father," Taylor responded.

"So?"

"He has rights."

Claire growled.

"Claire, I have to allow Dylan to see his son."

"You have a restraining order against him," Claire disagreed, her voice rising. She'd read somewhere that it took women up to seven times before they would leave their abusive partner. As far as Claire knew, this was only Taylor's second time trying to escape. She feared Taylor was thinking of going back.

"I..." Taylor sighed. "He said in the text it didn't include Zachary and if I kept him from him, he'd use that against me in the custody case."

"He's full of shit."

"Oooooo!" Zachary called out.

"Shit, sorry," Claire said, biting her lip and not realizing she'd cussed again until it was too late. "He won't get full custody of Zachary, Taylor. It's not going to happen. He pushed you down the stairs. He caused you to—"

Taylor put up her hand, not wanting to hear any more of it. Fresh tears had begun to fall down her cheeks.

"I know," she murmured. "Maybe you're right. Maybe I should try to rest again."

"You should." Claire cocked her head to the side. "You didn't text him back, did you?"

"No, I didn't."

"Good."

That evening, after Taylor had read Zachary his bedtime book, she sat on the couch, curled up and watching a romantic comedy. Claire joined her, adding some water to Taylor's glass before sitting down.

"Has he tried to contact you again?"

"No," Taylor answered. "Well, at least, I don't think so. My phone died earlier, and I've yet to plug it in. I don't know if I want to know if he replied."

"Is it because you're worried you'll go back to him if he asks you to?" Claire never shied away from the tough questions.

"No. I worry that he'll take Zachary from me," Taylor said. "I'm not going back to him, Claire. I know I did once before, but that was different...I didn't..." Taylor tightened her fingers around the glass. "I just want Zachary to be safe. I've read up on custody cases in domestic abuse situations, and they still get custody as long as there is no history of abuse towards the children."

"But..." Claire stammered. "We'll hire you the best lawyer, or...or my parents will be your lawyers." Claire sat up, drawing closer to her. "We won't let him have Zachary."

"You can't know that, Claire." Taylor's chin tremored. She pressed against her neck, turning her head away from Claire. A whimper left her before her body began to shake.

"I hate that he is Zachary's father. I hate that this is who I gave him as a father." Taylor's voice was barely above a whisper. "I can't protect him. I thought I was doing what was best for him by being with Dylan, but I now after Mia I know..." Taylor hiccupped.

Claire gently touched Taylor's shoulder, brushing some of her hair off her wet face. One stubborn strand wouldn't leave her cheek so

Claire gave up on it. She brought her arm carefully over her friend's shoulder and drew her closer.

"That boy adores you," Claire said, running her fingers through her friend's tangled hair. As it snagged, Claire withdrew her fingers, not wanting to cause Taylor any extra pain. "I know that you will do everything in your power to protect him, and you know that I will too, don't you?" Taylor nodded. "The judge will see, Taylor. They'll see that Dylan shouldn't be trusted to be around your son."

"I hope that's true."

"It is."

Ring! Ring! Ring!

Claire looked at her phone to see her boyfriend, Lucas, calling. She answered it, vaguely aware that she should be asleep because Zachary would be pounding on her door again early in the morning.

"Hi," she said into the phone, running her finger along the pattern of her duvet. Her grandmother had given it to her for Christmas, and she'd fallen in love with the texture and how it felt against her fingers.

"Hello, I haven't heard from you all day."

"Sorry, Taylor needed to rest, and so I had to help entertain Zachary."

"Right."

Claire tried to read what Lucas thought about this. The two of them had been dating for nearly nine months now. Like her, he had zero plans of having a family any time soon. They were enjoying the fun perks of being childless and still in the early stages of the relationship. When Claire took Taylor and her son in, it changed the dynamics of what they were. While Lucas said he was supportive of it, Claire did wonder.

"Should we do lunch tomorrow? I haven't seen you since last Sunday."

"I don't know. I really prefer not leaving Taylor here alone. What if he shows up?"

Lucas huffed on the other end.

"Don't you have to leave her when you go to work? What's a couple of hours?"

"Yes, I guess."

"And what exactly could you do if he did show up, Claire? Perhaps this is a bad idea, you letting them stay there. If he's that dangerous, he could hurt you, too."

"Hurt me?" Claire laughed. "Dylan wouldn't dare."

"He beats up women, Claire. Don't act like you're untouchable." Lucas's words were full of impatience.

"I'm not, but Dylan isn't stupid enough to come onto my property."

Lucas let out a long sigh, but he decided to change the subject.

"What if I came over tomorrow, finally met this old friend of yours and her little boy? See who has been taking all your time." Though he was trying to sound lighthearted, Claire noted the hint of resentment in his voice.

"Maybe not tomorrow," Claire disagreed with a shake of her head. "Taylor is still healing, but soon."

"Fine. I guess I'll see you next week, then?"

"Yes, I know everything has changed a lot lately, but I do love you."

"I love you." Lucas voice had softened. "You're a good friend, love. But do be careful. If you need me to come over, please let me know."

"I can handle it myself, but if anything happens, I promise I'll call you. Now, I should get to bed."

"It's just eleven," Lucas said, disappointed.

"And Zachary gets up with the sun. While Taylor is healing from her fall, I need to help her with him. But we'll talk tomorrow, all right?"

"Alright. Sleep well. Text me around lunchtime. Goodnight. Love you."

"Love you, too."

Claire laid back into her bed and quickly typed a note to Lucas.

Thank you for being patient with me, love. When this is all over, I promise I'll make this up to you.

Three dots came up to show that he was typing back. She waited to see his response.

No make-up needed. Keep doing what you need to do.

"What are you two up to?" Claire asked, stepping out onto her screened in back porch. Taylor sat in the corner, sipping on a tea, while watching Zachary run around the small area.

"Trying to stay quiet so you can sleep," Taylor said.

"Oh, don't worry about that."

"Well, it's nice outside, so it's fine."

Zachary ran past Claire with a toy airplane. He was making airplane sounds, jetting across the floor. Claire stepped back to give him more room.

"Have you eaten?"

"Not yet. Zachary had some muffins. I'm not hungry."

Claire went to sit down next to her friend.

"Well, you need to eat. I know you don't feel like it, but you need to."

"I don't need you telling me what to do, Claire," Taylor said, her cheeks flushing.

Claire fixed her gaze on Taylor, trying not to get upset. She knew Taylor needed time to find herself again.

"What if we got out of the house today? You haven't left since you've gotten here."

"No, that's alright. I'd rather stay here." Taylor took another sip of her tea. She brushed the back of her fingers over the bruising on her cheek.

"I can put some makeup right over that. No one will notice."

"I don't want to go out. I'm just...I'm not ready. I'm still sore all over." Taylor subconsciously covered her stomach, making Claire's heart drop.

"Alright. Maybe in a few days."

"Maybe," Taylor agreed.

"It's tough," Claire said, squeezing Taylor's knee. "But you are a survivor. You can't just give up."

"I...I'm not giving up." Taylor pinched the bridge of her nose and closed her eyes. "I'm just...tired. I need more time."

"I understand. Do you want to do anything special today? Order in? Watch a movie?"

"No. I just want..." Taylor pressed the heels of her hands into her face. "I don't know what I want."

"That's fine. You don't have to know," Claire murmured. "We'll just sit out here for a little while."

Claire could bake. It had always been one of her skills. As a young child, she'd spent a lot of her days at the counter with her Nana, baking. Even though Claire was the youngest of all of the grandchildren, her Nana made sure to give her special attention. Perhaps that's why she did, so Claire didn't feel forgotten.

As the smell of cinnamon rolls filled the air, Claire was taken back to when she was young and with her Nana. Closing her eyes, she could swear she could smell the light scent of the baby powder that her Nana always smelled of.

"Wow, this smells so good," Taylor said, entering the kitchen. Claire paused what she was doing to turn and face her friend.

"I wanted to make a nice brunch for us all. Are you sure you're not upset about Lucas coming over? I could always postpone it." After speaking with Taylor, they decided Lucas would come over for just breakfast so Taylor could meet him. It had been Taylor's idea. She was excited to meet the guy who had won Claire over.

Taylor shook her head. She'd pulled her dark locks into a low, side ponytail. Light makeup covered her face, nearly covering up the last bit of evidence of what had happened that fateful day.

"I can't hide away forever," Taylor said. She leaned forward. "I want to meet him. He's your boyfriend."

"Yes. He's a good guy. Smart. Hard worker." Claire grabbed the powdered sugar from the pantry to begin the icing for the rolls.

"And what does he do again?" Taylor picked at the edge of her nail with her thumb. Claire had noticed the redness from Taylor doing that often. It was a newer nervous habit of hers.

"He works with me as an event coordinator at The Ranch."

"Right," she said uneasily.

"Are you sure you don't want me to cancel?"

"I'm sure," Taylor said.

"Where is Zachary?"

"Watching the television. I really should try to take him to the park or something soon. He's getting stir-crazy."

Claire mixed her ingredients in the bowl. She kept her back to Taylor as she spoke.

"Just...don't go without me," she said carefully.

"Claire, I can take care of myself."

"If he sees you alone, he could do something to you."

Taylor gave a humorless chuckle.

"I can't just stay here, in your house, for the rest of my life. Also, he doesn't even know where you live."

"Why couldn't you live here forever?" Claire turned, smiling. "Well, I wish you could anyway. Back like the old days when we were room-mates."

"You need to live your life without a three-year-old and me in the way. I was thinking I'd find a job and a place to stay. There are shelters and you could..."

"You're not going to stay in a shelter, Taylor. You will stay here with me. Shelters are fine for people with no place to go, but you do. Don't take a bed from someone who needs it. As long as you stay here, you're safe. He won't dare step into my home."

Taylor gave a weak nod.

"I haven't thanked you for coming when I needed you and letting me stay here."

"No thanks needed. I know you would have done the same for me," Claire just said in return. "The best way you can thank me is by staying here, safe. Don't answer his calls. Do everything through the lawyers and the court."

Taylor let out a shaky breath before leaving Claire alone in the kitchen to finish preparing brunch. In the quiet, Claire tried not to think about what might happen if Dylan did come across Taylor out on the street. She didn't trust him, not at all.

"Hi."

"Hi," Lucas replied. He brought his arms around Claire's back before bringing his lips to hers. Claire melted against him, loving the taste of chocolate that always seemed to linger. His thumb brushed along her cheek as he deepened their kiss.

"That was a lovely hello," Claire said.

She took his hand, pulling him into her modest home. Thanks to her parents, she had been able to afford her first home nearly right out of college. Her parents gave every one of their children a down deposit for their first home and helped with a percentage of a mortgage.

When they stepped inside the foyer, Zachary ran toward Claire. He looked Lucas up and down before reaching out his hand.

"Hello!" he greeted. Claire watched as Lucas grinned and bent down to Zachary's level, reaching his own hand out to take Zachary's and shake it.

"Firm handshake, very nice."

Zachary squished up his nose.

"Zachary, this is my friend, Lucas."

"Hey," Zachary said. "That's Mommy!" Zachary pointed to where his mother was standing a bit further away. Taylor took a small step forward, forcing an awkward smile.

"Hi, um, nice to meet you."

"And nice to meet you." Lucas again reached out his hand, but Taylor didn't give hers for him to shake. Claire touched his lower back to remind him that while Taylor's arm was no longer in its sling it was still sore. Lucas quickly dropped his arm by his side. "You are the infamous Taylor. The one that got this one to finish college."

"I wouldn't say that," Taylor chuckled. Claire smiled, bringing her arm around Lucas's.

"Why don't we go and sit down to eat?" Claire suggested.

"Yes, Claire made my favorite. I can't wait for cinnamon rolls. Do you like cinnamon rolls, Zachary?'

"Yes!"

They went into the kitchen where Claire had already set up the kitchen table with plates, silverware, napkins, and food. With the cinnamon rolls, she prepared some bacon and fruit.

"So, Taylor, what do you do for fun?" Lucas innocently asked. Taylor placed her napkin in her lap, shaking her head.

"I don't...I don't really have any hobbies. You?"

"I like to ride."

"Like horses?"

"Oh yes, when I was younger I competed in competitions."

"He has so many first-place ribbons and trophies," Claire gushed. She searched for Lucas's thigh under the table.

"That sounds fun."

"It is. Have you ever ridden?"

"No," Taylor said. She bit into her cinnamon roll after helping Zachary with his. "But I'd like to."

"Claire will have to bring you and Zachary over to the barn sometime. I can teach you."

"Sure, that sounds fun."

"Thank you for coming by," Claire said, hugging him. His dark hair had no strand out of place since she'd convinced him to cut it. She reached out to stroke her fingers through it.

"Your friend is nice. Quiet. And Zachary is cute."

"He is," Claire agreed.

"But," Lucas began, "do you really think here is the best place for them? Your friend needs real help. Maybe a shelter for domestic..."

"You want me to kick them out?" Claire pulled away from him, chest heaving.

"No, not kick them out...just...help her. Get her in a position where she can take care of herself and her son. I doubt she wants to be here with you taking care of her."

"That's not what this is. She doesn't need me taking care of her. She needs a safe place to stay. This is a safe place. I am her friend. Eventually, she will be ready to move forward, but not until we know that Dylan is locked up somewhere, unable to get to her."

"So, instead, you keep her here, making you a target as well."

"I told you, Dylan wouldn't come here. He knows I'm not scared of him. It's why he made sure he didn't let us talk for nearly a year. I almost had her out of there. But he doesn't even know where I live."

"He could figure it out," Lucas said.

"Maybe," Claire agreed, biting down on the inside of her cheek.

"I don't like it. I worry, is all," Lucas said softly. He grabbed her hand and brought it up to his chest.

"Well, stop it. I will be fine," Claire said. "He won't hurt me. And I will not be sending Taylor out of this house until I know she'll be somewhere safe."

"Okay, fine." Lucas brought up his hands in mock surrender. "I won't mention it again."

"Good."

Lucas gave Claire's shoulders a loving rub, bringing Claire closer to him to kiss her.

"Let's not argue anymore."

"Yes, let's not."

CHAPTER 13

As Claire walked out to the back porch of her home, she found her friend sitting curled up on the small swing with a pad and pencil. Taylor kept so focused on what she was drawing that she didn't turn as Claire approached her. Taylor colored in with her pencil, with her bottom lip between her teeth and a long stray hair covering her cheek.

"Hey," Claire quietly said. Taylor's eyes didn't leave her drawing.

"Hey."

"Where's Zachary?"

"Taking a nap," Taylor answered. She tucked her pencil behind her ear.

"May I see what you're drawing? I don't remember the last time I saw you draw," Claire said.

"Sure."

Taking the pad, Claire saw the drawing of two hands. A baby hand and an adult hand. The adult's hand was curled protectively around the baby hand. Claire stared at the photo with a heavy heart.

"Are you thinking of painting this later? It would make a beautiful painting."

"No. I don't paint anymore. I just draw, sometimes," she murmured with a shrug of her shoulders.

"May I look at the others?"

"Sure."

Claire flipped to the front of the pad, realizing that Taylor was almost to the end of this particular book. The first drawing was of Zachary's smiling face. It always amazed Claire how Taylor could draw such a realistic portrait of someone when she could barely draw a stick figure. She turned the pages. With each turn, the pictures grew darker. One particularly daunting drawing made Claire's stomach flip. There was a fist pressed into a wall with blood gaping from the knuckles, bleeding out into the cracks that had been created by the hit. She shivered.

"You'll need to start a new pad soon," Claire said, trying to sound undaunted.

"Yeah," Taylor said. "I guess."

"Do you have all you need?"

"No, but I'll get to the store soon."

"Why don't we go after Zachary wakes up from his nap? You can get whatever you need. We could also grab some food and maybe a bathing suit for you and Zachary. The pool in the neighborhood opens soon."

"Okay."

Claire had expected Taylor to say no, so she was glad to hear her say yes. Since she'd left Dylan, Taylor had only left the house a handful of times. Taylor insisted on buying her own food, but Claire knew Taylor had a limited amount of funds and that she was running low on them. Dylan had only given Taylor a cash allowance each month which she had to use for groceries and any other needs. He paid all the bills and never allowed Taylor to see their bank account. She also wasn't allowed to work. Over the years, Taylor hid away some of the cash, giving her a few thousand dollars to carry with her when she ran off.

While Claire wanted to keep Taylor safe, she did believe finding a job would be good for Taylor. It might help her find the bit of herself she had lost.

"Grab yourself a few drawing pads," Claire said. She grabbed a couple of coloring books for Zachary, throwing them into the back of the cart and some crayons.

"You don't need to get him anything," Taylor stated, taking out the books and placing them back on the shelves. Zachary pointed his finger at the one coloring book at the front.

"Pwease, can I have it?"

Claire grabbed it again.

"I'm his godmother. I get to spoil him, plus it's only a dollar."

Claire handed the book to Zachary. He beamed. Taylor picked up two drawing pads and some coloring pencils to add to the cart.

"Alright, I need some apples. Let's walk over toward the food. What would you like for dinner?"

"Whatever you think," Taylor said.

Claire pushed the cart, smiling down at Zachary who kept showing her his new coloring book.

"I know, we'll color when we get home, won't we?"

"Yay!"

"Can we just hurry?"

Claire quickened her steps. On their way to the grocery section, they passed a toy aisle. Zachary's little hand grasped out toward the toys.

"Doggie!"

Claire noticed a stuffed, brown dog. She grabbed it and gave it to Zachary. He hugged it to him.

"What are you doing?" Taylor asked, her cheeks flushed.

"What? It's just a little stuffed dog," Claire said with a shrug.

Taylor snatched the dog from her son, putting it back where it had been. Zachary's eyes grew wide before he let out a loud cry.

"Taylor!"

"I don't need you buying me anything. You know what, just go get what you need. Zachary and I will go and wait by the car." Taylor lifted the now sobbing Zachary out of the cart, storming away.

Claire stood, stunned. She could hear Zachary's cries grow smaller and smaller as they got closer to the front of the store. Her eyes looked around her to see if anyone was watching. She saw one woman's eyes on her who turned as soon as Claire noticed. Claire lifted her chin, placed her hands back on the handle, and just kept walking forward.

Taylor struggled to keep her grip on her son with her hurt arm. He kicked and screamed, angry he wasn't getting his way. To keep ahold of him, she had to hold him like a football in one of her arms. She avoided all the eyes on her, only wanting to get to Claire's car.

Once she finally made it, she placed Zachary into his seat. As she buckled him in, he settled. Unlike most children, the car seat always had a calming effect on her son. Whenever he'd rile himself up, she'd simply place him inside his seat, and he'd calm down immediately.

Taylor climbed into her own seat, a harsh, unsteady breath leaving her. She was embarrassed with how she'd just reacted in the store. Claire had only been trying to be kind and nice. Taylor hated that she had to depend on Claire to survive. Dylan had taken all of her independence away.

She closed her eyes for a moment to calm down. Then she glanced back at Zachary, who'd fallen asleep in his seat. Her good arm reached back, brushing his cheek with the tips of her fingers. Zachary let out a little moan and moved his head to the side, but he remained asleep.

"I love you," Taylor whispered. She would figure out how to support her son on her own. She had the skills; she would become self-sufficient again.

When they reached the house, Taylor quickly took Zachary out of his car seat and went inside, not offering to help Claire with the groceries. Not that Claire was surprised. Taylor hadn't spoken a word the entire ride back to the house.

Once the grocery was put up, she decided to take the art supplies to her friend, who was closed up inside her room. She knocked on the door. There was no answer.

Instead of knocking again, Claire turned the knob to find it unlocked. She walked into the room that Taylor shared with Zachary. Zachary sat on the small cot with Taylor's phone watching videos, while Taylor sat on her bed, with her legs curled up to her chest, crying. Immediately, Claire rushed to sit beside her.

"I'm sorry," Taylor whispered. She wiped her cheek with her fingers. "I just...I can't take care of my son. I can't buy him the stupid little toy he wants. I have to depend on you to get me a drawing pad, which I don't even need. I hate this…"

"I understand," Claire said. She placed the bag of art supplies onto the night stand. "But you know I don't mind."

"But I do," Taylor said, touching her chest. "I do mind. Your money isn't infinite. Yes, your parents have helped you out in life, but I know you still have your own bills and life aspirations. I need to get a job. I need to pull my worth."

"You will," Claire assured her, "and once you're on your feet again, you can pay me back."

"And I will. A little while ago, I saw there was a work from home job posting online. It would allow me not to have to worry about care for Zachary."

"What type of job is it?"

"Telemarketing."

Claire made a face.

"I know. But I threw away my scholarship and I…"

"Shh, you'll be great at it. You're welcome to use my laptop as needed."

"Thanks," Taylor murmured, wiping beneath her eyes.

"But I want you to take time to sketch too, Taylor. You're truly talented. Maybe you could even try to sell some pieces online. Start a website or sell it on one of those websites," Claire suggested.

Taylor glanced up and rose her brows.

"No one wants to buy my artwork, Claire. It's subpar, at best."

"You're kidding me, right?"

Claire lifted up the worn drawing pad that Taylor had been drawing in for what appeared at least months. She turned to the picture of Zachary.

"People would pay you good money for such a drawing of their own children or their pets. But this," Claire said as she turned the pages to the picture of the hands, "this is poignant, Taylor. This makes people feel. They would pay for this."

"That isn't for anyone to have," Taylor snapped. She took it from Claire, slamming the pad closed. Claire sharply inhaled, but then forced a smile.

"That's the beauty of it," Claire said. "You get to decide what you sell and what you don't."

Taylor opened up to the picture of the hands again. Her finger ran along the baby's fingers, tears welling up in her eyes.

"I don't know if I can share any of my artwork anymore, Claire."

"Because of him?" Claire asked. Taylor nodded. "He doesn't control you anymore, Taylor. You get to take that control back now. I think your artwork could be a path for that."

Zachary crawled up into the bed, climbing into Taylor's lap. He placed his hand on her cheek.

"No crying, Mommy."

"See, Taylor. The both of us have your back," Claire said.

Taylor smiled. She turned the pages of the pad, showing Claire a drawing she hadn't noticed yet. It was the back of two women, sitting on a familiar couch, with a pint of ice cream between them. Taylor tore out the picture and gave it to Claire.

"Here, this one is for you."

"I love it."

"It's from our..."

"Dorm," Claire finished with her as a smile. "I love the touch of the pint of mint chocolate chip."

"Well, we ate far too much of it that year."

"Yes, we did."

A few days later, Taylor joined Claire on the couch after she put Zachary down for bed. She carried the drawing pad, holding it to her chest. She plopped down beside Claire before slowly putting the pad down and sliding it over to Claire.

"This was my lifeline," Taylor said. "Dylan didn't like me doing any of my art. He thought it was a waste of time. So I only had that one pad I bought one day while I was shopping for groceries. I even paid for it separately so I could throw away the receipt, just in case. He never actually checked the receipts, but still. I had that and only that. I drew in it while he was at work or when he went out with his buddies to drink. Then I hid it behind the cookbooks, knowing he would never even think to look back there. So I think that's why I got so upset the other day with you. Art has always been my escape. Even when I was younger and my dad came home drunk or, whatever. But in college, it was something else. Something more and I miss that. I miss who I was."

"Taylor, you're still you. And you get to do what you want to do now," Claire told her.

"I want to draw, for me," she said, "and maybe for others, too. I found an art studio about ten minutes away that needs teachers for part-time lessons. I was thinking since you have Monday's off, perhaps I could work there a few hours on Mondays. I would still do my telemarking job from home, but this would help me get out of the house. I do hate asking you to watch..."

"Stop right there," Claire said, putting up her hand. "You don't have to worry about it. Of course, I'll watch Zachary on Mondays for a few hours. I want to do whatever I can to help you get yourself back on your feet."

Taylor settled back into the cushions of the couch, drawing her legs up beneath her and pulling a fluffy pillow into her lap.

"I've done the math. This painting part-time job won't make much, but the telemarking job pays decently. I believe within a month or two Zachary and I should be able to move into a small apartment."

"Don't rush it," Claire said. "I like having you and Zachary here."

"And Lucas?"

Claire tugged at the edge of her sleeve.

"I didn't think he liked it."

"He is just..."

"Enjoying life as a carefree adult?"

"Yes," Claire chuckled. "But this is my home, not his. And I want you and Zachary to stay here as long as you need it. I also prefer you here until we know he can't get to you."

"Yeah," Taylor said. She then pointed to the drawing pad in Claire's lap. "You can keep it. I have a new one now to draw in." She smiled.

"You'd give me this?" Claire asked, surprised. "But this is like your journal, your personal thoughts."

"I know," Taylor said. "But it's time I start a new chapter. I did take out some of the pictures to keep, but outside of those. I'd like to keep the rest in the past."

"Alright. Well, thank you. I'll treasure it."

From upstairs, there came a cry. Taylor glanced up the stairs toward the noise before standing.

"I should go and check on him. Goodnight, Claire."

"Goodnight, Taylor."

Claire waited until Taylor walked up the stairs before opening the drawing pad to look through it in better detail. But before she did that,

Claire quickly went to the back, wondering if the picture of the hands was still there. She saw that Taylor had pulled it out. Claire ran her fingers over the edge where the left over pieces of the page had been left behind, glad Taylor had decided to keep that one.

Chapter 14

"Here," Claire said, placing paperwork in front of her friend where she sat painting on the back porch.

Since Taylor had decided she wanted to get back to her artwork, this was where Claire could often find her friend. She worked on the side of the porch, facing the backyard, always intense.

Today's piece had darkness to it. Most of them did. Gone were the bright, happy pieces she used to commission for their neighbors and friends in college. Now her work had become mature and somber. The ominous swirls on the canvas led to a small, tiny teddy bear in the middle with a torn arm and one of its eyes dangling near its nose. Then there were a pair of hands balled into fists near the bear.

Claire swallowed hard, the piece of art making her stomach hurt.

"What's this?" asked Taylor as she took the paperwork off the table in front of her.

"James sent it. It's a new temporary custody form since the other expires in a week. This still gives you emergency custody of Zachary. If Dylan wants to see him, he has to meet in public settings with a chaperone."

Claire's family had offered to help assist Taylor in her divorce and custody papers, with James as the one leading most of the work.

"What if he refuses to sign it?" Taylor asked. There was a smudge of paint across her cheek which momentarily took Claire out of the seriousness of the situation.

"Then you go to court," Claire said. "James thinks he'll sign it. He doesn't think Dylan wants to go to court and spend more money. Which reminds me, James asked if Dylan had sent anything in ways of child support?"

"No, he hasn't."

"Good, that's good for the case for you to get full custody of Zachary and he'll just get visitation."

"What keeps him from taking Zachary away?" Taylor's brows creased, her eyes still on the paperwork.

"We'll worry about that when the time comes. He won't be able to do it legally. And we'll have to make sure your home is safe, that he doesn't know where it is. James said that will all be a part of the paperwork, that you'll choose a public, well-lit location to meet. And I can come to every drop-off and pick-up."

"I doubt that will be necessary." Taylor lifted the pen and quickly scribbled her name.

"I wouldn't be so sure. He shoved you down the stairs, Taylor. He nearly killed you."

Taylor stiffened, clutching the pen.

"I know," she said, lowly. "I know what all he did."

Claire frowned. Over the past several years, her friend had been through far too much emotional, financial, and physical abuse.

"I'm sorry," Claire whispered, taking a seat next to her friend. "Want to tell me about it?" she asked as she pointed to the painting.

"Not really," Taylor answered.

"Does it help? Painting these types of pictures?"

Taylor nodded.

"Do you miss the brighter ones?" Taylor asked.

"Sometimes," Claire said, unable to lie. "But you are so talented, Taylor. Your talent has grown so much since we were in school together. And this is meaningful. Isn't that what art is, anyway?"

"I guess." Taylor lifted up her paint brush again, adding a line over the bear's stomach. "I'm the bear," she then whispered.

"Oh, Taylor..."

"No, don't pity me. I don't need it." She put the brush back down before standing. Her hands brushed over her thighs. "I need to wake Zachary. If I don't, he'll never fall asleep tonight."

Taylor went inside, leaving Claire alone with the painting. As she inched closer to it, she noticed there were words within the swirls of paint: worthless, ungrateful, helpless, and more. Sadness and anger burned in the pit of her stomach. She wished she could have just ten minutes alone in a room with Dylan. He'd never be able to hurt anyone again.

On Mondays, Taylor always came home much lighter on her feet. She stepped inside the house and bent down as Zachary ran into her arms. Taylor lifted Zachary, kissing his cheek. He giggled, burrowing his head against Taylor's shoulders and holding her tightly. These evenings were the longest he had ever been apart from her.

"What smells so good?" Taylor asked. She headed into the kitchen where her friend was mixing something in a bowl.

"Cake," Claire answered. "I'm making the icing now."

"What's the reason for cake?'

"No reason, but..." Claire paused. "Lucas is coming over for dinner. I hope that's alright."

"This is your house. You don't really have to ask me for permission to have your boyfriend over," Taylor said.

"Well, I still like to make sure. He's staying the night. But don't worry, we won't be loud."

Taylor made a face, making Claire laugh.

"And what's for dinner?" Taylor asked.

"Oh, I don't know. Lucas is picking something up for all of us. We know I'm useless when it comes to cooking. I just bake desserts."

"Desserts!" Zachary exclaimed, bouncing up and down. Taylor glanced at her son and then to the table. Claire had placed her nice, yellow tablecloth with the pink roses on it and her best chinaware was set out. She was planning on a nice evening with her boyfriend.

"Perhaps, Zachary and I should order something else and stay upstairs. I don't know the last time you had alone time with your boyfriend," Taylor said.

"Oh, don't be silly. I'm not forcing you and Zachary to stay upstairs. You can join us for dinner," Claire said before starting to ice the cake. "I insist."

"Okay, then what can I do to help?"

"Nothing."

Taylor felt as though she and her son were intruding on Claire and Lucas's plans, but she also knew her friend wouldn't let her hide away for the evening.

"I'm going to go upstairs and change. There is paint all over my top," she said. She took Zachary upstairs to change into something nicer.

Claire opened her front door before her boyfriend could knock. He stood before her with a big, goofy grin on his face. She tugged him inside and gave him a quick kiss.

"Lasagna for two and breadsticks," Lucas said, lifting up the bag from the local Italian restaurant.

"For two? What about Taylor and Zachary?"

Lucas's face fell.

"I thought...Claire, it's *our* anniversary."

"On *Friday*. We're going out on *Friday*. I told you to get dinner for all of us," Claire said. "And it's only our 10-month anniversary. It's not like it's a year anniversary or anything."

"I guess I misunderstood," he murmured. "You just eat this with Taylor. I guess I'll see you on Friday."

"Now, don't be like that," Claire said as she took in a deep breath. "I already told Taylor you were going to be over for dinner. She'll think it's her fault you're not staying. Stay, please. I invited you over tonight because I miss you."

"I miss you," Lucas repeated.

"I know it's been different with Taylor here, but that doesn't mean I don't want to spend time with you," Claire said. Then she added, "I made cake."

"What kind of cake?" Lucas playfully asked, his eyes brightening.

"Chocolate with buttercream."

Lucas grinned.

"Well, you know I can't resist that."

"Exactly," Claire said. She leaned forward. She kissed him languidly, tasting chocolate on his tongue. "Now, will you please run to the restaurant to grab some more food?"

"Sure."

The next morning, Claire woke up in Lucas's arms. His fingers grazed over her back, making her smile. She had missed this. She inched up, kissing him.

"Good morning," she whispered.

"Morning."

There were knocks on the door. Lucas sat up.

"Oh, don't worry about that," she said. "It's just Zachary. Taylor will get him."

"Alright. Want to join me in the shower? I have to get to work early. New client," Lucas told her.

"Sure."

As they climbed out of the bed, Zachary hit against the door some more.

"When will your friend get him?" Lucas asked, growing impatient.

"In a minute. She might still be asleep."

"It's just..." Lucas groaned. "We're childfree, Claire. This is supposed to be a fun time in our relationship. Perhaps you should stay over at my place in the future."

Claire took a moment to process what he said. She curled her hands into fists beside her.

"My best friend just left her abusive husband, and you're worried about having childfree time? She won't be living her forever, Lucas. Just until she can get on her feet."

"And how long will that be? A week? A month? A year? How long do we have to put this," he asked as he pointed between them, "on hold?"

"What?" Claire asked. "Are you serious right now?"

"She's been here for a while now. I *hardly* see you."

"It hasn't been that long. I thought you supported me on this," Claire said. "You told me you supported me helping her."

"I did—I *do*. I just didn't expect it to last this long. I thought after a week or two…"

Claire's eyes widened.

"I think you should leave," she whispered.

"Are you breaking up with me?" Lucas asked, shocked. He stepped forward, but Claire took a long stride back.

"No," Claire said, her voice trembling. "I can't do this with you right now, Lucas."

"Claire, you're being unfair. Maybe I was too harsh, but you know that I love you," Lucas said.

"And I love you," Claire replied, though her voice betrayed her words.

"What about Friday?"

"I'm not sure Friday is a good idea. I think we may need some time apart to figure out if this is what we really want."

Lucas remained in his spot. Claire struggled to read what he was thinking, which was a first for her. He opened and closed his mouth a few times, debating on what to say. In the end, he said nothing. He put on his clothes and grabbed his overnight bag, not taking a moment to brush his teeth or go to the bathroom.

When he left her room, Claire thought she might cry but she didn't. She slowly settled back onto her bed. In a way, it was actually kind of freeing, no longer having to worry about appeasing him in all of this. But her heart also broke in wondering if this was really the end.

"Oh, James is coming over to stay for a few days," Claire casually mentioned after breakfast a few days later.

Taylor, who had been eating a bowl of cereal, looked up. Her friend was leaning forward with a sly grin on her face.

"Why?"

"Well, he's helping with your divorce. It's easier for him to be here to go over some of the stuff with you. He'll stay in the room downstairs," Claire said.

"Oh," Taylor said as she took another bite of her food.

Claire smiled.

"Did you have a crush on him like he had on you?"

A blush rose in Taylor's cheeks. She dipped her head down, hoping that Claire hadn't noticed.

"No," Taylor said. "And I have zero plans on dating anyone ever again. I am in the middle of a divorce."

"Of course," Claire sympathized. "I shouldn't have—I was only teasing. James always did have a crush on you."

"No, he didn't," Taylor disagreed, though her cheeks only brightened in color. "And even if he did, I'm sure he has new crushes now. Doesn't he have a girlfriend?"

"Had," Claire corrected. "They broke up a few months ago."

"Oh." Taylor looked over to Zachary, who was pinching his marshmallows from his cereal with his fingers. "I should shower. I have to get to work."

"You are okay with James staying here, right?" Claire asked. "I can ask him to stay somewhere else if it makes you uncomfortable."

"He doesn't make me uncomfortable," Taylor assured her. "I like James. He's nice. It'll be nice to have someone else here for a while."

Chapter 15

James despised the hustle and bustle of the road down where his sister lived. Traffic seemed to be more stop than go. He swore it took ten minutes just to turn into her neighborhood.

When he finally arrived at Claire's house, he realized he hadn't seen Taylor in over a year, since the 4th of July party at his parents' house. That day remained etched in his memory, wishing he'd done more to protect her from that scum.

He grabbed his overnight bag from the side seat and got out of his car, heading to Claire's front door. Before he could knock, it opened to reveal Claire. She clucked her tongue against the roof of her mouth and rose her eyebrows at him.

"You're late."

"The traffic around your place is atrocious," he replied.

"It is not that bad," Claire said with a roll of her eyes. "You can be so dramatic."

James scoffed, but he didn't say anything. Instead, he stepped inside his sister's home.

"She's out back, painting," Claire told him.

"And?"

"I just thought you might want to talk to her."

"Well, I will need to speak with her," he said. "But it can wait. I don't want to disturb her."

"Right." Claire stepped out of the way, tapping her fingers along the side of the door before closing it. She crossed her arms over her chest and her face fell. "I *really* hate him."

"Yeah, me too. How is she doing?" His eyes shot to the back, hoping to see a glance of Taylor. All he could see was the corner of a canvas and a splash of red paint.

"Better. She seems lighter. Of course, she still has her days," Claire said. "It's only been a little over a month since everything happened. But she's finding things that make her happy, like painting again."

"That's good."

A cry came from upstairs.

"Oh, that's Zachary. I'm going to run up and get him before he gets Taylor out of her moment."

Claire dashed up the stairs, leaving James all alone. He went around the corner to go to the guest room downstairs. He'd only stayed at Claire's house one other time when he had come down for a party she'd thrown and drank a little too much, deciding not to drive the two hours back home.

He knew his sister had high hopes that something new would spark between him and Taylor; he wasn't an idiot. However, he also knew that Taylor had just left her abusive husband and had been through some very traumatic experiences. He doubted she was anywhere ready for anything new. He was also sure his sister knew this, deep down.

Once he placed his bag down, he walked back out into the foyer. Right as he did, Taylor stepped in from outside. Immediately, James's breath left him. She was just as stunning as he remembered her, only her hair was a dark brown—no longer the red she had all those years ago.

"Hi," he greeted.

"Hi," Taylor said, blushing.

Claire and Zachary came down the stairs and stood between them.

"Hi!" Zachary excitedly said next, jumping up with a wave.

"Well, hello," James said to him. "I'm James, Claire's brother."

Zachary eyed him carefully before stepping closer.

"Wanna play?"

"Maybe in a little bit," James promised. His eyes moved back up to Taylor, who was reaching out toward her son.

"Let's let James settle in for a bit," she said. "Come on, why don't you get a snack?"

The word snack had Zachary rushing to his mother and taking her hand before nearly dragging her into the kitchen. Claire chuckled.

"Isn't he fun?"

"Yes," James agreed. "She looks..." He couldn't find the words he wanted to say so instead, he let his words fade into the air, shaking his head. "Where can I set up my laptop?"

"Oh, um, my desk, I guess. The office area would be the best place for all of this. It's in that front nook. Zachary has managed to stay out of there so far. There's also a printer for when you need to print anything out."

"Perfect, thanks."

James went back into the guest room to grab his laptop from his bag before taking it into the office. It was a tiny space, and James was unsure how they would all easily fit in here to discuss all the paperwork he'd done up for the divorce.

When he walked back out, Taylor was there again. She stood at the bottom of the stairs, her fingers on the banister as if she were about to head up but had forgotten what she needed. He walked up to her.

"Brain fart?"

"Huh?" she asked as a small laugh escaped her lips. Her dark locks fell over her cheeks before she brushed it behind her ear. "Actually, yes. But now I remember what I was going to do. Zachary wants his stuffy."

"Stuffy?"

"It's his stuffed bear," Taylor explained. "He can't survive twenty minutes without it."

"Then you better hurry up," James said with a smile. Taylor took another step before pausing and looking at him again.

"I haven't had a chance to thank you for all you've done for me, James. I will find a way to pay you for your service. I..."

"No, you won't. You're my friend. I like to help my friends when they need it," he said, his smile softening. Taylor blushed and ducked her head, allowing the hair to fall back over her face.

"Thank you," she mumbled before she continued up the stairs.

James went into the main living area of the house. Toys were strewn all over the room, and a children's cartoon blared on the television. He chuckled at his sister sitting on the couch as Zachary climbed over her lap before sitting beside her and dropping crackers along the way.

"I know, right?" Claire laughed with him. "My entire downstairs has become a playset for this little one right here," she said, playfully pinching his cheeks. "He's lucky he's cute, and I love him so much."

Zachary looked up at her and brightly smiled. He grabbed another cracker, taking a big bite that made more crumbs fall.

"You aren't this nice to your nieces and nephews," James pointed out. He found a seat on the loveseat, which was the only place not covered in toys.

"James, you know I'm not really a children person. Zachary's just different. He's sweet."

"Our nieces and nephews are sweet too," James said.

"I know. I just..."

Zachary stuffed a cracker into her mouth.

"Hungry?" he asked her. Claire coughed, and James let out a howl of laughter as his sister continued to sputter out pieces of the cracker.

"What's happened?" Taylor came in, concerned.

Claire stood up, shaking her head.

"Nothing," she said.

Taylor walked over to Zachary and gave him his stuffy. The little boy brought it to his face, hugging it. Then Taylor's eyes went over the messy room.

"I need to clean this up."

"It's fine," Claire brushed off.

"It's a disaster," Taylor disagreed. "You've bought him too many toys."

James gave his sister a look.

"Well, you had to leave most of his toys behind. Plus, it's my job to spoil him," Claire added. She tapped Zachary's nose with her finger. "Don't you like it when Auntie Claire buys you toys?"

Zachary eagerly nodded.

"I think there are plenty for now," Taylor said. She cleaned up a small pile and sat down on the couch next to her son. She looked to James. "When do we hand over the divorce papers?"

"You've officially been separated for a month now so that means you can begin the divorce proceedings. The hope is he'll allow a few meetings to go over everything, then sign the papers, and this is all over in a month."

"And if he doesn't?"

"Then we'll take it from there. I thought tomorrow we could go over the paperwork I have, what you're asking for from him."

"All I want is custody of Zachary."

"I know," James said. "But I think he owes you more. At least some sort of alimony and child support."

"No," Taylor said. "No alimony. I don't want it. And I will forgo child support if he'll give me full custody of Zachary. He hardly spent time with him when we were together, but he'll want custody just to hurt me."

A stray tear slid down Taylor's cheek. She quickly wiped it away with the pad of her thumb.

"I wish I'd given Zachary a better father," she whispered. Suddenly, she seemed to realize she was speaking to both him and Claire, curling inwards to hide herself.

"He'll be safe," Claire promised. "And who's to say that one day in the future you won't find a father for Zachary?"

Taylor glanced up, crinkling her nose.

"I don't foresee that happening, Claire. I've given up on happily ever afters. They seem a bit silly now, don't you think?"

The next day, James found Taylor and Zachary on the back porch of Claire's house. Taylor sat with a drawing pad in her lap, looking up every so often at Zachary, who was sitting on the ground attempting to place the correct chunky puzzle pieces in their spaces.

"Claire's at work," Taylor said the moment he stepped outside. She tucked a hair behind her ear and looked up at him, closing her drawing pad to set it beside her lap.

"Yes," he said. He caressed his neck. The heat from outside had already made beads of sweat form there. "How do you manage to stay out here so long? It's hot."

"Oh, I don't know. It doesn't bother me."

"Would you like to get ice cream?"

Zachary excitedly glanced up upon hearing about such a treat. He jumped up, pointing at James.

"Ice cream? I wike ice cream!"

James realized it may have been better to ask Taylor alone than to say it in front of her child, who now would be disappointed if she told him no and making her the bad guy. But when he looked over at Taylor, she smiled and nodded.

"Why don't we go? Sounds good." She paused. "You do have a space for a car seat in your car, don't you? I don't have a car."

"Yes," James quickly answered.

They went outside where Taylor hooked in Zachary's car seat and then buckled him in to it. She turned, and James realized how close he was to her. Their eyes met. He stepped back, licking his lower lip.

"So, you still don't drive?" he asked, trying to make sure his words didn't sound judgmental.

"He...um, he never would let me," she said. Her eyes fell to her shoes. James felt like the biggest jerk. He never should have brought it up. Taylor continued, "I mean, he pretended he wanted to teach me once. But instead, he just made me more terrified of getting behind the wheel."

"I could teach you," he offered.

Taylor laughed, shaking her head before walking around the car to take a seat. He got in too.

"Maybe one day, but for now I can catch rides from others or take the bus. I mainly work from home, well, Claire's home now. Whenever I move, I'll have to see what I can manage without a car."

"What work do you do outside of the home?"

"I work at a painting studio," Taylor said. "It's just about a ten-minute walk from here. Claire always offers to drive me, but I like the walk. It's quiet and mainly busy, so I don't have to worry about some weirdo coming near me." Though she spoke of it as some random person, James had the impression that she was actually speaking about Dylan.

"Do you like the job?"

"I love it. It's my favorite day of the week."

When they reached the ice cream shop, he attempted to get Zachary out of his seat but the buckle was too difficult to open. Taylor gently pushed him aside, easily popping the buckle.

"You have to be a bit stronger than that," she teased. She lifted Zachary into her arms and kissed his pudgy cheek. Zachary then reached out to James.

"Oh, you want me to hold you?" James asked. Zachary nearly jumped out of Taylor's arms, launching himself into James's arms.

"Sorry about that."

"Doesn't bother me at all," James said.

"He usually doesn't like men," Taylor added. They walked up to the shop. James opened the door for Taylor to go through first before following in behind her.

After they ordered their food, Taylor started to pull out cash from her wallet. James stopped her.

"I invited you."

"Oh, alright," she conceded.

After the three of them sat, Zachary dug right into his ice cream.

"You're going to give yourself brain freeze," James said.

Zachary licked at the edge of his spoon. James grabbed a spoonful of his own sundae, making sure to get plenty of whipped cream on his spoon. Apparently this amused Taylor, because she laughed at him.

"What?"

"Are you eating ice cream with whipped cream or whipped cream with a side of ice cream?"

James looked at his spoon.

"I do not see a problem with it."

Taylor continued to smile, and James realized he would never tire of her looking happy. He brought his spoon to his mouth, savoring the taste of the ice cream and whipped cream coming together on his tongue. Again, Taylor laughed.

"Why do you eat your ice cream like that?"

"Like what?"

"Like you're..." She paused, blushing. Then she lowered her voice and said, "Like you're making love to it."

"I don't eat ice cream like that!" James opposed, unable to keep himself from grinning.

"You do. There are children here. Mine is at the table."

Their laugher continued. Zachary joined in, even though he wasn't sure what, exactly, they were laughing about.

"Thanks for inviting me out for ice cream," Taylor said a beat later. "I don't get out much, except for work. Claire does try, but I feel bad."

"Why?"

"Because she's already sacrificed so much for us. I hate taking up more of her time."

"My sister never does anything she doesn't want to do."

"I guess that is right," Taylor said. She took a bite of her ice cream. "This is really good. I can't remember the last time I had ice cream just because."

"I have it all the time," James admitted. "It's my favorite treat."

"All the time and you have abs like that? What's your secret?" Taylor asked. Zachary nearly dropped his ice cream in his lap, so Taylor had to help him to adjust it. Then she looked back at James.

"I don't know. I work out, a lot. I also have an unhealthy obsession, probably."

"Why do you say that?"

"I don't know. I do it too much. My doctor actually told me that I should work out less. My knees are giving out."

"That sounds painful, do you...?"

Taylor's words stuck in her throat, and all the color drained from her face. James turned his head to follow where her eyes were tracking. There, through the window, stood Dylan, his eyes stuck right on Taylor. He stayed there for a moment, his cheeks sunk in before disappearing back down the road. As James looked back at Taylor, he saw her body trembling.

"Are you okay?"

"I..." She trailed.

"Why don't we go back to Claire's?" James offered.

Taylor glanced down at the table as she spun her spoon around in her ice cream.

"No," she whispered. "He's just trying to frighten me. He does this every so often."

"He's been following you around?" James asked. "That's against the rules, isn't it?"

Taylor looked up, meeting his eyes. "Yes. But no one cares. The police don't care, James. They never have. He'd have to physically hurt me, again, for them to even look into it."

"Taylor..."

"Can we not talk about it anymore? We were having a nice time. I don't want him to ruin the rest of our day."

James nodded, though there was an odd feeling in the pit of his stomach. With Dylan following Taylor around, did he know where Claire's place was? Were Taylor and Zachary no longer safe there? He shook his fears away and gave Taylor a grin, wanting to ease her own fears.

"Of course."

CHAPTER 16

Taylor's phone kept buzzing on the table next to her. She looked down at it briefly before reminding herself not to let it trouble her. However, it seemed to bother Claire, who swooped it up into her hands.

"Who is texting you like this?"

"Hey!" Taylor called out. "That's my phone."

Claire ignored her friend's pleas. She slid the screen and saw a wall of texts from Dylan. Taylor glanced down at the screen at the same time as Claire did.

I saw you with your boyfriend, James.

Is that why you left? Cheating on me?

I always knew you were a whore.

Did you tell our son that was his new daddy?

Don't worry, I don't want you back after you fucked another man.

Slut.

I'll get custody of him, just wait.

Is this why you 'fell' down the stairs? Needed to make sure your new boyfriend didn't have more children to take care of.

Taylor watched as a flash of anger covered Claire's face.

"Oh my god, these are vile, Taylor, absolutely vile."

"I know," Taylor whispered.

She received texts like those on a daily basis. Even though she wanted to block them, she couldn't. They could be used in the upcoming case. She needed whatever possible to keep Dylan from getting custody of her son.

Taylor reached out and took the phone back from Claire, reading over the final text. Her chin began to tremble. She let out a harsh sob, and Claire's arms wrapped around her instinctively. Since the hospital, this was the first time she had allowed herself to break down like this. Taylor had been compartmentalizing the pain for so long, focusing on getting away from Dylan.

"Oh, Taylor," Claire murmured, brushing the hair off Taylor's face. "He's an asshole. He's just saying that to hurt you. That is all it is. Don't respond to him. Put him on mute. Don't block him, because we need the messages, but you don't have to read them. All right?"

"Mommy?"

The sound of Zachary's voice made Taylor sit herself up and wipe the tears off her cheeks before looking down at her son.

"Hey," she whispered.

"What if you and I went outside and played?" Claire offered. He looked up at her with a squished-up nose.

"I want Mommy."

"It's alright," Taylor said.

She bent down, swooping her son up with ease. He giggled, resting his head on her chest. She cradled him to her, kissing the top of his head and breathing the scent of him in. Everything she did was for him.

"Your birthday is soon. What should we do to celebrate?" Claire asked.

"I don't need a celebration. All I want is the divorce papers signed. I want to be free of him."

"Yes, I know you do. But you're turning 24, surely we should celebrate."

"No," Taylor firmly said. "I don't want to."

"But…"

Taylor stood from the chair, nearly knocking it over and keeping Zachary tucked at her chest.

"I said, I don't want to celebrate. Just leave it alone," Taylor growled.

Claire's eyes grew wide. She sat back in shock before nodding her head.

"Alright, if that's what you want."

"It is," Taylor said, glancing up at the ceiling to keep her tears at bay. "I just…my birthday isn't a day I like to celebrate anymore."

"Not even go out to dinner?"

"No. In fact, if we can avoid even saying it's my birthday, that will be best," Taylor said.

"No presents?"

"No presents."

"Okay."

Claire got home later than normal the next evening, so the house was quiet. All the toys were put away and the kitchen was cleaned up, but there was food with a message on how to heat it up on her island from Taylor.

Claire unwrapped the food and placed it into the microwave. As it heated up, she walked outside to sit with Taylor, leaving the door open to listen out for her food.

"Thanks for dinner."

"Thank you for helping me."

"Of course," Claire said. The microwave beeped. She walked back inside, hearing Taylor walk in behind her. A knock came at the door. She looked at the time. It was eight at night. "Who could that be?" she asked, nervous. Could it be Dylan?

"Oh, yeah, you see..."

Claire had already made it to the door before Taylor could finish her sentence. She opened her door to find her brother standing on the other side. Her face brightened before turning to look at Taylor. James had just been here a couple of days ago.

"I asked him to come and help me sort through some custody stuff. I hope that's alright."

"It's more than alright," Claire said, a bit too brightly. "I think I'll take my food upstairs. Will you be staying tonight?" Claire asked as she saw the overnight bag James held. "Oh, well, how fun. Yes, I'll take my food upstairs. I'm sure you have lots to speak about."

Claire grabbed her food from the microwave before beginning to make the walk up the stairs. She paused halfway where they could no longer see her, but she could see them. The two stood awkwardly across from one another. She leaned down more. Her fork fell from her plate making a loud plop on the stairs.

"Are you all right?" James called up.

"Uh...yes! Sorry." She quickly grabbed the fork and rushed up the stairs, hoping the sound hadn't ruined anything.

Around ten, Claire realized she hadn't filled up her nightly water cup. She grabbed it and took it downstairs. She paused when she saw Taylor and James on the couch. They weren't touching, but they were smiling at one another. As she grew closer, she could hear them chatting and it was not about the divorce.

"You played in the band?" Taylor asked.

"Yes. Trombone."

"Can you still play?"

"Not a chance."

Claire made her steps heavier so they would know she was coming downstairs. Their voices quieted.

"Is everything going alright?" she asked them both. "It's ten o'clock."

"Is it?" Taylor sat up, glancing towards the kitchen to see the time on the stove. "Oh."

"Yes, it seems time has gotten away from us."

"Well, don't mind me. I only needed to get some water."

"I should probably go to bed," Taylor said, standing up. "Zachary will be up early." She turned to face James. "I have to work from 10-1 tomorrow. But at 1, perhaps we could get lunch like you suggested."

"Sure."

Taylor told them both goodnight and went up the stairs. Claire listened out to make sure Taylor was out of earshot before saying anything.

"Lunch tomorrow?"

"It's not like that," James said, standing. He lifted his arms with a yawn. "She said she likes getting out of the house."

"Especially if it's with you."

"Even if there is something there, Taylor isn't ready for anything serious. So please don't put that pressure on her. For now, she and I are friends."

"Right," Claire agreed. But she smiled. James really was what her friend needed right now. He cared about what she'd been through and was taking it slowly. "Well, I'm getting water and going to bed. How long are you planning on staying?"

"A few nights. I'll still have to go into work, but I have tomorrow off."

"Alright. Well, you know you're welcome to stay as long as you'd like."

"I know," he said. He grabbed his overnight bag from the floor. "I do wish I had about an hour with that guy."

"Oh, me too, you don't even know."

"I think I do."

Taylor had called James because she needed something important done. It was something she couldn't tell Claire, not yet. Because she knew if she told Claire, her friend would grow more concerned than she already was.

"I need you to write up some more paperwork for me," Taylor said as they sat together at the booth at the restaurant.

Zachary sat beside her and colored nondescript marks on his children's menu. She touched his soft hair, her eyes glistening.

"Sure, what's that?" James asked. He grabbed a chip from the basket, dipping it into the queso.

"A will. If anything were to happen to me, I need to know that Zachary will be okay," Taylor said.

James's brows knitted.

"Has Dylan threatened you, Taylor?"

Taylor exhaled. She shook her head, not quite meeting his eyes.

"Not in so many words," she answered.

"What did he say?" James asked sharply.

"I-I don't know," Taylor murmured.

"You do know, Taylor. What did he say? Have you told the police?"

"He just said I would regret leaving him and that...that he'd never forgive me for leaving him for you," Taylor told him.

"But you didn't leave him for me," James said. "Why would he even say that?"

"He's never liked you."

"Yeah, well the feeling is mutual," James muttered.

James unlocked his grip on the table, sitting back. He pushed his plate away from him and let out a loud sigh.

"Before I left him, he had warned me he would kill me if I ever did," Taylor admitted. She glanced over at Zachary before reaching up to stroke his cheek. "Sometimes I worry he'll come after me."

"You have to tell the police," James said.

"I have. All they gave me was a restraining order," she said. "Will you please help me write up a will?"

Her heart was heavy. Deep down, she was terrified of what might happen to Zachary if anything happened to her.

"He's not going to hurt you, Taylor. I won't let him," James promised.

Taylor could only give him a weak smile, knowing that it wasn't really something he could promise her.

"Will you write up a will for me?" she asked again.

"Of course I will."

"The only thing I have is Zachary and my paintings," Taylor said. "And I want Claire to have both."

"Claire?"

"Yes," Taylor replied. "She's like my sister. She's family. I know she'd take care of Zachary if anything ever happened to me."

"But it won't," James insisted.

Taylor averted her gaze from James, unable to say anything else. He didn't know Dylan and what he was capable of.

The ride home back to Claire's was silent. James didn't know what to say since Taylor asked him to write her up a will. He'd known that Dylan was a dangerous man. However, he hadn't realized he was one of those men who still went after their women when they left them.

When they arrived, Taylor lifted her sleeping son from his car seat.

"I can carry him for you," James offered.

Taylor smiled up at him, her brown eyes bright.

"No, that's okay. He's not too heavy. Just open the door for me."

He did as she requested, finding there was a letter on the door addressed to Taylor. James tore it off the frame and eyed it carefully.

"May I read this?"

"Yes." Taylor continued inside, taking her son upstairs to lay him down so he could finish her nap.

While she was upstairs, he opened the letter. As he suspected, it was from Dylan. The words scribbled on the page were tough to read. Since he'd never read Dylan's writing before he couldn't know if they were frenzied or his typical writing.

Taylor-

This is enough. I miss you. Zachary needs his father. Stop being selfish. Come home.

Dylan

James refolded the paper, placing it back into its folder. He looked up at the camera his sister had installed above her door, hoping it got evidence of Dylan being within so many feet of where Taylor was staying so they could use it against his restraining order.

"What does it say?" Taylor asked as she came back down the stairs.

"Just that he wants you to come home."

Taylor didn't ask to see the letter. She instead went to sit down on the couch and brought her legs up beneath her.

"Will that letter help my case for custody?"

"It could," James answered. He sat down next to her. "It isn't threatening, which is a good thing. But him bringing the letter has him breaking his restraining order. We can take that to the police."

"I doubt he stepped on Claire's property," Taylor said. "He probably had one of his buddies bring it. Dylan might not be smart, but he's not stupid enough to get near anything Claire owns."

"Why is that?" James asked, amused.

"He is scared of Claire."

That made a loud yelp of laughter escape him. Scared of his sister?

"And what, exactly, did my sister do to terrify him?"

"He's intimidated by strong women," Taylor said with a shrug.

"You're strong."

"Not like Claire."

"You are," James disagreed.

Taylor's lower lip came between her teeth, making his heart skip a beat. Her dark hair fell perfectly over her shoulders, and her eyes were bright and wide. James scooted himself back slightly, knowing he was walking on dangerous ground. It had only been a little over a month since Taylor had left her relationship. She wasn't even divorced yet.

"It's already three," Taylor then said, changing the subject. "Maybe I shouldn't let Zachary sleep any longer. He'll stay up later and then not sleep as well tonight."

"We didn't have to go to lunch and mess up his schedule."

"I wanted to," Taylor said as he moved so she was closer to him. "I enjoy spending time with you, James."

"And I enjoy spending time with you," he replied.

"I have to take things slowly. For now, I can only be friends," she said. "And I understand if that isn't enough for you."

"Taylor, being friends for now sounds amazing."

She smiled. Her finger curled through her hair.

"Do you remember when I was a redhead?"

"I do."

"I'm thinking of going back. Dylan didn't like it. He said he preferred my hair darker, but I think he really just knew it made me happy."

"Well, I say you should do it. It suited you."

"I think so, too."

When he got home the next day, he looked over the paperwork for Taylor's will. She had little to her name outside of her son. In her will, she'd written that if she were to pass, she'd like for Claire to have custody of Zachary. James had to explain to Taylor that this paperwork only would show her wishes and could be used in the court for that purpose, but that in the end if she was dead and Dylan was alive, he'd get custody.

"What if he's in prison?" she asked.

James hadn't had an answer for her.

The cameras showed that Taylor was right. Dylan did not step onto Claire's property, so calling the police on him wouldn't work. They would have to wait.

James kept a file of records. Any type of contact from Dylan was noted. Since Taylor left him, he'd asked to see Zachary, but he never followed through in seeing him. That would be helpful when it came time to ask for full custody. He hoped the police report on Taylor's fall would also be enough to keep him away from them both.

His phone rang. It was Taylor.

"Hello?" he said into his phone.

"Hi. I hope you don't mind me calling you. I know it's late."

"It's fine." James checked the time. It was nearing midnight. He hadn't even realized how late it had become. "Shouldn't you be asleep?"

"I should," Taylor agreed.

James closed his laptop and then moved over to his bed, to sink into the mattress. His head hit the pillow and he glanced up at the ceiling, watching as the fan spun around above him.

"Why aren't you? Can't sleep?"

"Tomorrow was my due date," she whispered.

His face fell.

"Oh, Taylor."

"I don't...I don't want to talk about it," she said. "I just couldn't sleep, and I didn't want to wake up Claire."

"Well, I'm sure she wouldn't mind if you did," James said.

"I know."

"But I can talk to you as long as you need. What do you want to talk about?"

"I don't know."

"Have you dyed your hair yet?" James asked.

"No, Claire insists she wants to take me to the salon to have it professionally done. I've never had my hair done professionally before," Taylor said, her voice animated.

"Are you excited?"

"I kind of am. Does that make me sound lame?"

"Not at all."

They spoke for two hours until he no longer heard Taylor talking. He checked his phone and saw they were still connected. He smiled when he realized she must have fallen asleep. He hung up the phone and turned to his side. Even though he'd have to be awake in just a few hours, he had enjoyed his talk with Taylor.

Chapter 17

As she adjusted her godson on her hip, she came over to the chair where Taylor had just finished getting her hair done. If she wouldn't let Claire do anything for her birthday, she was going to do this randomly for her.

With her new trimmed and red hair, Taylor looked brighter than she had in a long time. It was almost as though the red hair was her. She'd even took the leap to get bangs. Claire had to admit they looked amazing; she could never pull them off like Taylor could.

The red was an auburn red, less bright than she'd had when they were in college, suiting her better.

"So, what do you think?" Taylor asked, still looking at herself in the mirror, running her fingers through her hair.

"Me? I think it looks wonderful, Taylor. Perfectly you, I'd say. What about you, Zachary, what do you think?"

Zachary leaned forward, running his fingers through his mother's hair. He grinned.

"You look pretty, Mommy," he said. Taylor brightened even more. She turned, taking Zachary from Claire's arms.

"Yes? You like it?"

"Yep!"

Taylor kissed his cheek before looking up at Claire.

"Thank you, truly."

"It's nothing," Claire said, though she knew the thank you held a heavier meaning than just her getting her hair done. "I'm going to go and pay. Why don't you go on out to the car?"

Taylor got up from her chair with Zachary. She nuzzled her nose against his cheek, making him squeal with laughter. As they walked out, Claire went up to the front to pay. She put in her card and gave the lady cash for a tip.

Turning around, she froze. There *he* was, standing at the window. Her eyes darted in search of both Taylor and Zachary. She couldn't see them. Quickly, she made her way outside and stormed up to him.

"What are you doing here," Claire asked, placing her hands on her hips.

"It's a public space. You can't tell me where I can be," Dylan said with a smirk.

"You're not allowed this close to Taylor. I can call the police right now."

Dylan didn't flinch. He chewed obnoxiously on his gum, looking over at Claire's car where Taylor was putting Zachary into his seat.

"Can't tell me I can't be in a public space."

"Yes, I can. You have to leave immediately if Taylor is near," she countered, crossing her arms over her chest and widening her stance.

"Call the cops. See what they say," he said. "But if you do, just know they'll believe me that I didn't even realize my wife was here. I just so happened to be in the area, but you are the one who kept me here."

Claire tapped her foot, trying to quell the anger within her.

"You've stolen four years from her. Just let her go."

Dylan's nose flared.

"Never."

He turned and walked away. Claire kept her eyes on him the entire time until he was out of view.

When she reached the car, she sat down and took a moment to compose herself. Her left hand clutched hard around the steering wheel.

"What's wrong?" Taylor asked, spinning back around from playing a game with Zachary in the backseat.

"You didn't see..."

But Claire stopped herself from saying his name. She wouldn't ruin Taylor's good day by mentioning that he was around. Instead, she shook her head.

"Nothing, just thinking of this event coming up."

"Could I help? Maybe you could talk it through?"

"No, that's alright."

They got onto the road, and Claire looked around the car and through her mirrors to make sure they weren't being followed. Dylan knew where she lived, but he wouldn't dare step on her property, would he? Was he following them? Was she being followed to know when Taylor and Zachary were home alone?

"So, I was wondering if you'll keep Zachary next Friday night. Um, James was going to take me out to dinner," Taylor asked, drawing Claire out of her thoughts.

"What?" Claire happily gasped. "On your birthday?"

"Well, it's just a dinner, not for my birthday. I warned him if there are any mentions of my birthday that I'll leave the restaurant."

"Sure," Claire said. "I can keep Zachary for your date."

"It's...it isn't really a date," Taylor clarified. "Just dinner."

"Okay. Well, I'll happily keep Zachary. Not a problem."

"Do you think it's wrong that I want to go out with him for the evening? Is it too soon? Will people think...?"

"First of all, tell anyone who has an opinion on it to fudge off," Claire said, proud of herself for censoring her language around Zachary. "Second of all, you know what's best for you. If you are comfortable going to dinner with James, then you should go. As you said, it doesn't have to have a title. I know James is more than willing to take his time and do what's comfortable for you. He won't pressure you to name it anything until you are ready nor will he pressure you to do anything until you're ready."

"Well, I won't be ready for anything like that for a while," Taylor said, sitting back in the seat. She pulled down the visor to look at herself in the mirror. "I really do like my new hair. It's gorgeous."

"Good. I love it, too."

Two months away from Dylan had brought out more and more of the old Taylor. She smiled much more, she acted less like a prisoner and more like a young mother who was ready to see the world ahead of her.

"Have you thought about going back to school?" Claire asked as they pulled into her garage.

"I don't have the means for school, Claire."

Taylor's demeanor changed from bright to solemn in an instant. She unbuckled her son from her car seat, placing him down to run inside.

"I could help you, you know? You can stay here as long as you need, take a few classes here and there."

"I know you would," Taylor said. "And I appreciate it, I really do. I've been thinking about going back home."

"Home?" Claire asked. "But you haven't seen your dad since..."

Claire tried to do the math in her head.

"Do you even speak with your dad?"

"Sometimes."

Taylor grabbed her purse out of the car before shrugging her shoulders.

"Would you stay with him?" Claire asked, feeling uneasy about the whole idea. She didn't want to lose her best friend, again.

"No, but there are cheap apartments. I could easily get a job somewhere for decent pay, or I could even do the job I have now there."

"I thought you hated where you grew up," Claire said.

"I didn't hate it. Everyone there is very nice. It just wasn't what I wanted for myself. However, now I don't have any other choice."

"Sure you do," Claire disagreed. "I'll help you find a place nearby. Don't jump to moving back to your hometown just yet."

They stepped inside the house and paused when they saw bright red paint splattered on the windows. Taylor tensed beside her.

"Take Zachary upstairs," Claire said.

"What?"

"Upstairs."

Taylor picked up Zachary, doing as Claire asked. Once they were gone, she walked up to her front door, opening it. She stepped outside and closed the door back for a full view of the front of her house. Her whole body froze. The word slut was painted over the front door, and there were splatters of red paint thrown over the windows. Her eyes moved up to her camera to see it had also been sprayed.

Claire went in search of her phone. It was time to call the police.

For what seemed like over an hour, the police scrutinized the paint outside. They took some photos and asked a relentless stream of questions. Taylor paced back and forth between questions, trying to calm her nerves. Despite all her efforts, her hands still shook at her sides.

"Shouldn't you arrest him, already?" Claire asked.

"We can't know for sure he was the one who painted your door," one of the policemen said.

"But he was around Taylor today, following her. That was against his restraining order."

"It was a public space," the policeman said. "Did he specifically say he was following you?"

"He lives over an hour away! For what reason would he be at a female salon? And he's supposed to leave immediately even at a public place if Taylor is there," Claire angrily said.

"No need to get angry, Ms. Donahue," the policeman said condescendingly. "We can't know he was there to see her. And he left her alone, right? He left the place?"

"Yes," Claire said between clinched teeth. "But..."

"I understand how this is frustrating, but we cannot arrest someone without cause."

"Then what *can* you do?"

"We keep this on file and try to find the perpetrator who sprayed the camera, though it's not a clear picture. We will also note that you saw Mr. Montgomery today. If it happens again, you call us. The more it happens the more we can have a case against him for arrest."

"Oh, okay," Claire sarcastically said. "You'll just let him continue to harass Taylor, but you'll maybe arrest him next time. But how long will you even keep him locked up, a day, or two? He almost killed her!"

Taylor reached out to take her friend's hand. Claire met her eyes and slowed her breaths, giving Taylor a small nod.

"Fine, whatever," Claire said.

"We do take this seriously," the other officer said.

"Uh-huh. Do you need anything else from us?" Claire asked.

"No."

"Then please leave my home."

The police gave Taylor their card before a nod to them. Claire stood, walking them to her front door. Once they were outside, she closed it, locking the door behind her.

"This is unacceptable," she growled.

"It's how it works," Taylor sighed. "They need proof."

Taylor ran her fingers through her hair, leaning over to process it all.

"I'll never escape him," she whispered. "I'm going to go upstairs."

"Taylor—"

"I-I'll be all right," Taylor lied. "Don't worry about me."

CHAPTER 18

When the time came for Taylor's 'not date' with James, Taylor stood for a long time, eyeing every piece of clothing in her closet. She had only a few options, but none of them stood out to her. Claire reached in and pulled out a simple black dress.

"This one," she said, holding it up to Taylor's chest. "Yes. You'll look stunning."

Taylor slipped off her shirt, leaving her in a simple black bra, which was a stark contrast to her pale skin. She caught Claire's eyes on the harsh C-section scar above her panty line from when she lost Mia. Before Claire could say anything about it, Taylor brought the dress up and over her head, covering the scar.

"Gorgeous," Claire said, helping to zip up the back. The zipper caught on the back, making Claire have to hold the zipper together to help it make it the rest of the way up.

"I still haven't lost the weight."

"Taylor, you look amazing," Claire said in response.

"It doesn't seem fair, does it? Going through all of that, still having reminders, but no baby?"

"Oh, Taylor."

However, Taylor just shook away her thoughts before meeting her own eyes in the mirror before her. Today she wasn't going to wallow in her self-pity; today was going to be a good day.

"How should I do my hair?"

Taking the cues from her friend, Claire stepped up behind her and twisted her hair into a low bun.

"Bun?" she asked before she dropped the hair and did a simple braid to the side. "Braid? Or my personal favorite, down? I can curl it."

Claire undid the braid and allowed Taylor's auburn locks to fall over her shoulders.

"All right. Let's do down. Will you do my makeup too?"

"Absolutely, I will."

James stood still when he saw his sister and Taylor walking down the stairs. He adjusted the right sleeve of his lavender button-up top before stepping forward to them.

"Doesn't she look gorgeous?" Claire asked.

"Y...yes," James said, trying not to gape.

Nervously, he lifted the small bag he had brought for Taylor. He'd made sure to place it in a nondescript bag to make sure it didn't look like it was for her birthday.

Taylor reached for it curiously.

"Is this a birthday present?" she asked, lifting a brow playfully.

"No," James said with a smile. "No birthday presents here. I was told under no certain circumstances could we celebrate a birthday today. I just saw it, and it made me think of you."

"Do I open it now?" she asked. Her tongue jutted out of her mouth and ran along her lower lip.

"Oh yes, please. I want to see what my brother brought," Claire said, stepping closer.

Taylor pulled it back, chuckling. Then she dug into the bag, lifting out the simple silver necklace with a small, star pendant.

James held his breath. He never considered himself fashionable or to have good taste when it came to jewelry. His last girlfriend teased him relentlessly about his horrible sense of gift giving.

"Oh, it's beautiful," Taylor said.

"Nice," Claire commented. "Very Taylor."

Zachary came around them, interested. He glanced up at the silver necklace, pointing.

"For you, Mommy?"

"Yes, a present for Mommy," Taylor said with a wink. She bent down, showing him the necklace. "Look at the pretty star pendant on the bottom."

"But why a star?" Claire asked. "You said this reminded you of Taylor. Why did that remind you of her?"

"Um..." James said as hadn't expected to be caught off guard by his sister asking questions. "It just reminded me of her."

Taylor still looked at the necklace, her eyes staring wistfully at the piece of jewelry. She unlatched the clasp, bringing it around her neck to wear for the evening.

"Here," James immediately offered, stepping forward. "I can help."

Claire stepped out of the way to let him do it. His fingers brushed along Taylor's skin, making a feeling run through him that he couldn't quite explain. Then he quickly latched it back, pulling away from her.

Taylor's fingers ran over the star, smiling.

"I love it. Thank you, James."

"It was nothing."

"Oh, this is too nice," Taylor said as they entered the steak restaurant. "Am I even dressed up enough?"

Her eyes widened while she took in the dim lighting and quietness of the location. The maître d took James's name, and Taylor realized it had been a long time since she could recall eating somewhere that took reservations. "You look lovely," James assured her.

"Follow me," a waitress said.

As they walked toward the table, James reached out for Taylor's hand. She took it, grazing her thumb over the top of his knuckles. He let go, only for her to get into her seat. It was an intimate, corner booth. As they slid into their sides, the two came together at the corner.

"This is a lot for a dinner with me," Taylor said.

"It's not much, at all," James disagreed. "I wanted to do this for you."

"I do love my necklace," Taylor said after they ordered their drinks.

"I'm glad you like your necklace. I'll be honest, I was worried you wouldn't like it."

"Why?" Taylor asked as she continued to twirl the end of the necklace around her finger.

"I don't know. I've never been good at picking out gifts for others, especially women. I usually ask my mom to help me."

Taylor chuckled at that. She took a sip of her water.

"Well, to be honest, I don't have good taste either. But I like the necklace and that's all that matters, right?"

"Absolutely," James said, grinning.

"But why the star? Is there some meaning behind it I don't get?"

"Oh." James laughed. "Don't you remember?"

Taylor shook her head, causing a lock of hair to fall down onto her cheek. James reached out to brush it away. As his fingers touched her skin, their eyes met and Taylor's breath hitched. They remained with locked eyes for a moment before Taylor finally broke their gaze.

"No," she murmured. "I don't."

"We looked up at the stars one evening when you came to visit."

"Oh right," Taylor said. "I do remember that."

"I was impressed. You told me all about the stars and different constellations. So when I saw this necklace I thought it was nice and well, it reminded me of you."

"That's sweet," Taylor said. "You *really* think about me every time you see a star?"

"Pretty much."

Taylor could feel the familiar blush rising up to her cheeks, and she hoped James didn't notice. In an attempt to hide them, she looked down at her menu and changed the topic.

"This is nice. Not worrying that I'll say or do the wrong thing that leads to a blow up later. I'd forgotten not everyone has that switch in them."

"Switch?"

"That can turn them into a monster," Taylor whispered. She glanced back up at James to see horror looking back at her.

"Taylor—"

"I feel so foolish for ever dating Dylan, like what was I thinking, you know? The signs were there from the beginning."

"Hey, don't be hard on yourself. Men like Dylan know what they are doing," James said.

"But Claire saw it."

"Yeah, well, that's Claire. You can't blame yourself for what hap-pened. He's the abuser. He's the bad guy. And now, you've escaped him. Now, you get to take your life back."

Taylor smiled up at him. It was so different with James. It was easy, fun. She reached across and touched the skin beneath his sleeve, biting down on her lower lip.

"What do you want to take back first?" asked James.

"My birthday."

"Oh, so we get to call tonight your birthday then?" he playfully asked.

"Maybe. He had a way of making my birthday all about him. And then last year he..." she trailed off, deciding not to talk about it. "But that's all behind me. Today I turned 24."

"24. Happy 24th birthday to you," James sincerely said.

He lifted up his drink. Taylor did the same. They clinked their glasses together.

"I feel so old. I have a three year old."

"You're not old. You're still very young. You have time to start over, Taylor. Plenty of people do it at all stages in life, and many aren't nearly as young as you are. You can go back to school, start a new career. Really, you can do anything."

"You sound an awful lot like your sister."

"Well, we are related," he reminded her.

"True."

"So what do you want to do?"

"I'm not sure. I want to find a place for Zachary and me to live. My telemarking job is decent enough money. I do hope to get more hours soon. And maybe in my free time I could try and sell some portraits."

"I think you should get back into your artwork, Taylor. You're so talented."

Again, she blushed.

"I do enjoy it. I have a painting I did for my dad. It's of a shrimping boat. He shrimps, or used to. I just haven't sent it to him yet. I haven't told him I've left Dylan," Taylor said.

"And why not?"

"We don't talk much. I send him cards every so often. Sometimes, he'll call me. But he's not...well, he tries," she said with a shrug. "I've learned to keep the lines open between us. One day, he could do better, and he could have a relationship with me or my son. But I'm not doing all the work. I just do what I can do."

"That's a good idea."

It was late when they got back to Claire's house. They entered the home quietly, not wanting to wake Claire or Zachary, though there was a part of James that expected to find his sister sitting on the couch and waiting for them. To his surprise, she was not.

"I smell cake," Taylor said, sniffing the air. "Claire must have made cakes or cupcakes with Zachary. She must have the patience of a saint."

"Claire? Doubtful."

They entered the kitchen, where Claire's cake stand held a freshly made cake. It was obvious she'd allowed Zachary to help her decorate with the uneven piping of the icing and the random sprinkles on top. James was also pretty sure he saw a small finger swipe along the top. Next to the cake sat a piece of paper that said: *Eat me, please. It's a non-birthday cake.*

"I think she was going for unbirthday," Taylor said. She grabbed two plates from the cabinet, giving one to James. "Would you like some milk?"

"Let me," he offered. "It is your birthday. You're taking it back, remember? That means getting waited on hand and foot."

Taylor smiled up at him as he searched around the kitchen for the glasses. He kept opening doors, finding anything and everything except for cups. Taylor giggled behind him. He turned to her.

"Well, can I at least tell you where the glasses are?" He nodded, and she pointed.

He gave a thankful head shake before opening the correct cabinet door. As he grabbed the two cups, he saw Taylor cutting them large slices of cake. He opened his mouth to protest and then decided better against it.

"Here," Taylor said as he sat down next to her. "I took the piece with Zachary's finger swipe." She laughed. "I doubt Claire noticed. She wouldn't have left it there. She can be a perfectionist with her cakes. Though, it seemed she let Zachary do his thing. She's so great with him."

"Surprisingly," James said.

"Why do you say that?"

"I just never thought of Claire as the nurturing type."

"Yes, I guess I do see that."

They decided to take their cake into the living room to watch a movie. Taylor sat on one side of the couch. James tried to decide where he should sit, but before he could, Taylor patted beside her.

"Come on and sit. What movie should we watch?"

"You have to decide. It's your birthday."

In the end, she chose an early 2000s teen movie. Even though the movie was on, they didn't watch it. Instead, they chatted most of the time. It wasn't until the final twenty minutes that Taylor grew interested in it.

"Oh! This is my favorite part!"

James tried to give the movie his full attention, but he was drawn to look at Taylor as she enjoyed the movie. She leaned forward, watching the scene eagerly.

"Wasn't that wonderful?" she asked him when the scene ended.

"Yes," James agreed. "Wonderful."

Only a few minutes later, James saw Taylor was curled up against the side of the couch, asleep. He leaned over, gently touching her shoulder.

"Taylor," he whispered. "You should probably go to bed."

She only stirred.

"Taylor," he tried again.

When she wouldn't move, he decided to leave her where she was. He picked up a blanket, placing it over her.

"Goodnight, Taylor. Happy birthday."

CHAPTER 19

Taylor hung up the phone and sat at the edge of her bed. She watched her son stack blocks up at the edge of the cot, only to knock them down after he got them so high. Each time the stack hit the ground, it made a thud, causing her to flinch.

When she looked up, she spotted Claire in the doorway. Her dark brows were knitted together with worry.

"He won't grant me the divorce," Taylor whispered.

Claire entered the bedroom, sitting down next to Taylor.

"Did he contact you today?"

"No, his lawyer did," Taylor said. "Basically told me I should rethink this divorce because Dylan has offered to go to therapy."

"Oh, he did, did he?" Claire huffed. "I hope you told him to kiss your ass—I mean, butt." Her eyes cut over to Zachary, and she gave Taylor an apologetic smile.

A humorless chuckle left Taylor, and she shook her head. Sometimes she wished she was as brazen as Claire. If she was like Claire, she'd never been trapped in Dylan's abusive web.

"I told him it's been promised before. I told him that I'm going through with the divorce. Then the lawyer said Dylan will get custody of Zachary, because he has more to offer him. It's true. I can hardly support myself."

"That's not true," Claire disagreed. "And he never comes around to see Zachary. He's a deadbeat, Taylor. He only wants to control you. Once he realizes he can't, he'll move on to someone he can."

Taylor let out a low moan, soothing herself by rubbing her arms. Every time she thought things were getting easier, Dylan would pop back into her life to remind her he still held all the cards.

"James is coming up for the evening to help me with moving some things around downstairs. Why don't you two go to dinner? I'll watch Zachary," Claire offered.

Just the thought of seeing James made Taylor smile. She sat up taller.

"Really? We could all go out together," Taylor said, though she liked the idea of another evening alone with James.

"No, you both go out. Something simple. Grab burgers or something. Oh, and grab ice cream for all of us on the way back! I'm craving some ice cream."

"Okay."

Once James and Taylor left for their dinner, Claire helped Zachary with his plate. She settled him at the table and sat down beside him before pulling out her phone and opening up the security app on her phone. Since Dylan's latest attempts to bother Taylor, Claire had more cameras installed. Any time the cameras detected any type of movement, it sent her a notification.

"Are you watching a movie?" Zachary asked innocently. He ate a bite of his food, looking over her arm to get a better view of her phone.

"No. I'm just looking at our cameras from outside."

The little boy inched closer to her to see.

"Do you see mommy on it?"

"No, Mommy is out with James right now."

"Oh."

Claire stood, walking over to the front of the house to look out the window. An indistinguishable car showed up on the camera, parked across the street. She widened the blinds to get a better view.

Part of her wanted to go outside and see if anyone was inside. But she couldn't leave Zachary in the house alone, and she definitely wasn't taking him out there if it was Dylan. She couldn't call the police, because the car wasn't on her property.

She sunk down onto her couch, pulling back up her app. She rewound from when the car pulled up just after Taylor and James left. However with the way the car had parked, she was unable to tell if someone had gotten out or in.

She opened up her social media app, searching for Dylan's name. They'd never been friends online or in real life. When she found his page, she saw he didn't keep his settings at private. His profile picture was one of him and Zachary by the water.

"Rich," Claire said beneath her breath as she scanned through his page, appalled.

Nearly every other post was about how he was doing everything to get his wife back, how she'd been poisoned against him. Even worse were the comments supporting him. Claire wanted to throw her phone across the room.

A loud crash made Claire jump. Zachary cried out. She jumped from the couch, rushing to the kitchen. Her heart raced in her chest. Had Dylan broken into her home?

When she reached the kitchen, however, she found Zachary on the floor with his foot stuck inside the chair. He was still crying, holding onto his biscuit. Claire let out a sigh of relief before lifting him up into her arms. She helped unlatch his foot from the chair, checking it over to make sure he hadn't hurt himself.

"Thank god," she said, when she saw he was just fine. It seemed the fall had only scared him. She rocked him close to her, pressing a kiss at the top of his head. "What if we got some cookies?"

Zachary's tears stopped. He looked up at her and smiled.

"Cookies?"

"Yes, would you like some?"

Zachary eagerly nodded. Claire smiled. She kept him in her arms, walking over to her pantry in search of the cookies. Zachary pointed to the ones he wanted. She grabbed the entire package of them. Then she walked the both of them to the couch, turned on Zachary's favorite show, and sat down beside him.

While having a child in the house all of the time wasn't easy, Claire would miss him terribly when he and Taylor moved out. It would make her house almost too quiet. She ran her fingers through his hair. He glanced up at her and smiled. She smiled back.

"It's almost time for bed," she told him. "But your mommy shouldn't be out too late. Would you like to wait until she's home?"

He nodded. His eyes searched around for something on the couch.

"Oh! I'll run upstairs and get it," Claire said. She knew he wanted his stuffed bear. "It's in your room."

As she stood, Zachary stood too, tugging on her arm. She looked at him and shook her head.

"I'll be right back," she promised.

"No, I wanna be with you," he said.

"Oh, alright."

As they walked up the stairs, Zachary remained right at her side. They went into the bedroom and there, right on his cot, sat his bear. He grabbed it, hugging it to his chest. Claire decided to walk to the window to see if the car was still there. It was.

"Daddy?"

She hadn't noticed Zachary following her to the window. She saw him also looking out the window and at the car. This wasn't a car she recognized. Of course, Dylan had access to plenty of cars where he worked.

"Does that look like your daddy's car?" Claire asked.

"Daddy likes cars." The only time Zachary ever brought up his daddy since his arrival to Claire's was in relation to cars. Taylor told her Dylan only gave Zachary attention when he showed interest in vehicles.

"Yes," she agreed. "But is this one of your daddy's cars?"

The three year old inched himself up onto his tiptoes as he held onto the ledge of the window to get a better view. He shrugged.

"I dunno."

"Alright," Claire said. She lifted him up onto her hip, helping him not lose his bear in the process. "Let's go back downstairs."

She took one last look at the car before turning away. Again, her heart raced in her chest. While she wasn't terrified of Dylan hurting her, she was terrified of him hurting Zachary or Taylor. Men like him were unpredictable.

They'd eaten at a local burger joint. Taylor got a simple burger with fries, and James got the same but with onion rings. They sat at the sticky booth and chatted about everything but Dylan.

"Maybe next time we should stay in and let Claire go on a night out with some of her friends," Taylor mentioned, digging her French fry into the ketchup.

"Yeah, not a bad idea," James agreed.

"She's always watching Zachary for me. She's been a good friend, a *great* friend really. Maybe I can set up some sort of evening for her with some of her friends," Taylor said before squishing her nose. "Um, do you know who her friends are?"

James laughed, making the skin beside his eyes crinkle. He leaned forward and reached over, taking Taylor's hand within his own.

"We can figure it out. That sounds like a great idea."

Taylor turned her hand so they could link their fingers together. His hands were smooth and rough at the same time. She knew his hands would never hurt her.

When they finished their meal, James helped her out of the booth. As she stood, their eyes met. She took a few steps forward before inching up onto her toes. Her nose brushed against his before they kissed. It was short and chaste, but everything she ever could have wished for.

"I-I..." she stuttered.

James only grinned. His hand caressed her cheek, and he kissed her once more.

Claire kept checking outside the window to see if the car was still sitting there across the street. It was. She had a hard time remaining focused on her godson, too worried about what it meant if Dylan was sitting there spying on them. She ended up making a call to the nonemergency number, telling them her concerns. They promised to drive by and take a look, but they couldn't give her a time when they'd be able to make it by.

By the time Taylor and James came back, Claire noticed the car had left. She stared in the blank spot for a moment before searching down the street.

"What are you looking for?" Taylor asked.

Claire lifted her phone, showing both her and James a screenshot of the car.

"Does this look familiar to you?"

"Maybe," Taylor said, knitting her brows.

"It sat outside the house the whole time you were away. Does Dylan have a car like this?"

"It's possible there's one at the shop," Taylor said. "I can't know for sure."

"Right, of course. Maybe I'm just on edge. Do you still follow him on all your social media accounts?"

"I guess," Taylor said. "I don't actually get on my social media anymore. I try to avoid any way he can contact me."

"That's smart," James chimed in. Claire didn't miss how his hand brushed over Taylor's shoulder.

"Well, I stalked his page. It is all about how you left him, and how he's fighting to get you back."

Claire pulled up the page on her phone and gave it to James.

"Couldn't this help with the divorce?"

Her brother scanned over it, making a face that got progressively more disgusted the more he read.

"Maybe."

Taylor reached out for the phone, but Claire stopped her.

"Don't read it. It's just ramblings of a madman. You don't need any of that swirling around in your head."

"I agree," James said.

"But then why did you tell me about it?" Taylor asked.

"I...I was only wondering if you had seen it. Now, I know you haven't."

"I guess," Taylor trailed off. "Where's Zachary?"

"He fell asleep while we watched a show. I put him on his cot."

"Thanks. I should probably go to bed myself. I have early morning telemarking calls tomorrow," she said, looking to James and giving him a small smile. "When do you have to go back?"

"I have work tomorrow," he said. "But I could come back on Friday?"

"Alright."

Taylor's cheeks turned a crimson red. James only brightened his smile; his fingertips brushed along the back of her hand. Taylor turned her palm and squeezed his fingers. Claire was unable to tear her eyes away. Then they unlatched, and Taylor went up the stairs.

"Well," Claire began, "looks like you had a good dinner."

"We did," James said. "Nothing serious. Just friends."

"Right, of course you are."

After Taylor checked on her sleeping son, she approached her window and opened the blinds. The spot where Claire said she saw the car was still empty, but it didn't keep Taylor from feeling uneasy. Why couldn't Dylan just let her go?

She plopped onto her bed, kicking off her shoes, when her phone buzzed. She froze. But as she lifted the phone, her body relaxed. It was a message from James.

I had a nice evening with you. I don't leave until after lunch tomorrow. Could you and Zachary join me for lunch?

Taylor bit on the inside of her cheek.

Sure. That sounds fun.

CHAPTER 20

"What do you think?" Taylor asked, looking to her friend for approval.

Taylor watched as Claire took in the new apartments they had found. They were only a quick bus ride from Claire's house and the art studio where she worked.

"It's quaint," Claire said with a nod.

"You hate it."

"No, I do not. I'm just sad you are going to leave me soon," Claire replied. "But it's nice, really. And it comes furnished." Claire walked over to the small table by the small kitchenette and ran her fingers over the top of it. "And best of all, you'll be here and not far away."

"Yes," Taylor agreed, smiling. "You were right. I don't really want to move back home. I like it here near you."

"And James?" Claire rose a brow. Taylor's cheeks burned.

"Maybe."

Zachary, who had been quiet until now, ran from the back of the apartment and up front where they were. He zoomed his plane up in the air and then under the table where Claire stood. Claire bent down to his level and began playing along with him. As Taylor watched, her heart grew full.

"You'll always be there for him, won't you?"

Claire stood back up.

"Of course, I will. I adore Zachary, just as I adore you," she said.

"Good," Taylor replied. She knew she should mention the will she'd written, but she didn't want this joyous moment about getting back on her feet to be darkened. She would bring it up to her soon. "Now, let me show you the bedrooms."

Taylor now counted down the days when James would be back in town. She felt like a school girl falling in love. He just left the day before. Now it would be over a week before she'd see him again.

"Why are you blushing?" Claire asked Taylor playfully as she braided Taylor's red hair into two side plaits to then pull into a bun, so it'd keep her hair out of her face that evening for her painting class.

"Am I?"

With her fingers, Taylor played with the trinket on her necklace that James had given her. Her mind went to him.

"I heard you on the phone late last night. Speaking with James?"

"Perhaps."

The blush on Taylor's cheek deepened, making Claire laugh.

"I knew it! You'll be exhausted if you continue that."

"It's the easiest time to talk. If I try to speak on the phone when Zachary is awake, he's like a moth to a flame. So I have to wait until he's asleep, and you too."

"Me?" Claire asked playing innocent.

"Yes, you. You'll listen in, if I'm not careful."

"I am not listening in," Claire assured her. "I have zero want to know what you and my brother are talking on the phone about."

She made a face and forced out a fake gag.

"We don't speak about anything inappropriate!"

"For now," Claire teased. "But once the divorce is final, then perhaps you might."

Taylor rolled her eyes before standing. She began messing with her bun. Claire tugged her hands away.

"Stop, you'll mess it up. You look cute."

"That's not the look I'm going for, but thank you."

"What look are you going for?" Claire asked.

Taylor shrugged and chuckled.

"I actually don't know. I mean, it's just painting class."

"But you enjoy it, don't you?"

"Oh yes, I love it. It's my favorite part of the week," Taylor said with much enthusiasm.

"Outside of spending time with James?" Claire asked, leaning a bit closer to her.

Again, Taylor rolled her eyes. She tugged at the bottom of her shirt.

"Enough of that. We're friends who may have kissed...once."

"Wait...what?!"

"I have to go," Taylor said, skirting around Claire with a smile on her face.

"You can't just leave now! When? Where? How?"

"How did I kiss him? You want details?" Taylor asked as her eyebrows danced. She enjoyed teasing her friend.

"No...that's not...When?" Claire sputtered.

"I really do need to go. My class starts soon."

"Tonight, you are filling in all the blanks for me, except the details of how."

"Understood." Taylor said as she kissed the top of Zachary's head, caressing his cheek. "Be good for Claire. I love you so much."

"I love you, too!"

Taylor waved at the both before she exited the house. She giggled, thinking about Claire's face, and how it was going to kill her to know the details all afternoon. Taylor bounced on her feet, feeling freer than she had in a long time.

While Taylor was off at work, Claire and Zachary drew with chalk on the small concrete stairs that went down to the grass outside. Zachary asked her to write his mommy's name, requesting hearts around it. They played outside for nearly an hour when Claire realized it was time to feed Zachary something for dinner.

"We should go in and wash up now," Claire said.

"But it's still bright outside."

"Yes, because it's summer. Come on."

They went inside to wash up. As Claire glanced down at her black shorts, she saw they were covered in chalk dust. She made sure Zachary was content and went upstairs to change herself, deciding to go ahead and put on her comfy clothes for bed.

When she got back downstairs, Zachary was playing quietly on the couch with a chunky puzzle she'd found with his favorite cartoon characters. She sat down beside him before her phone dinged.

It was a message from Lucas.

I miss you.

Claire stared at the text, surprised. Lately, if he texted her, he did it under the pretense of it being work related. Her fingers tapped against the side of her leg, as she debated how to respond to him.

What do you want me to say?

She didn't mean to sound rude, but she didn't know what to say to him. They both wanted very different things.

Three dots showed on the screen, showing that he was typing. They then disappeared, before reappearing again. Finally, his response came through.

That you miss me too.

Claire sighed.

"Are you sad?" Zachary asked. He climbed over the pillow on the couch before sitting down beside her, resting his head against her arm. She smiled down at him, deciding she would message him back later.

"No, everything is just fine."

"Oh, okay," he said as he jumped up next to her before moving down to the floor. Then he walked over to the window to look outside. "Where's Mommy?"

Claire checked her watch.

"She should be arriving anytime soon."

Nearly an hour later, Taylor still wasn't back. While it didn't happen every week, sometimes she'd get asked to stay later by one of the customers to help with a question they had. However, Taylor usually messaged Claire when she was running behind.

She lifted her phone to text Taylor. There was no immediate response. Not quite the worry for alarm, but she did call. Zachary would need to go to bed soon. He preferred when Taylor did it. There was no answer.

"Strange."

This time she called the studio. The owner, Margaret, answered right away.

"Art and Stuff, this is Margaret speaking."

"Margaret, this is Claire, Taylor's roommate. Is she still there?" Claire asked, hoping to hear she'd just left and would be back here soon.

"She never showed up."

"What?" Claire asked as her heart fell within her chest.

"Yes, I tried to call her several times, but she never answered. I assumed she was sick or something had happened with Zachary."

"She...she left for work at the same time she always does."

Her body began to shake. She brought her hand up over her mouth; a worry sob escaped her and she whispered, "Dylan."

PART THREE

CHAPTER 21

The dark clouds in the sky filled the ominous feeling in Claire's chest. The clouds were heavy, but had yet to open up and allow the rain droplets to fall to the ground. Claire knew when that happened it would be hard, painful drops that stung as they hit her skin.

Her song skipped a beat, drawing her attention to her radio in her car. With her palm, she hit against her dash, making the CD play correctly. Even though she had an iPhone and a way to connect it to her car, she needed to listen to this particular CD all the time lately. The CD was an old mixed tape made by Taylor. It had been scratched and blemished over years of use. But when she listened to it, it took her back to when it was first given to her and road trips back home singing the songs at the top of their lungs.

As Claire pulled her hand away from her radio, she noted her nails that had been bitten down over the past several days. Her paint was chipped and unkempt, unlike how she normally kept her nails.

Again she stared out her car window toward the clouds. It seemed in the past several seconds they had already grown darker.

"Just rain already," she whispered.

She sat back in her chair, accidentally seeing her reflection in her rearview mirror. She usually twisted her raven thick hair up in a way so her beautiful curls framed around her face. But now, it was just drawn up into a weird, askew bun. Claire brought her hand up to her hair and attempted to flatten the top. She ignored the bags under her eyes and the lack of makeup on her face.

When she finally gathered the courage to leave her car, Claire remained outside for several minutes. Her eyes judged the building in front of her. It was a small house that had been turned into a business. There was a flimsy sign hanging from the banister which was halfway dangling from the edge as the wind blew it up and down. The light blue house's paint was chipped and most of the shutters were missing.

Claire began to walk up the stairs toward to the first door. The second step had a creak in it so loud that Claire was sure the stair would collapse beneath her feet. She quickened her steps until she was on the wrap-around porch.

She clutched her small sweater around her shoulders, and she wondered if she had chosen the wrong person. This did not appear to be the office of the best private detective in the area. She creased her forehead, unsure.

"Hello?" a voice said. She glanced over to see a young woman out through a window. She had a bright smile that did not match the weather. The tip of her nose and her cheekbones were rosy against her fair skin. She wore her light blonde locks in a braid that fell over her shoulder. "May I help you?"

"I..."

"Do you have an appointment with PI Evans?"

The girl's bubbly personality made Claire uncomfortable. There was nothing happy about this appointment.

"I do," Claire answered.

The woman disappeared and shut the window. Before Claire could even realize what was happening, the door in front of her opened to reveal the young woman. She was shorter than Claire and was likely only eighteen or nineteen. She wore a purple, flowery sundress and silver flip-flops.

"Hello," the young woman greeted. "I'm Liliana. You're Claire Donahue?"

"Yes," Claire said.

"Great! My brother is just through that door right there," Liliana said as she pointed down a long hallway.

Claire stepped inside the house and a chill ran down her spine. It was cold and damp in the building, not homely at all. They had made the living room into a waiting room and an area for the receptionist. There was one small desk, a fireplace, and two rickety chairs.

"I know, it's not much," Liliana commented. "We're going to do some remodeling soon."

"Where is the PI?" Claire clipped. She had no interest in the plans for this establishment. She just wanted to speak with Evans.

"Oh, yes," Liliana said. She again pointed down the long, dark hallway. "Last door, straight ahead. Just walk in. He's expecting you."

Claire gave Liliana a curt nod. Then she made her way to the door. Before she could knock, the door opened. A tall man stood before her.

"Come in," he said. He spun and walked around back to his desk, sitting down. He pointed to the chair across from him to tell her to sit as well. Claire did. Then she eyed Evans.

He had blond hair like his sister, but it was a darker blond. It was in a gentleman's cut that brought out the blue in his eyes. His skin was tan from time at the beach, which she could tell from the hints of red sunburn on his pale white ears. He was dressed to the nines in a suit and tie, definitely his professional wear. Claire noticed his tie was purple, and she briefly wondered if his sister had insisted they match.

"I've come to hire you," Claire cut to the chase. "I'm sure you have heard of the missing woman, Taylor Montgomery?"

"Yes," Evans said as he cleared his throat. "Tragedy. Or, perhaps, she left on her own accord?"

Claire's jaw tightened.

"She didn't. She has a three-year-old son. She never would have left him," Claire told Evans. Her blunt nails dug into the side of her palms as her thoughts went to Zachary.

"Perhaps," Evans answered.

"She wouldn't," Claire stated once more. "Her husband did it."

"I'm sure the police will come to that same conclusion, Mrs....."

"*Ms.*," she corrected. "Donahue, but you can call me Claire. And no, the police will not come to that conclusion. They believe my friend left of her own will. I know that is a lie. They have proven time and time again to be useless when my friend asked them for help. That is why I have come to you."

"Alright, Claire," Evans stated. His sky blue eyes stared right back at her. "I'm pricey."

"I don't care. I have savings," Claire answered.

The previous night, she had counted up how many hours she could afford. With her savings and the inheritance from her grandparents, she could hire him for a few weeks if it was needed. After that, she would no longer have a backup in life, but that didn't matter.

"Alright."

"I need you to find my friend, Mr. Evans. I know her husband had a hand in her disappearance. She left him, and he didn't like that. You need to follow him, prove that he..."

Her resolve faded then. Two tears fell down her cheeks and onto the top of her black pants, making a small splash.

Evans grabbed a tissue from his desk. He stood and gave it over to her. Claire gratefully took it and dabbed her cheeks. She hadn't come here to cry.

"Thank you," she whispered.

"What is his name?"

"Dylan Montgomery," Claire answered. She watched Evans scribble the name down on the small pad on his desk.

"He did it," she then whispered with much intensity. More tears came. "I know he did it. He killed her. He *killed* her."

Max Evans never knew what to do when the person before him started to cry. He always held tissues on his desk, because despite that, his job often came with crying clients. The woman before him was no exception. She kept wiping under her eyelids, trying to keep the tears at bay.

"So," Max began, with a tight smile.

Claire glanced up at him. Her dark eyes stared at him, intense with grief. It unsettled him. He cleared his throat.

"What can you tell me about Dylan Montgomery?"

"He's an abusive asshole," Claire said as she tapped her fingertips against her knee.

"Where does he work?" Max asked.

Claire's fingers tapped harder.

"Um... Mike's Garage, it's a couple towns over, about an hour away. He repairs cars."

"Alright. Does his family live in the same area?"

"No," Claire said with a shake of her head. "He doesn't speak with his family, from what I know. Taylor said that anyway. I don't...he and I didn't really get along."

Bending over, Claire dug in her purse. Max waited patiently, checking the time on the clock over his door. There were still twenty-five minutes left of this thirty-minute session.

"Here," Claire said, dropping a thin manila envelope onto his desk. "There is everything I know about Dylan Montgomery and Taylor. Taylor and I have known each other for nearly five years. She's been with Dylan for four of those."

Max took the envelope and opened it. He pulled out all that was inside. There were a few photos, some letters, and a list of names, but the most valuable piece was a timeline of events that Claire had already written down in great detail from the moment Taylor left her husband until today. There was even a map of the route Taylor took from Claire's house to the art studio where she must have been taken.

"Why are you not giving this information to the police?" he asked her.

His eyes remained on the timeline. Taylor left her husband three months ago and just a week prior she went missing.

"I did. They made a copy. But they are useless. Do you know how many times Taylor asked for their help while she was still with him? Dozens. Do you know how many times they helped?" Claire paused, waiting for Max to guess.

"None?"

"Close, once," Claire said with much venom in her voice. "One time they listened to her cries for help, but it was too late. I don't trust them to do the right thing. It's why I am hiring you, Evans. From what I've read about you, you're the very best."

Pride bloomed in Max's chest. He was the best in this area as well as the surrounding ones. Even though he was one of the youngest, he'd never allowed that to stop him. In fact, it was what pushed him to work harder. Just last month he'd been in the local magazine's top 40 under 40 you need to know. He'd made number 3. Next year, his goal was number one.

"I am."

Claire's eyes rolled, making Max bristle.

"I am the best private detective within 100 miles. My record speaks for itself."

"I know that," Claire said with a huff as her arms came across her chest. "I just didn't expect you to be so arrogant about it. I should have guessed with that picture of yours in the magazine."

"Ah, so you saw it?"

"You do know that I am here because my best friend is missing, right? That she was likely killed by her abusive husband, correct? Not to talk about how great you are?"

"I know," Max said solemnly. "I apologize, Claire."

"Here," Claire said as she sat her phone down in front of Max, showing a picture of a little boy with bright green eyes and messy brown hair. "This is Zachary. He is three years old. Taylor is his mother. Remember this face when you are working on this assignment."

"Of course."

The room fell silent for a moment.

"What else do you need?" Claire asked, breaking the silence.

"I see you have a list of names. Who are they?"

"People who work with Dylan, neighbors, and his friends."

"Alright. Do you happen to have Taylor's phone? And a list of her friends?"

"She didn't have any, outside of me," Claire said. Another tear slipped down her cheek. "Dylan didn't like her to have people to lean on. Before she called me a few months ago, I hadn't spoken to her in nearly a year. She had a neighbor next door that sometimes watched Zachary and called the police from time to time when she heard screams."

"And Taylor's phone? Do you have it?"

"No. She had it on her the day she went missing."

"What about the number?"

Claire wrote it down quickly before sliding it over toward Max.

"Here. How can that help?"

"I can possibly track it down. I can't promise, but this will help," he said, adding it to the pile of information about Taylor and Dylan. "And you're sure your friend didn't just take off? She's young, so she had her son young. Bad relationship, life stolen away..."

"Taylor didn't run off. She adores her son, Zachary. If she were to leave, she'd take him along with her. She'd never leave him behind. Zachary is why she finally left Dylan. She knew she needed to protect him. There is no way she'd leave him where Dylan could have complete access to him."

Max pondered this. His eyes looked down at the photo of Taylor that sat within the pile. He slid it over so he could see the entire picture. She held a small child in her arms, but his head was buried in Taylor's shoulder. Her eyes weren't on the camera; they were on her son, bright and full of love. Yes, he had to agree. It was unlikely the woman in the picture would leave behind her son.

"I'll find her," Max promised. "I'll find your friend."

When Claire left his office, Max poured over everything he and Claire had spoken about. He kept staring at the photo of Taylor with her son. Suddenly this job felt much heavier than all the others he had done. It wasn't his first missing person's case. He'd had a few of them. But those were all teenagers who had run away from home with their boyfriends or girlfriends. Each easily found after he had access to their social media accounts.

Most of his cases were affairs. Following cheating men and women was also a fast and easy deal. That was often when he had the crying across his desk as he showed the person on the other side the evidence he'd found. Of course, sometimes, the person would be thrilled because of a prenup. Those were the most fun. It didn't feel as though he was destroying lives then, but instead making them better.

But he didn't feel there would be any happy ending when he found Taylor Montgomery.

"She's pretty."

Max groaned. He quickly placed the paperwork back into its file before glancing up at his baby sister. His mother insisted he give Liliana a job. She was fresh out of high school, needing to make some money before college started in the fall.

"What does that matter?"

"I was just saying that she is pretty, is all," Liliana said, stepping further into his office. "So, is it another affair case? Is her husband cheating on her?"

"No. Her best friend is missing."

"Oh! Did she run off with her man?" Liliana giggled. "Let me guess, you're going to tap into his phone? See who all he's been texting?"

Max's expression hardened.

"I told you it's not an affair case."

"Alright, her best friend is missing. But where'd she go?"

Liliana plopped into the chair where Claire had just been. She tugged on the edge of her braid before throwing it over her shoulder.

"She believes the husband killed her."

"Woah, that's deep."

"Yeah," Max murmured as he rubbed the back of his neck.

"So, what does that mean? What do you do?"

"I find the friend," Max simply answered. "Hopefully, I find her alive. Likely, I will."

He offered his sister a soft smile, trying not to show that he was lying. Liliana was too innocent to be working here with this type of job.

"Sure, of course."

"Now, get back to work."

"But what if..."

"Back to work," Max said.

Liliana groaned. She did what he said, though, and exited the room. Right as she closed the door, a loud clap of thunder made Max jump. The power cut out. Liliana let out a shriek.

"Are you alright?"

"Yes," she answered from down the hallway. "It just freaked me out for a moment. I'm fine."

"Good. Get the flashlights. I'll go to the box."

As his sister did as he asked, he lifted the picture of Taylor and her son. A flash of lightning gave him a better view of the woman.

"Alright, Taylor Montgomery," he said to himself. "What happened to you?"

Chapter 22

After she pulled into her garage, Claire spent ten minutes trying to pull herself together. On the ride home from meeting with the private investigator, she couldn't stop crying. The tears came, and she couldn't find the strength to stop them.

She wiped beneath her eyes. Then she pulled down her visor and lifted up the door to the window, groaning. She looked like shit.

Quickly, she searched for her lipstick, hoping that some color on her lips wouldn't give away to the fact she'd been crying. Once she stepped through the door, she had to put on her brave face.

With a deep breath, she finally stepped out of the car and walked into her home. The patter of little footsteps ran toward her. She forced herself to smile.

"Cwaire!" Zachary happily called out. She bent down, immediately swooping him up into her arms. "Mommy coming home today?"

Her smile faltered.

"Not yet," was all she managed to get out.

As she walked around and into the living room, her sister stood from the couch. Simone held her baby in her arms while her older son was on some device on the loveseat. Since Taylor's disappearance, her sister had really stepped up to help Claire out with Zachary. They never had been really close, the two of them, but Simone was temporarily a stay at home mother and Claire still had to go to work. And she was not about to give Zachary over to Dylan (not that he'd asked for him) or social services.

"How'd it go?" Simone asked.

"It went," Claire answered simply. "Thank you for watching him again."

"It's no bother, really. He's a sweet kid. Anthony, come on, we need to go."

Claire's five-year-old nephew jumped up from the couch.

"I like it here at Aunt Claire's. Why can't I stay?"

Claire and Simone met eyes. Any other time and Claire would have said he could, but she didn't have the energy for another child in her home right now. She was struggling just to stay upbeat enough for Zachary, unable to tell him there was a chance his mommy may never come home.

"Not today," Simone said, turning to face her son. "But another day."

"Yes, you guys can come over here any time when I'm at work if it's okay with your mom," Claire said.

"Oh, okay," Anthony sighed.

Claire walked her sister and nephews to the front door. When Simone was stepping out, she gave Claire's shoulder a supportive squeeze. Her chin began to quiver, and she could feel the tears springing to her eyes.

"Thank you," Claire managed to say as the lump formed in her throat.

"Let me know if you need anything else, alright? I'm just ten minutes away," Simone said. She smiled down at Zachary. "I'll see you in the morning."

"Okay," he said shyly, hiding his face away into the nook of Claire's neck.

She waited until her sister was in her car and had begun to drive away before closing the door.

They went back into the living room. It was immaculate. Claire didn't know how her sister did it, but toys were always put away when she was in charge. How did she manage all three boys and keep the house spotless?

"Want to play?" Claire asked Zachary.

"I want Mommy," he said.

Claire rubbed Zachary's back in an attempt to soothe him.

"Me too," she whispered. "I'm doing everything I can to bring her back home."

Last she'd heard, Dylan had been called in for questioning but wasn't taken into custody. Apparently he had an alibi for the time of Taylor's disappearance. Whoever it was, Claire was sure they were lying to the police.

Every day, she called and asked for more updates about the case, though there was little they could tell her. Every time they spoke with her, they had an air about them that said they were sure Taylor had left of her own free will, and that she hadn't been taken. They didn't know her friend, at all.

She made Zachary something to eat, setting him down into his chair to do so. She focused on making him a grilled cheese and not all the thoughts swirling around in her head. The toasted bread came out perfectly golden. She placed it on the plate and cut it into four triangles. It was strangely domestic. She realized that overnight, she'd become a single mother to the little boy sitting at her table.

Her eyes closed. No, she wasn't his mother. She never would be his mother. His mother was bright, cheerful, and loving. And she, Claire, was someone who always saw herself as a childless being, at least for another five or so years.

More tears came then. It wasn't fair.

She quickly placed the sandwich in front of Zachary and left the room, not wanting him to see her cry. There she searched for her phone, wanting to call the police station to ask and see if they were anywhere closer to finding her friend.

A knock came at her front door. She paused. Now anytime someone knocked, she worried it was Dylan on the other side coming to ask for Zachary. She'd tell him no, of course, but just one phone call to the cops and she'd have to hand him over. She had no rights to him.

Worried, Claire peeked through the blinds. She calmed. It was only Lucas. She opened the door. He stood, rocking on his feet.

"I heard," he said.

"You heard?" she asked.

"About Taylor. I've seen you at work. I didn't realize...Taylor is really missing?"

Claire nodded and wiped beneath her eye.

"I wish I had known sooner," he said, stepping forward.

"It's been on the news," Claire rebutted, taking her own step back.

"I don't watch the news."

It was true, he didn't. Claire knew he got most of his news online and none of it was local. Taylor's disappearance hadn't left the local news.

"How are you holding up?" Lucas asked as he touched her elbow. He gently drew her closer to him, staring intently into her eyes. She hiccupped before sobbing. Quickly, Lucas wrapped his arms around her. "Oh, Claire. I'm so sorry."

"He did it," she murmured against his chest. "I know he did it."

"Who? Her husband?"

Claire nodded. He tightened his hold of her. She was grateful for his support. More tears came.

"She left for work, but never showed up. He must have taken her somewhere between here and there. I retraced her path multiple times trying to figure out where he could have grabbed her," Claire cried.

"Has he been arrested?"

"No. He had an alibi."

Claire brought her palms up to Lucas's chest and pushed him back, because she was starting to feel claustrophobic. With the tips of her fingers, she wiped beneath her eyes.

"I'm glad you're here," she said, surprising herself.

For weeks, she hadn't missed him, but right now she was grateful to have Lucas here with her, to not be dealing with Taylor's disappearance on her own. James wouldn't even answer her calls. He was dealing with Taylor's disappearance in a completely different way. Anytime she called all she would get was a text asking if they'd found her yet. When she would reply with a no, she wouldn't hear from him again.

"May I come in?" Lucas asked.

Claire hesitated for only a moment.

"Sure."

They entered her home. Lucas took her hand and she allowed it, weaving her fingers in with his.

"Zachary is eating in the kitchen. I should probably check in on him."

"You're keeping Taylor's son?" he asked, surprised.

"Yes, who else would?"

"I...I don't know. I mean—" Lucas paused, then he smiled. "I think that's great. I'm sure he feels more comfortable here with you."

"He does," Claire agreed.

They entered the kitchen where Zachary sat at the table, still munching on his grilled cheese sandwich. Upon seeing Lucas, he paused. He placed the piece of sandwich he was eating back onto his plate.

"Hi," Lucas greeted.

Zachary didn't respond. Since Taylor's disappearance, he'd become more withdrawn to strangers.

"Zachary, do you remember my friend, Lucas?" Claire asked. Zachary stared Lucas down, not saying a word. "Well, he's just come by to say hello. Is your food alright?" Again, Zachary didn't say anything.

"What are you eating there, bud?"

Lucas's attempt to try and get Zachary to speak with him failed. Zachary looked down at his plate.

"We'll let you finish up," Claire said. "Come on, we can sit in the living room while he finishes."

They went to sit on the couch. From here, Claire could see Zachary, but they weren't standing over him and making him feel uncomfortable.

"So what happens now?" Lucas asked.

"I hired a private detective, um...Max Evans. Supposedly, he is the best within so many miles from here."

"And what do you think he can do that the police can't?"

"Prove that Dylan is lying, find my friend, anything really will be better than what they have done."

"Right. Well, I do hope he finds her."

"I do too," Claire said. "I want her back."

Lucas wrapped his arm around her and she rested her head on his shoulder. In that moment, she only remembered all of the good and wonderful things about Lucas. She closed her eyes and breathed him in.

"I missed this," she whispered.

"I did, too."

Zachary wouldn't go to bed. Nothing Claire did or said would calm him down. He stood on the edge of the cot and flung his arms toward her, not wanting her to touch him. She backed up, trying to give him space through his tantrum.

"You're tired," she said between his screams as she sat down on the edge of the bed in the room.

"I want Mommy!" he yelled.

Tears fell down his little cheeks. Claire swallowed hard.

"I know," she murmured. "Would you like to sleep up here in Mommy's bed?"

The little boy shook his head. He brought his right leg up, crossed his arms over his chest, and then hit his foot against the cot.

"I. Want. Mommy."

"I know you do," Claire tried to remain calm.

This was the first tantrum she had to deal with on her own. When Taylor was here, she could watch from afar or just leave the room. He'd never had one while Taylor was at work or when she went out to eat with James. But it seemed Claire's time was up, and now she had to learn how to deal with one.

"Why don't I read you a story?"

"Want. Mommy!" he yelled; his cheeks were red.

Claire struggled to try and find a way to make him happy. She grabbed her phone and quickly found a picture of Taylor on it to offer him. He looked at it for a split second before chucking it across the room. It slammed against the wall.

"Zachary!"

The little boy fell down onto his cot and cried harder, kicking his legs against the padding. She covered her face. This further showed how inept of a parent she would be one day.

Zachary continued to cry. She slid off the bed, down to his side. Gently, she patted his back before rubbing big circles on it. He didn't push her away. Eventually, his cries settled, and he fell into an uneasy sleep.

Once he was out, she sat back, resting her back against the bed. Zachary needed Taylor. *She* needed Taylor. Again, the tears came. She shook them away and stood, going over to reach for her phone. By some miracle, it appeared undamaged.

She walked out of the room and went back downstairs where Lucas still sat on her couch.

"I hadn't expected you to be here," she said. "I thought for sure once you heard the tantrum you'd flee." She let out a half-hearted chuckle.

"Of course, I wouldn't. You need me right now. You can't do this alone."

"No," Claire agreed with a low sob. "I can't."

Lucas bent over, cupping her cheek.

"Then don't."

Claire couldn't explain what came over her, but she leaned forward to him. Her lips pressed against his. He deepened the kiss, and she let him. It was nice to have someone here in her corner with her again.

When they pulled apart, she met his eyes and smiled.

"I guess I really did miss you."

The next morning, Claire had to rush to get everything in order. She'd overslept. Somehow Zachary didn't wake up early that morning, and she'd forgotten to set her alarm. Now she was in a rush trying to get all of his things ready to take him to her sister's house. Going to her sister's always added at least twenty extra minutes to her morning routine. She looked at the clock, she was already running five minutes behind.

"Here."

She gave Lucas a to-go coffee cup. He had stayed the night. He kissed her cheek, stepping outside the door.

"I can cover for you," he told her. "Don't rush and get in an accident or something."

"I'll be fine," she assured him. "I can make it."

"Well, if you don't, don't worry, alright? We don't have any important events this weekend."

"Right. Okay, goodbye. I'll see you shortly."

She kissed him, pressing her hand on his cheek. He smiled, nuzzling his nose against hers for a brief moment. He walked over to his car. Though she should have been getting Zachary cleaned up from breakfast, she followed Lucas. That's when she spotted James. He was parked in front of her house.

As Lucas pulled out of the driveway, James began to walk toward Claire's front door.

"I don't have time for whatever this is, James. I have to get to work."

The closer James got to her, the better she could see how much his cheeks had sunken in and the circles beneath his eyes.

"Wow, you look like shit."

"I thought you broke up with him," James said instead of responding to her. His hands were deep in his hoodie pocket.

"Not break up, just a break."

"Huh," he muttered. "So tell me about this PI you've hired. Is he any good? Will he find her?"

Admitting defeat that she wouldn't make it to work in time, Claire motioned for her brother to come inside. He did. When he spotted Zachary, his eyes lit up before the pain grew deeper.

"He needs her," he whispered.

"He does," Claire agreed with a whimper.

"So this PI..."

"Right. He's supposed to be the best. I've given him all of what I know about Dylan and the day Taylor disappeared."

"He has a girlfriend," James said.

"Evans? The PI? What would that matter?" Claire shrugged.

"No, Dylan. I saw him out with her last night."

"Oh. Of course he does, the snake. Taylor's body isn't even cold, and he's chasing another woman."

Claire made a low sound. Beside her, James paled.

"She could still be alive."

"I hope so," Claire said quickly. "I want that, of course I do. But men like Dylan...they..." she murmured, shaking her head, not able to say it. "I wonder if this is some new girlfriend, or if he's been dating her for a while. I'll mention it to Evans. Not sure if it will help, but it could."

"Maybe."

Claire glanced at her watch. She was supposed to be at work in ten minutes.

"I have to go, get to work."

"Who watches Zachary?"

"Simone, for now."

"Oh."

Claire went to get Zachary and his bag for her sister's. James walked outside with her and waited until she had gotten Zachary into the car before saying anything else.

"You were 'on a break' for a reason, Claire. You've always had a decent gut feeling, follow that."

Claire frowned.

"Are you talking about Lucas?"

"Yes."

Claire rolled her eyes.

"He won't hurt me, James. He's not an abusive asshole like Dylan."

"I never said he was. Have a good rest of your day," he said before heading back to his car.

"Oh!" Claire called after him. "Answer the phone sometime."

James just waved again before getting into his car and driving away. Claire climbed into the car. She looked back at Zachary who had this thumb in his mouth and was kicking the seat in front of him.

"Are you ready to go?"

The little boy shook his head.

"I want my mommy," he repeated for the hundredth time.

"Me too, kid. Me too."

CHAPTER 23

From a distance, James could see Dylan standing in front of the auto shop, drinking a soda and talking on his cell phone. Anger coursed through his veins. He wanted to walk right up to him and demand to know where Taylor was. But he knew Dylan wouldn't tell him. He knew he had to watch and wait for him to slip up.

For the past several days, he'd not shown up for work. His parents called several times worried about him. They also cared about Taylor and understood why he was distraught. But James was unable to talk to them about it. He ignored most of their calls.

Dylan finished his drink and turned. He met James's eyes. The heat rose in his chest. He knew he should have hidden himself so he wouldn't be seen, but he had been hoping for a confrontation. He needed to see him face to face.

Dylan dropped his soda by the trash can, missing the opening by close to a foot. Then he walked over toward James.

"I should call the cops on you," Dylan said. "You here, just watching me like this."

"It's not a crime to stand in front of a restaurant," James said as he pointed to the diner behind him. "I can stand here all day. You are at work. I'm not on your private property."

"You know," Dylan began, "I should call the cops. I bet they'd like to know you were dating Taylor, who is my wife. Bet they'd like to know you were cheating with my wife and now she's gone missing."

"Where is she?" James asked.

"How should I know? You were the one sleeping around with *my* wife."

Dylan stepped forward, pressing his finger against James's chest. James was a good few inches taller than Dylan, so he stood up straighter.

"Don't touch me. Where is Taylor? What did you do with her?"

"I don't know," Dylan said with a snarl. "She left me for you."

"She didn't leave you for me," James said. "You pushed her down the stairs."

"I never hurt her!" Dylan yelled now. "I will call the cops, and tell them I suspect you of taking my wife!"

"Good luck with that," James said. "I have a real alibi. God, I wish I had been with her. I could have protected her."

A look flashed over Dylan's face that was akin to pride. It made James feel increasingly uncomfortable.

"You couldn't have," Dylan quietly said.

Something took over James then. He brought his arm up and punched Dylan straight in the nose. Then as Dylan tried to lean forward, James grasped at the lapels of his shirt.

"Where is she?!" he screamed. "Where is she?! What did you do to her!? Where is she!?"

An hour later, James sat in a cell at the local police station, still fuming. Dylan's words, *you couldn't have,* kept running through his head.

"Your sister is here," an officer said, unlocking and opening up the door. James stood. He walked out to find his sister, Claire, waiting for him out front. James retrieved his bag of things before they went outside to Claire's car.

"What were you thinking?" Claire seethed. "You are so incredibly stupid!"

"I..."

"It's bad enough you are following him around. Now here you go getting yourself arrested! How does that help Taylor?"

"I didn't mean—he came up to me and I...I couldn't control myself. All I could think about was her and what he did to her."

Claire's face softened. She nodded, then pointed to the car to say it was time to get in. But as they sat down, Claire didn't turn on the car.

"Did it feel good?"

"Hm?"

"To punch him in the face. How did it feel?"

"Satisfying, in the moment," he added.

"I bet it did," Claire said. "What I wouldn't give for five minutes alone in a room with him. Did he say anything about Taylor? Give any inclination of where she might be?"

"He said I couldn't have protected her."

Claire let go of the wheel and sat back. She pursed her lips and flared her nostrils.

"You'll tell the police that," Claire said. "I'll drive you to the station where the detectives are. That has to be enough to prove he did this."

A tear slipped down his sister's cheek. He sat awkwardly beside her, not knowing what he could say to make this any better for either of them. They'd never been an overly affectionate family.

"I keep trying to hope that she's still alive out there somewhere," Claire murmured, "but it's hard to keep that hope."

"I know," James whispered. "I know."

James didn't get back home until much later that evening. His parents called him several times after learning of his arrest. He finally answered his mother's call and assured her he was taking care of it.

After he got off the phone with her, he sat down on his couch. With his phone, he looked at pictures of him and Taylor. There were only a few. She was camera shy. He'd had to convince her for the few he'd gotten. Now he was glad he had. He laid down, still looking at the picture on his screen. It was on Taylor's birthday. Her smile was bright; she was mid-laugh. He couldn't help but grin as he thought of the memory.

The picture disappeared, and his sister's name covered the screen before a loud ring. He wanted to swipe away from the sound, but he told himself he probably should answer.

"Hello," he said, trying not to sound annoyed.

"He took him!" Claire cried, her voice desperate and heartbroken.

"Took him?"

"Zachary! Dylan showed up at my house with the police, saying I had no rights to keep him."

"Oh my god," he murmured.

"He...and now..."

James heard harsh gasps and sobs on the other end of the phone.

"I'm sorry. That bastard."

"I mean...he's right. I don't have rights to him, but..."

"Do you want me to drive down there?" he offered.

"No," Claire said, a bit stronger. "I'll be fine. I'm just...Dylan took him. I can't protect him anymore!"

He flinched at his sister's anger.

"I'm sorry," he said once more.

"I'm going to go," Claire said. "I need to clean up or...I don't know. I just need to do something right now. Goodbye."

Before James even had a chance to say goodbye, the phone line was cut. He stood then, going off and into his office where he kept the will Taylor had asked him to make for her. Taylor owned very little outside of her paintings, but she had him add a clause that gave his sister custody if she were dead. The caveat, of course, was that Dylan had rights to his son. This only worked if Dylan was also dead and hadn't written up a will of his own. But still...

"A-ha!" he said triumphantly.

There it was. The envelope was nestled between another file and his clock on top of his desk. He opened it. There inside was Taylor's signature. His finger ran over the letters. Her penmanship was beautiful. She took care to write each letter, never rushing to make it go by quicker.

He called his mother.

"Hello?"

He could tell she was annoyed. He checked his clock. It was after nine. By now, she was usually on her second glass of wine and watching one of her reality television shows.

"If someone dies and they wrote in their will for their child to go to a friend, can that be used in a custody case if the other parent still is alive?"

"James, you know that can't, not unless that parent is proven to be unfit. Even then, it's not clear cut as all that. What is this referencing? I don't recall any cases like that coming into our offices."

"It's about Zachary," James said.

"Oh," his mother murmured. "It would be a fight, and not a fight easily won. But we would fight it. Do you have paperwork from Taylor?"

"Yes."

"Bring it in tomorrow, and I'll look over it."

James hung up the phone and placed it onto his desk, holding the file protectively in his hands.

CHAPTER 24

Dylan Montgomery's social media page had little to it. It wasn't private, so Max could see every friend and every post made on the page. He mainly shared pictures of cars. There were none of his family, though, and Max did find that telling. He didn't have a picture of them anywhere on his page. And when Max delved deeper, he saw most of Dylan's friends were women, and they all liked his posts. Several wrote messages. He noticed that Taylor wasn't his friend.

So he searched her. Her page was private. He looked at her friends. There was another account for Dylan.

"Sneaky bastard," Max said.

His adrenaline was pumping. Men like Dylan were all the same. None of them really hid any of their shenanigans. They put stock in knowing that their wives wouldn't try to find them out and that those he messed around with would never reach out to their wives.

His second page also wasn't private. It had one picture he'd posted: a profile picture of him with his son. It was clearly just a page he kept to make Taylor believe it was his only one.

He went back to the other page. That one would have the answers he needed. Was there one female making more comments recently? Would that lead him to find who had been Dylan's alibi the afternoon of Taylor's disappearance?

As he searched through them all, he did see one particular female liking every post going back an entire year. She'd also commented on most of them, as well, and Dylan had liked those comments. He clicked on her name: Ally Wilbur.

Her profile picture was only of her, but her cover picture had Dylan.

"Bingo," he said. "Well, well. Are you his girlfriend?"

Max scribbled her name down on a piece of paper. He doubted she was the only woman Dylan was sleeping around with. He seemed the type to have a wife, a girlfriend, and many side quests. Max was sure the girlfriend had been told all sorts of lies about Taylor, and how he was leaving her soon to be with her. These men were all the same.

There was a knock on the door, and he glanced up.

"What?" he said with a huff to his sister.

She tugged on the edge of her braid and stuck out her tongue, acting more like she was twelve instead of eighteen.

"That lady, Claire Donahue, is here."

He checked his watch.

"She's not supposed to be here until this afternoon."

He rolled his eyes. He'd had clients like Claire before, too. They all thought they were more important than his schedule.

"I told her that," Liliana said. "But she said it's important."

"Fine, let her come back."

Liliana disappeared back down the hallway. The click of heels sounded down the hallway. He saw Claire. She was much more put together than the last time he saw her. She wore her hair down in its tight curls, and wore a suit jacket with a straight skirt that stopped a few inches above her knee.

"You're early," he said.

"I know," Claire said, taking a seat. "Do you have any leads? We need to have Dylan put away. Zachary is now in danger. Taylor's son! He's taken him back from me. Don't you see? He's in danger as long as he's with his father. We have to get him locked up and away from his son."

Max folded his hands together before placing his arms on his desk, leaning forward.

"You know what's interesting?"

"What?"

"Your brother, James. He was dating Taylor, wasn't he?"

"Well, not officially," Claire said. "They spoke and had gone out a few times. Why?"

"He was just arrested for physical violence. Are we absolutely sure it was Dylan who took her? Could it have been your brother?"

"That's absolute nonsense. James never would hurt her."

Max chuckled. He shook his head.

"So many sisters, mothers, even wives say the same thing."

"James didn't do it," Claire said with anger in her voice. "He was working that night with a client. He's already been questioned by the police who followed the same thought pattern you did. But I thought you were smarter than them. Aren't you supposed to be the best? Or am I wasting my money on you?"

Again, a chuckle left Max. He had to give Claire credit. She was ballsy.

"I am the best. I think I've found the girlfriend, likely the alibi. I'm going to contact her, see if I can get her to change her tune, prove he wasn't with her when Taylor went missing."

Claire shifted in her seat.

"What's her name?"

"I think it's best I don't tell you. I don't need you interfering. Your brother has already done enough with that," he said pointedly. "How long were your brother and Taylor not officially dating?"

"Not long, why?"

"So it started before or after she left Dylan?"

"After," Claire said. "They hadn't even spoken in years before that. As much of an ass Dylan was to her, Taylor never would have cheated. She was too pure for that."

"Okay."

"I almost forgot why I was here. Yesterday, when my brother confronted Dylan, he made a comment that alluded to the fact that he killed Taylor."

"Oh? Has he told the police?"

"Yes. Not that anything's been done about it," she huffed. "I don't know if that helps you or not, but I wanted to tell you."

"Alright. Do you need anything else?"

"Just find my friend and find the evidence to put her husband away for the rest of his life," she said as she stood. "You know, do your job."

She brought the sunglasses that were sitting on top of her head down and over her eyes.

She walked out of the room, not saying anything else. Max could hear her steps all the way until she exited the house. A moment later, his sister's head poked back through his door.

"She's pretty," she commented, now stepping into the room.

"You should be working up front."

"I was," Liliana said. "You have a long list of people requesting you. All I do now all day is tell people you're busy."

"And I am," he said with a shrug. "This case could change everything for me here, Liliana. It is my first potential murder case. If I solve this, it will make me the local hero."

Liliana crossed her arms over her chest and frowned.

"You think she was murdered?"

"Yes. It checks all the boxes on domestic violence. He was abusive, she left him, he couldn't get her to come back home, and then she went missing. All signs point to him."

"Then why isn't he arrested?"

"He has an alibi," Max said. "Girlfriend, I think."

"So, you think she's covering for him? Why would she do that?"

"Believes he's innocent. You'd be surprised what people will believe when they want to."

Liliana sunk into the chair in front of Max's desk, her face forlorn.

"Why would he kill her? Why not just let her go?"

"I don't know," Max said. "Shouldn't you be working?"

But his sister didn't move from her seat, she just sat there, staring over his shoulder and sighing. He didn't have time for her dramatics right now.

"Liliana, go back to work."

"Doesn't this bother you?" she asked, though she did finally stand. "A woman could be dead."

"It's part of the job. I can't get attached to the people I work for or the stories that I hear every day."

"But she could be dead, *murdered*."

"Yes, I know. So, why don't you let me get back to work?"

With a loud huff, Liliana walked out of his office. Max shook his head, hoping she wouldn't be back anytime soon. He had work he needed to do.

He went back to Ally's page. For a moment, he debated sending her a message, but then he saw that she'd put where she worked under her about me area on her page. It would be much better to see her in person. When you went to speak with someone face to face, it was much harder for them to avoid you.

He wrote down the address and the location. Then he stood. He walked up front where his sister was reorganizing her desk for the fifth time this week.

"You can go home," he told her.

"But it's only eleven."

"Don't worry, you'll still get paid. I'm working out of the office for the rest of the day. Go on home."

Liliana didn't have to be told again. She dashed up, grabbed her purse, and headed to the front door.

"And Liliana? Don't tell Mom or Dad about my case, alright? Remember it's all confidential."

"I know."

Max stood outside the nail salon, trying to see if he could spot Ally Wilbur from the window. There were several people inside, but he couldn't make out if Ally was inside or not. He'd have to go in.

He was pleasantly surprised to see she was the woman at the front desk. She looked up at him and smiled.

"Hello! Can we help you?" she asked, brightly.

She wasn't exactly what Max expected. Her dark gray eyes were kind. She had a sweetness about her. He guessed he expected someone who was shallow, not that he could really know. Though he usually got a good reading off of someone within the first few moments of meeting them. That's when he saw the ring on her finger. She wasn't just the girlfriend. She was the backup wife. Dylan had already proposed to her.

He gave her a tight smile.

"I actually wanted to speak with you. You are Ally, correct?" Her smile faded, and she looked at him suspiciously while tucking her light brown hair behind her ear. Her hand ran over her pale cheek before dropping it by her side.

"Yes, why?"

He grabbed his business card out of his front pocket.

"I'm Max Evans, a private detective. I'd like to speak with you about a missing person: Taylor Montgomery."

"Why? I don't know what happened to her."

"And yet, you're dating or might I say *engaged*," he said as he pointed to the ring on her finger, "to her husband."

Ally hid her hand below the desk.

"They're getting a divorce. Dylan's been trying to get her to sign the papers for a while now," she said. "She's just run off, left him to care for their son, like she always does. She'll show back up when she needs something."

"Oh, so that's what he's told you."

Typical, he thought. People like Montgomery knew how to manipulate others into believing him even if the evidence was damning against them.

Another client walked in. Ally let out a relieved sigh.

"Keep my card, call me when you're ready to hear the truth about Dylan. And if you don't call me, I'll be back. Taylor Montgomery was taken. She didn't run off."

With that, he left the nail salon.

That night, as Max sat alone in his apartment eating his dinner, he saw Taylor's face flash across the television screen. He knew that picture. It was one Claire gave him the first time she stepped inside his office.

He reached across the couch to grab his remote and turn up the volume.

"Tonight," the announcer began, "we have Claire Donahue."

Then there she was: Claire. Although she looked perfectly put together, her eyes were red rimmed and her lips were tight with distress.

"Please," Claire pleaded as she stood there. "If you have any information that could help us find my friend, Taylor, please let us know. She's a mother. She has a three-year-old son. She's an artist. She's kind. She's my *best* friend. *Please.*"

Her voice shook as she wiped tears off her cheek.

Max turned off his television. He sat back and brought his hand over his lips. For a moment there, it was heavy and real. He couldn't allow himself to be drawn into the realness of the situation. No emotions could impact his behavior. He needed to remain focused on solving this case. That was what mattered.

CHAPTER 25

Without Zachary, her home was too quiet. She'd gotten used to hearing his little footsteps, his little voice, or his shows on her television screen. All of his toys had been put into boxes and placed in her small storage space. So as she walked through her home, it was almost as though neither he nor Taylor had ever been here.

But upstairs, their room had been left untouched, as well as all of Taylor's paintings. Claire couldn't bring herself to go through any of it. It felt like an invasion of privacy. She needed to keep it all the same for when Taylor returned.

"Hey," Lucas whispered, coming up behind her. He wrapped his arms around her waist and kissed her cheek. "You did great." Claire had been so grateful to have Lucas come with her to the news studio. She wasn't sure she'd been able to drive herself home with how upset she was. She leaned against his touch.

"I don't know if it'll help," she said, "but I have to try everything possible to find her."

"I know."

Lucas turned Claire around to face him. He pressed his forehead lovingly against hers as his fingers caressed the back of her neck. Claire closed her eyes, appreciating his comforting touch.

"And I miss Zachary," Claire murmured. "I worry about him, and if Dylan is making sure he's fed and taken care of."

"You can't worry about that."

Claire popped her eyes open, taking a step back.

"What do you mean, *I can't*?"

"I meant...I *just* meant you have so much on your mind. You're doing all you can."

"Oh, right," she murmured.

Again, Lucas moved closer to her. He brought his arms around her back and allowed her to rest her head on his shoulder.

"Why don't you let me order us some take-out? It's been a long day. We could eat and watch a movie."

"Yes, that sounds nice," Claire said as she stood up straighter, attempting a smile, but her mouth only quirked up. "Thank you."

Lucas made an order on his phone before sitting down on the couch and bringing Claire down with him. She curled up against his side, accepting his comfort. Claire didn't know what the future held between her and Lucas, yet she did know that right now, he was what she needed.

Claire thought about how beautiful the weather was this particular day as she stood outside of the bus stop. It was the type of day where Taylor would be sitting outside to paint, because she said she found more inspiration from the fresh air and life around her. A tear slipped down Claire's cheek. She wiped it away just in time for the bus to pull up.

It stopped, the door opening to let the passengers out. She stood awkwardly. She'd invited Taylor's father up to speak with the police on his daughter's behalf. Claire hadn't met Larry Smith, and she wasn't even sure what he looked like.

A man stepped off. He wore an old, worn-out t-shirt and a battered baseball hat on his head. He turned and smiled at Claire; one of his teeth up front was missing. Though he was only in his early 40s, he looked much older. Claire assumed the alcohol had a hand in that.

"Hello, Mr. Smith?"

"Claire?"

He stepped closer, reaching out his hand. She met his hand halfway and gave it a shake.

"It's so nice to meet you. Taylor's always telling me all about you."

"Yes, it's nice to meet you, too. Why don't we go and grab a bite to eat? I'm sure you're starved. It was a long ride."

"It was," he said. "Still no news on my Taylor?"

"No," she murmured, "there hasn't been."

They got into her car, this moment reminding her of the time she picked up Taylor from this exact same bus stop all those years ago.

"She'll show up," Larry said. "She's my strong girl."

Claire's body froze. He had no idea, she realized, just how horrific Taylor's relationship with Dylan had been.

"I do hope she does," Claire managed to say. "You didn't pack any clothes?"

"I'm only staying for the night," Larry said.

"Only for the night?"

"Well, I have work I need to do. I do want to see the boy. Um..."

"Zachary," Claire said, her jaw tightening.

"Yeah, my grandson. He's a fine boy."

"Well, I can't promise you'll be able to see him. He's with Dylan. I wouldn't be surprised if he won't let you come over."

They parked in front of the restaurant, and Claire turned to face Larry.

"Taylor didn't tell you anything about her marriage with Dylan?"

"What do you mean?"

"Did she explain why she moved in with me?"

"She did?" Larry asked.

Claire frowned as stepped out of the car. Larry knew absolutely nothing.

When Larry got out of the car, Claire met his eyes again.

"Dylan was abusive and controlling. Taylor left him. She and Zachary were staying with me when she disappeared. I am very sure it was him who had something to do with her disappearance. And I don't think she's alive, Mr. Smith. I think he killed her."

The man before her paled. He held on to the top of her car and swayed on his feet before shaking his head.

"Taylor never said anything like that to me. Dylan was good to her, gave her a home, and took care of her."

"At the price of controlling everything she did, treating her like shit, and throwing her down the stairs causing her to lose their daughter."

"But..." Larry said as his voice trembled. "Why didn't she ever tell me? I didn't even know about the baby."

"Because, she didn't like to worry you. She didn't like to worry anybody," Claire added. "You need to stay here, fight for the police to keep searching for her, speak to the reporters, and plead for her. It's how we protect the most precious thing to her: Zachary."

"I don't know," Larry said with a shake of his head. "I'm not good at any of that. I still think she'll come home. You can't know for sure she's gone. Maybe she just got overwhelmed. Her mother did. It...it happens."

"Taylor is not her mother, Mr. Smith. She never would have left Zachary. *Never*."

Suddenly, Claire no longer felt hungry. Instead, she was frustrated with the man standing before her. This wasn't how she'd expected this meeting to go. He didn't really know his daughter and how much she loved that little boy.

"I just..." Larry said as his shoulders slumped. "I love my little girl, Claire. I know I'm a shit father, but I do love her. I didn't know...If I had known..."

"We'll eat," Claire said, softening. "Then we can go by the police station, alright?"

"Alright."

Once they'd gone to the police station, Claire was defeated. They didn't care Larry Smith was there to ask about the case. They told him the same thing: the husband had an alibi and the friends all had alibis. Either she was taken by someone randomly, or she'd run off. They were still searching, but they had no leads.

"It's bullshit," Claire said as they stood outside of the hotel. "But I have hired a PI. He's supposed to be the best. He told me he found the alibi."

"But what if it was some random person who snatched her?" Larry asked.

"It wasn't," Claire said with a shake of her head. "It was Dylan."

"How can you be so sure?"

"Because I know who Dylan is. He didn't like that she left. He didn't like that she was finally happy."

"Right."

"Here's your key. It's booked for three nights. We can always add more. Do you need me to take you shopping for some more clothes tomorrow?"

"Nah, I'm all right," he said. Claire gave a weak smile, trying to hide her disgust. "Do you know if there is a liquor store nearby?"

"I...I don't," Claire lied. "You should stay sober, for Taylor and Zachary. Now I'm going to go home. Tomorrow, I'll meet with the PI. Would you like to tag along?"

"Sure. Not sure how I'll help, though."

"Just showing another face who cares helps, Mr. Smith."

"Hey," a whisper said in her ear.

Claire tucked her head further into the mattress, not wanting to wake. She'd finally gotten a decent night's sleep. It was the first night since Taylor's disappearance that she hadn't been plagued by nightmares.

"Hey," it whispered again.

Claire moaned. She brought her pillow over her head, hearing chuckles coming behind her. Arms wrapped around to her stomach and a kiss pressed against her cheek.

"You have to wake up. You have to get to work."

"But why?" she asked.

"Because you have to afford your house, pay bills."

Claire made a face, but she did push her pillow off her head and turn onto her back. Lucas now had himself perched on his elbow while his fingers ran along her bare arm.

"You're only working half a day, anyway," he reminded her with a smile. "I wish I could come with you to meet that private detective. He sounds like a piece of work."

"He is."

"I don't want him trying to pull anything," Lucas said.

"He's not dangerous, Lucas. He's just full of himself. You have nothing to be concerned about. Plus, Mr. Smith is coming along with me today."

"And do you feel safe with him?"

"Yes. He's harmless."

Claire swung her legs over the side of the bed and stood. She ran her hands over her face, yawning. She really did hate mornings. That was part of the reason it took her longer to finish college. Her first year she'd missed half of her morning classes, choosing to sleep in instead of attending.

"Are you sure?"

Claire turned to look at Lucas.

"Why are you so worried about who I am with all of the sudden?"

"Well, Taylor..."

She sharply inhaled.

"Taylor was taken by her abusive ex-husband. Neither Evans nor Mr. Smith are him. Plus, at Evan's office, his sister is there. We aren't all alone. And Mr. Smith is so thin I could probably make him fall over by blowing on him," Claire said with a laugh. She scooted over the bed to be closer to Lucas. "It is adorable how you worry, though. I promise I'm safe."

"It's because I love you."

Claire felt that feeling again in her chest, one she couldn't explain when he said such words. If he hadn't been here for her with all of this and Taylor, would she still be with him? She shook that thought away and leaned forward to give him a quick kiss. Lucas gently laid her back to deepen it. Gently, Claire pushed him back.

"I really need to hop into the shower. Maybe later?"

"Later sounds good."

When Claire stepped out of the shower, she peeked into her bedroom to see that Lucas was no longer in her room. She grabbed her clothing for the day and put them on. Then she spent an ungodly amount of time on her hair, making sure it looked perfect. The client she was meeting with today was one of their reoccurring clients who was very particular about whom they allowed to work with them.

Once she made it downstairs, she saw Lucas in her kitchen. He'd run out for breakfast because there were fresh bagels and coffees sitting on the counter. He grabbed the bag of bagels and her coffee, walking them over to her and kissing her.

"I knew you were going to be in a rush this morning," he said.

"This was very kind."

She took a sip of the coffee.

"I do miss your cinnamon rolls," Lucas mentioned with a smile. "Do you think maybe this weekend…?"

"I'm not baking," Claire said, tears building in her eyes. "I just don't have the energy for that right now. Perhaps another time?"

"Of course," he said, kissing her temple. "I'll get you breakfast every morning if that's what you need."

She patted his cheek.

"You're too sweet to me, Lucas."

"Because I love you."

It was the second time this morning he'd said that.

"Yes, me too," she said back. "I should get going. Do you want to ride with me?"

"I should take my own car. I have to work all day."

"Right, right, of course. Well, lock up? I'll see you later?"

"Absolutely."

Claire was glad when her meeting with the client was over. The client was always so particular about every single detail. Sometimes that could be nice, because they had a clear path to follow for the event. However, this particular client would make a fuss if something was off by the smallest amount. She'd be coming over several times before the event to make sure everything was just right.

Claire entered her office and sat down. She checked the time on her wall clock. Her meeting with Evans still was a few hours away. She'd have to do some actual work until then.

She took her phone out of her top drawer in her desk and turned it off of silent. That's when she saw she had a text from Larry. She opened it up.

I have to go back home. I'm sorry I couldn't do more. Let me know what they say and when they find my baby girl.

"Shit," Claire said, wanting to throw her phone across the room.

Her head shook. It all made so much more sense now why Taylor hardly had any relationship with her father. He couldn't deal. He may have been the parent who stayed, but he wasn't really there either. Taylor had to deal with this all on her own. And Dylan knew that. He took advantage of the fact her friend didn't have a family to force her into this relationship with him.

With a heaviness on her chest, Claire placed the phone down. She wouldn't respond now, because if she did it wouldn't be kind. Taylor wouldn't want that.

Her phone dinged again. Claire thought it might be Larry, but it wasn't. It was Evans.

I have a meeting with the alibi in an hour. Let's push back our meeting an hour just to be safe.

Claire read over the text a few times. How she wished she could go with him to this meeting. She wanted to look the alibi right in the eyes, then force her to look at pictures of Taylor, and see if she would still try to cover for that bastard.

Alright, I will see you at two o'clock.

CHAPTER 26

Max met with Ally at a coffee shop right outside of the town where she lived. She chose the place, and Max wondered if it was because she feared Dylan. Meeting Ally and learning more about Dylan made it clearer to Max that this was not a case of Taylor running away or being snatched by someone random. All the signs were pointing to Dylan. He didn't know how the police couldn't see it. It was as clear as day.

They found a seat further inside and not by the windows, also chosen by her. Ally looked around them, and then adjusted her glasses on her nose.

"I was with him that night," she started. Max eyed her carefully.

"Has he threatened you, Ally?"

"What? No, of course not! He and I were together that night. He stayed over with me. You can even ask my roommate."

"Alright, but at what time did he arrive?"

"I don't remember."

"Then you are saying there is a possibility he wasn't with you at the time of Taylor's disappearance."

"No," Ally quickly said. "He was there, at my house."

Max opened up his briefcase. He pulled out the picture of Taylor and Zachary that Claire had given him. He slid it over to Ally.

"That is Taylor. Have you ever seen a picture of her?"

"No," Ally said. "But I don't know why…"

"Did Dylan happen to tell you about the baby?"

"His son?"

"No, the baby. The baby Taylor lost a few months ago."

"I don't know what you're talking about. They've been separated for a while now. Dylan never mentioned another child."

"There was another. Dylan shoved Taylor, forced her to lose her footing, and then she fell down the stairs. She lost the baby."

"You're lying," Ally said, pushing the photo back over to Max. "Dylan would never hurt anyone. He loved Taylor, but she left him for another man. And now she's abandoned her son."

Max clucked his tongue in his mouth before narrowing his eyes.

"If you're so certain Dylan is this wonderful guy, then why do you keep looking around you? Are you worried he'll know you're out at a coffee shop with another guy? Does he get jealous easily? Funny, since he's been with you for a while and he's the married one."

"He's not the jealous type. He is wonderful. I'm just nervous. I've never spoken to a PI before, is all. And I do have to go soon, I'm watching Zachary while Dylan has to get to work."

Max made note of that in his phone. Ally tried to get a look of what he was typing, but he turned his phone upside down and looked back up at her.

"I have proof."

"Proof?"

"About the baby. About the amount of times the police were called from neighbors when they heard screaming at the house. About the restraining order against Dylan."

"None of that is true. Why should I believe you?"

Max didn't answer right away. He opened his briefcase and pulled out the files. He went through them to find the copy of the restraining order.

"Here," he said, setting it down. "You can look through all of these. There are even medical files from when Taylor was in the hospital after she lost the baby. She had all sorts of fractures, cuts, and bruises."

"How would you even get these types of records? That's not legal, is it?"

"I have my ways."

Max just shrugged. He never told anyone how he got the information he did. That could lead to people getting fired or his credibility being ruined when those people no longer wanted to help him.

"Now, take a minute to look through them."

Ally paused a moment before lifting the first file. As she read through them, Max sensed the horror she was feeling. Her shoulders tightened and her brows would knit as she read over certain words.

"I don't know how to know this is true. And it doesn't matter. He was with me that day," Ally finally said.

"Well, it is true. I have no reason to lie to you. I was hired by her best friend, Claire. She was staying at her place before she went missing. If you remember anything about that evening that could help the police, I ask you tell them and me."

He stuffed the paperwork back into his brief case, stood, and then looked back at her.

"Men like Dylan don't stop. If he gets away with this, he'll think he can get away with it again. You will likely be his next victim of abuse.

And if you try to escape like Taylor did, you'll also be his next victim that disappears."

With that, he walked away, reminding himself not to look back at her. He hoped his words were enough to get her to think on if it was worth covering for Dylan Montgomery.

When Max arrived at his office, Claire Donahue was already waiting for him outside. She stood on the large wrap around porch, clutching a coffee cup and leaning against the railing. Once she spotted him, she took her sunglasses off, tucking them into her purse.

"About time," she said.

He checked his watch. He was ten minutes earlier than they had even discussed.

"It's not two, yet."

"Thirty minutes before is early, fifteen minutes before is on time, on time is late," Claire said.

"Oh god, you're one of those people."

Max dug his keys out from his pocket, unlocking and opening the front door of his office building. He turned on the lights.

"You mean punctual people? You should try it sometime," Claire said as she stepped inside the door and glanced around.

"I am punctual. I'm always early."

"Where is your sister, anyway?"

"I gave her the rest of the day off. With me only working this one case, she's been bored."

"You're only working one case. Why? Have people decided not to use you anymore?"

"No. I'm dedicating all my time on this case."

"Oh," Claire said, pausing her steps. For a moment, Max thought she might be impressed, but she added, "Can't juggle too much at once, can you?"

Max narrowed his eyes.

"Let's go to my office."

The two of them walked back to his office. He took off his jacket and hung it on the coat hanger by the door. Then he walked around to sit in his seat. Claire slowly took the seat across from him, placing her coffee cup at the edge of his desk.

"What did this...woman say?"

"She's sticking to her story," Max said, "*for now.*"

"Why on earth would she lie for him?" Claire growled.

"I'm not sure. I told her the truth about Dylan. I explained who he really is. I do think this will get her thinking about it and about how he acts. Hopefully, it means she'll go to the police and tell them he wasn't there with her during the time Taylor disappeared."

"And if she doesn't?"

"I keep searching for her. I keep searching for things that prove Dylan was involved in her disappearance."

Claire sat before him, silent for a moment. She rubbed her hands together before bringing them up to rest right in front of her mouth. She blinked, taking in a deep breath, and then dropped her arms by her side.

"Do you really believe you can do that?"

"I do," he said.

And he did. He shuffled some papers over his desk before he found the map he'd been making notes on. He then stood and motioned for Claire to do the same. On the map, he had a few marks and lines between the marks.

"Here," he started, "is where he works. We know, for a fact, he was there until one. Around here was where Taylor was taken. Since she did not show up at work, we know she disappeared sometime between 2:30 and 3:00. Then here is where the woman lives. We don't know what time he showed up at her place, but we know he did. If we knew the time, it would make it much easier to pinpoint how long Dylan was with Taylor and possibly where he took her."

Claire's fingers touched the map. She followed the path between where Taylor disappeared to where Ally lived. Then she made a circle around it with her finger.

"There's plenty of bodies of water along that path. Also, the woods. Where do you even start?"

"We hope she takes back her alibi, and the police use their resources to look. But I'm going to try and narrow it down."

"He'll never admit what he did with her, even if they discover the truth. He'll make us search and wonder," Claire said, her eyes misty.

"I will find her," Max said strongly.

"I need you to. I need to know. And I need Zachary to come home. He's probably so scared," Claire said as she inhaled sharply.

"Yes, about Zachary…" Max trailed off, wondering if he should tell Claire this. Claire looked up. "The woman said she watches him for Dylan while he's at work."

"He lets that woman watch Taylor's son?!" Claire screeched. "That son of a bitch!"

"She has an engagement ring," Max added.

Claire's eyes widened. She fell back into her chair and brought her fingers up to pinch the bridge of her nose.

"She won't tell the police the truth. He's either lied to her or threatened her. Then in a few years, we'll hear a similar story with her. It's hopeless."

"It's not hopeless," Max said in disagreement. "Men like Dylan always screw up. They get too cocky. We will catch him off guard. We will put a stop to him and find Taylor."

He walked around his desk and moved down to his knee, looking up at Claire.

"I'm not giving up, and I know you aren't one to give up. Now, you hired me to do my job, remember?"

"Yes."

"And I'm going to do it. I'm not finished with my work for today. The woman was just part of my goals for the day. I'm not giving up until Taylor's found."

Claire nodded, her eyes shining with tears. He stood before helping her stand. She grabbed her coffee cup and gave him a nod of thanks.

"You'll call me later this evening? Give me an update."

"I will."

"Good. I'll speak with you then."

She walked down the long hallway. Max noted how there was less determinedness in each of her steps. She moved slower, with less purpose. He knew it was because her hope was waning.

Once the front door closed, he sat back down in his office chair. His chest felt—*heavy*. He'd had plenty of women and men sit across from him and cry. He'd even had Claire cry in front of him before, so why did it feel so different this time? What made this different?

Death. Murder. He did have to admit that those elements to his case made the stakes that much higher. An uneasy sound left him. The picture of Taylor sat rested against his computer screen to remind him what this case meant.

A mother, a friend, and an artist was missing.

While Max watched Dylan Montgomery at his workplace from afar, he noted how often Dylan walked outside to make a call or take a smoke break. Sometimes these were at the same time. Max sat back in his car, making sure he wasn't noticed by Dylan. Though Dylan was too self-involved to notice anyone could be watching him.

This last time Dylan walked outside, he had an intense conversation. His face turned red, and he appeared to be screaming into the phone. Max tried to pull a bit closer to hear what he was saying, but, by the time he got close enough, Dylan went back inside the shop.

Watching Dylan for the past couple of hours proved to give him nothing. He'd have to wait until he was off work to follow his car, see if where he drove gave him any indication of where Taylor might be.

He checked the time. It should be soon. Waiting was often the worst part of his job. But it was also one of the most important ones. If he didn't wait, he could miss something important.

Finally the time came when Dylan climbed into his car. Max followed behind by a few cars. He'd been following him for the past several days. Each time came up with no leads, as Dylan would drive straight home.

Tonight, however, they made a right turn, surprising Max. They ended up on a back road, making it harder for Max to follow without being suspicious. Max turned into a small drive and watched Dylan's car continue to head straight ahead.

Max pulled out his phone to look at a map. Ahead of him was a pond and some woods. He waited.

About half an hour later, Dylan came back out and turned out toward his home. Max decided to now travel down the path. It was getting darker outside.

The path ended at the large pond. From his headlights, he could only see the pond and trees for miles and miles. He parked the car and grabbed his flashlight from the compartment, still leaving his headlights on for extra light.

He stepped out of his car, hearing a squelching sound as his foot went into the wet mud below him. His eyes glanced around the area. There was the one dirt path he'd driven down, but he couldn't spot any other paths. He lifted his flashlight and began to search for footprints.

Closer to the pond, he noticed some prints that appeared to belong to someone with thick boots like Dylan's. He followed along the steps, but it was cut off when he got to the grass.

As his flashlight's light moved over the ground, he saw something shining in the dirt. He leaned forward, thinking he might find some trash, but it was a chain. He grabbed his pen out of his pocket, using it to lift the chain and not put his fingerprints on it. He brought it closer to him, realizing it was a necklace with a small star pendant.

He grabbed a small plastic bag that he had and placed the necklace inside.

His eyes moved to the pond; he shuddered.

After searching around a little while longer, he decided he would have to come back in the daylight for a better look, as well as bringing in detectives to help search the area. He placed it into his briefcase before getting into his car. He'd have to ask Claire about it this evening when he spoke with her.

Ring! Ring!

He nearly jumped. The silence and darkness had made him more aware of every sound. He grabbed his phone. It was Ally.

"Hello?"

"I'm going to tell the police that he wasn't with me until later that night," Ally said, her voice shook with emotion.

"Are you safe?"

"Yes. I just left his house. He…he's not in a good mood."

"And he really wasn't with you when Taylor went missing?"

Ally didn't answer right away. Max held his breath.

"No," she whispered. "He...he came to my place that night, muddy. Said he wasn't there when Taylor went missing."

"Thank you, Ally. You're going to help us find her."

CHAPTER 27

It was becoming harder for Claire to face each day. Even though Lucas lay beside her on her bed this evening, she felt alone. Her heart ached for Taylor and for Zachary. Every waking moment was filled with thinking about what her friend went through the day she went missing.

A ding on her phone made her turn. Lucas moved closer to her, lifting up his head to rest it on her shoulder. She shrugged him away, not wanting him to look at what her phone said. He frowned, but did slip away and get off the bed.

"I'm going to go and figure out something for dinner," he said.

Claire replied with a noncommittal grunt.

She swiped the screen to see the text. Everything within her body froze before her fingers tightened against the screen.

I found this out in the woods near a pond tonight. Does it look familiar?

At first, Claire could not respond. Her mouth went dry.

Since she didn't respond right away, her phone began to ring. She answered it, holding the phone to her ear.

"Claire?"

"I..." she started, but she found her words stuck in her throat. "Where..."

"Near Dylan's house, a few miles away. It was Taylor's, wasn't it?"

Claire weakly nodded, forgetting that Dylan couldn't see her.

"Yes...my brother...he...he gave it to her," Claire managed to say.

"I'm taking it to the police department. The woman is also going to tell them that Dylan was not with her when Taylor went missing. This is all a good step toward finding Taylor."

Claire pressed her palm against her beating heart. A lone tear slipped down her cheek.

"She's dead, isn't she? Oh god," she cried, leaning forward.

"We can't know that, not yet."

"I've tried to keep some hope but..."

Her voice caught; she let out a low sob.

"Let's focus on finding her, Claire. Let's focus on putting Dylan away for a really long time."

"Yes," she agreed.

The tears continued falling down her cheeks.

"I'll call you after I leave the station."

"Thank you."

She hung up, not having the energy to say much more.

She remained in her own misery for a while, ignoring Lucas calling upstairs for her to come down and eat. He even poked his head into her door to check in on her, but Claire told him she wasn't hungry. Thankfully he slipped back downstairs, leaving her alone.

She finally gathered the courage to call her brother.

"Oh, hi," James answered.

She could hear the faint sound of his television on in the background as she tried to remain focused on the reason for this call.

"Claire?"

"The PI found Taylor's necklace, the one you gave her, James. She..." Claire said as she rubbed her forehead with her palm. "And the girlfriend or whatever she is confirmed Dylan wasn't really with her when Taylor disappeared. She's going to go to the police."

The line was silent.

"There's a real lead now, James. It's...well, it's not good news, but it's..."

"News," James said, his voice strained.

"Yes," Claire agreed. "News."

"Was it my fault?" James asked at a near whisper.

"*What*? Why on *earth* would you ask that?"

"I wasn't there. Men like Dylan don't like..."

"It's *not* your fault," Claire said strongly. "And it's not mine. It's that bastard's fault, only *his* fault."

"But I promised her she would be safe, Claire. I promised her he wouldn't hurt her again. I..."

"No, you cannot blame yourself for that sicko's behavior. You did protect her, but we couldn't keep her in a bubble. She would never allow that."

"I..."

"Why don't you come here? You can stay in the guest room," Claire offered.

"No. I'm fine. Thank you for calling. I know this is just as hard for you, if not harder. I'll speak with you when we know more."

"Alright. Goodnight, James. I love you."

"Love you, too."

Claire held onto her phone before making her way down the stairs in search of Lucas. She found him in her kitchen munching on some overcooked popcorn. The burnt smell filled the air, making her squish up her nose in disgust.

"Yeah, I forgot I was making it," Lucas said.

He slid the bowl closer to her offering her a bite. She shook her head emphatically.

"I'd rather you throw it away and spray something to rid my kitchen of that god-awful smell," she said, making a face.

"Alright."

Lucas picked up the bowl and tossed it into the trash. Then he opened up the windows in the kitchen to allow some fresh air inside, as well as turning on the microwave fan.

"Is that better?"

"I guess," Claire said. She slunk down onto one of the barstools around the island. "Evans found something of Taylor's out in the woods near Dylan's house. This could be the break we've needed in the case."

Lucas sat back down beside her, touching her thigh.

"And he's taking it to the police, correct?"

"Yes. Once they arrest him, I hope they'll bring Zachary back here, where he belongs."

"With you?"

"Yes," Claire said. "He belongs here with me."

"Until they find Taylor, that is, right?"

"Well, if she's alive, then of course he belongs with her."

"But if she's not, then what? Surely she has family that would want Zachary, Claire. You aren't seriously thinking of keeping Zachary if something's happened to her, are you? He's a young child. You can't raise a young child. You aren't his mother."

Claire immediately saw red.

"Stop talking. Don't say anything else on this matter, you're up-setting me more than I already am. My best friend is missing, and you're lecturing me on whether or not I'm cut out to be a parent to her child?"

"Claire..."

She put her hand up to stop him.

"Don't," she warned. "Just don't say anything else."

Claire walked around to her refrigerator and grabbed a drink. She opened it before leaving Lucas behind and going to sit outside on the back porch. It was dark out now, the only lights coming from the full moon, the stars, and the neighbors' house lights. Even though it was warm outside, the wind caused a chill to run up her spine every time it blew.

Every few minutes, she checked her phone, hoping for an update from the police or Evans. She wanted to know if the woman really had gone through with it and told them the truth. She was also curious about what led her to tell the truth. Had Dylan done something to her?

The door to the back porch opened slightly, making a loud creaking sound. She needed to get some WD-40 for the door, but it hadn't been a high priority for her. She refused to turn to look at Lucas.

"I'm only looking out for you," he said quietly. "I love you, Claire. This—all of this—is so hard, Claire. You've been holding all of the cards. You can't shuffle them all."

"Sure I can," Claire said with a shake of her head.

She stood, bringing her arms over her chest as she walked to the screen of her porch. She turned her head toward Lucas.

"And if Taylor is dead, I will fight for Zachary. Taylor's only relative is her father, who is nowhere near competent enough to take in his grandson. And if Dylan has any living relatives, I wouldn't trust them with him for a minute. If you are not okay with me fighting for Zachary, then you better leave now."

Lucas stood in the doorway, his hand resting on the frame by his head. His face fell with defeat.

Claire turned back away from him, closing her eyes. Her fingers tapped against her arms. She could hear Zachary's laughter in her mind with Taylor's giggles surrounding him. Visually, she could picture the two of them happy and free.

"Claire—"

Her eyes popped open.

"Are you staying or going?"

It was all she could ask. She couldn't face him, not right now. Not if he was about to walk away.

Footsteps came up behind her before Lucas's arms went around her center and his head rested on her shoulder. He kissed her cheek, tightening his hold.

"I'm staying," he promised.

Claire turned, then, something taking over her. She realized she needed to feel something other than pain and worry. She needed to take her mind off of what the next couple of days may bring. She cupped Lucas's cheeks as she brought his head closer to hers and kissed him languidly. He moaned in appreciation.

"Let's go upstairs," she whispered.

They quickly made their way upstairs and into Claire's bedroom. Lucas led her to the bed, helping her to sit down. His hands ran down to the edge of her shirt and began to tug it up and over Claire's head. She allowed it before pulling him on top of her to kiss him one more. She just needed this deep and passionate make out session right now to drown out all the voices and thoughts in her head. Lucas didn't seem to mind.

As her own fingers moved down to help remove Lucas's shirt, her phone rang. She paused.

"Let it ring," Lucas whispered into her ear.

It rang again. Claire pushed him off her.

"I can't just let it ring. It could be news about Taylor."

She grabbed her phone that sat next on the bed, ignoring the hurt look on Lucas's face. She was half tempted to tell him to go and take a cold shower, but decided against it.

"Hello?" she asked into the phone.

"I've spoken to the police. They can't tell me too much, but from what I gather, they'll be arresting Dylan tonight. They are also going to start searching the area where I found the necklace. We're close, Claire. They should find her soon."

Claire exhaled. Then a sob passed through her.

"I'm so scared," she murmured.

"I know," Evans said. "But this is good news. Remember that. I'll call you when I know more."

Claire hung up her phone. Her breaths grew heavy.

"This could be it," she whispered. "I don't know if I'm ready."

CHAPTER 28

After Max showed the detectives exactly where he found the necklace, he was told to get out of the way. While he tried not to disturb anything, he did follow behind. They were searching for patches of dirt that looked disturbed. Another set was searching around the pond. He kept looking between the two, hoping to help.

"Over here!" a gruff voice called out.

Max turned and quickened his steps to the sound. With his flashlight, he had a limited view of everything around him. As he got closer to the detectives around the water, he saw what appeared to be a dark sheet covering a body. His stomach lurched.

The detective who had called out began tugging the mass out of the pond. It was heavy and unrelenting. Max, though he was terrified, found himself drawn closer to get a better look. A large part of him began to pray it was just trash. He'd never seen a dead body before.

Another detective moved beside him. They undid the rope around what appeared to be the neck. Max inhaled sharply in anticipation, knowing he should look away before they removed the sheet, but unable to do so.

"A body," the detective said as the sheet was removed.

All Max could focus on was the red hair. He covered his mouth and turned around, unable to look anymore.

"It's likely the girl," the detective said. "She's been in here for a few days at least. I found this anchor over by the side. The murderer must have tried to sink her, but whatever he used failed."

Max took a step backward, nearly losing his footing. *Dead*. Taylor was dead. Even though a large part of him had known that was the most likely outcome, it didn't make it any easier standing here and seeing her body pulled from the water.

Around him there were shuffles and shouts from the detectives, speaking about what came next. Max remained frozen. His thoughts went to Claire, who would have to learn the truth and learn it soon.

He found her address on the paperwork she'd filled out in his car. He wanted to be the one to tell her. She had hired him to solve the case and to find her friend. He had to finish his job.

By the time he made it to Claire's house, it was nearly three in the morning. He should have called. Perhaps, he should have waited until the morning. He sat in the car, debating whether or not it was a good idea to tell her this news when she was likely asleep.

His eyes scanned over the house. All the lights were off. He sighed and turned off his engine. He pulled the charger off his phone and clicked on Claire's name. If she answered, he would tell her. If she didn't, he'd let her sleep and come and tell her in the morning.

It rang once. The upstairs light turned on.

"Hello?"

"You're awake," he said.

"I can't sleep."

"I'm here," he told her. "Can I come inside?

"Yes. It's bad news, isn't it?" Claire asked, her voice strained.

"I'll be at your door in a minute."

Max hung up his phone. He saw more lights in the house being turned on, but he couldn't step out of his car just yet. He hadn't slept since the night before. The tiredness filled him to the core.

When he saw the downstairs light come on, he knew he had to go and tell Claire. He opened the door, got out, and then closed the door behind him. His hands came together in front of him, and he took a moment before walking up to the front door and knocking.

Immediately, Claire opened the door. She wore a pink, silky robe and brown slippers on her feet. Even distressed, she was beautiful, he thought fleetingly.

"Come on inside," Claire said.

She had a nervous energy about her, walking with quick steps over to the couch. She pointed for him to sit down. She sat down next to him.

"Claire," Max said, "they found a body in the pond."

Claire inhaled sharply before glancing up at the ceiling.

"Now, they don't know for sure that the body they found is Taylor's. The body still needs to be identified, but it was a woman and she did have red hair."

"Was...was it in braids?" Claire asked, moving her dark brown eyes to look at him intensely.

The image of the body being pulled out of the pond remained sketched in his brain. Her hair was the most prominent feature.

"I...I'm not sure. I couldn't really tell how her hair was done. It was pulled back, off her face."

"Oh god," Claire cried.

She turned away from him, leaning forward and letting out a low sob. Her breaths came out in harsh pants as her body began to shake.

"It's her—oh god—it's her! He did it. That bastard. He...Taylor...he killed her..."

Max inched forward. He didn't know what he should say in this moment, so he remained quiet, just letting her know that he was here. She surprised him by turning toward his touch and wrapping her arms around him, pressing her head into his chest. Instinctively, his arms moved around to her back. As Claire's tears continued, he could feel his shirt growing damp.

Unlike he had believed he would, there was no joy in solving this case. Only darkness. A man had killed a woman. A son no longer had his mother. A friend no longer had her closest confidant.

The sound of footsteps made Max glance up. A man came down the stairs. He drew his brows together, causing a deep crease above his nose upon seeing Claire in Max's arms.

"What's going on?" the man asked.

He yawned, but didn't make a move to get to Claire.

"I'm Max Evans," Max said. "The PI."

"Oh," he said, his lips curling into a tight o. "I'm guessing Taylor is..."

A loud moan left Claire at that, and she moved her face deeper into Max's chest.

Yes, Max mouthed.

"Oh, Claire," the man said, moving quickly to Claire's side.

He sat down beside her, bringing his hands to her shoulders in an attempt to get her to turn to him. But Claire didn't move. She remained stuck to Max as though he was her life force, the tears never yielding.

"Claire," he tried again.

"Leave me alone, Lucas," she managed to say, turning her face slightly for him to hear her before hiding it back.

Lucas sat back, hurt covering his face. He didn't say another word, standing and walking over to the kitchen.

This was awkward. Max was in a space where he didn't really belong, yet he couldn't get up and leave. Claire's fingers clung to his back, unrelenting. He wasn't sure he could pull her away if he tried.

"Taylor," she cried, her body jerking with every harsh sob. "Oh, Zachary."

From the corner of his eye, he saw Lucas making coffee in the kitchen. The smell finally wafted into the living room area, making Max's mouth water. He would happily take a cup of coffee if it was offered to him.

A few moments later, Lucas walked back, carrying two cups. He sat them down onto the coffee table.

"Claire," Lucas tried. "Why don't you drink some coffee? I'm sure Evans here would like to go home."

"I'm in no rush," Max said.

Lucas shot his eyes up at him in what seemed like a warning.

It took a minute but Claire sat herself up, wiping beneath her eyelids with the tips of her fingers. She grabbed a cup of coffee, taking the smallest of sips. Then she pointed to the other.

"Drink some," she offered to Max.

"I'm not..."

"Go on," Lucas said.

Max took the other cup, his eyes not leaving Lucas. Had he just scowled at him?

"I wonder if I'll be asked to identify her body," Claire said then, drawing both of their attentions back to her. "I've never identified a body before."

More sobs came.

"Most people don't," Lucas said, "and you can always say no."

"Say *no*?" Claire asked, offended. "They have to know to charge that bastard! I'll do whatever they need to do to put him away."

"That's not—" Lucas started before he stood up and ran his fingers through his hair. "It's early in the morning. We should let Mr. Evans go home. He looks like he's been up all night."

While that was true, it did make Max wonder about his appearance. He glanced down at his shirt, now wet and disheveled from Claire's cries.

"He's right. I should leave. I have been up all night."

Claire remained at her spot on the couch. Her eyes rimmed red from all the tears she had shed. She stared off to a spot on the wall, not directly looking at anyone or anything. Every few moments, her body would tremble from the aftershock of her tears.

"I'll just be going then," Max said.

He tentatively reached his hand out to give Lucas a handshake. Lucas met his hand in the middle. It was an uncomfortable moment, both avoiding the other's eyes and probably both hoping never to see the other again. He then headed to the door, ready to leave, when Claire stood and spoke up.

"Wait!" she called out.

She quickly moved over to him and gave him a grateful nod, taking his right hand into both of hers. She brought it up to her chest, holding it there and meeting his eyes.

"Thank you," she said gratefully as her eyes shined with fresh tears. "Thank you."

"I was only doing my job," Max said. "Get some rest. I'm sure the department will be calling you soon. I'll let you know if I am able to find out anything else for you."

"Alright," Claire said.

She let go of him. Her lips attempted to curl up into a smile, but instead they shook with the weight of the truth.

Max tossed and turned, the image of the body being pulled from the pond always there whenever he attempted to close his eyes. He sat up, wiping his sweaty forehead. This case had shaken him to his core.

Unable to sleep, he turned on the television, hoping for some noise to drown out the thoughts inside his head. As he turned the channels, he paused when he saw Taylor's face on the screen. His eyes moved to the clock. It was six in the morning. Time for the morning news. He was curious to see whether the news was going to report on the finding of the body or just speak about her being missing. He turned up the television.

"Early this morning, a body was found in Grant Park Pond, assumed to be the body of missing person: Taylor Montgomery. Her husband was arrested just hours before after his alibi proved to be false. Tune back later for more news on this horrific case."

Max turned off his television. His head leaned back against the headboard of his bed. The old him would have been upset they hadn't mentioned his name or even asked him for an interview to speak about his part in finding Taylor's body. Where was the part of him that wanted the fame of it all?

Ding!

He moaned, wondering who would be messaging him this early in the morning. It was his sister, Liliana.

You did it! You found her! How does it feel?

I'm not sure, he answered honestly.

Have you told the friend, Ms. Donahue?

I have. It's harder than I thought it would be, he admitted.

Do you want me to come over? Bring you some breakfast?

No, thank you. Take today off. There are no cases. I need to try to sleep.

He clicked the button on his phone to make the screen dark. Part of him wanted to put the phone on silent, but he worried Claire may need to reach out to him. The police department also may try to contact him about the case, so it was best to leave it on.

After placing his phone onto his bedside table, Max laid himself back down, unsure that he would actually be able to fall asleep. But he would try. He had a feeling the next few days would be hard.

CHAPTER 29

The morgue. At her age, Claire never imagined herself standing outside of a morgue. The only funeral she ever attended had been ten years ago after her great-uncle passed. They hadn't been close.

She reached out to the doorknob, pausing before it could touch the metal. Her fingers shook as her eyes glanced down at her nails, noticing it was time to get them redone. She brought them up to her face to get a better view, debating which color she should do next. It was still summer. So, something bright and cheerful? Or should it be solemn after all she now had to face. Would it look strange to have a soft pink on her nails as she spoke at her friend's funeral?

"Claire?"

She blinked, not removing her eyes from her nails.

"We don't have to go in, not yet."

Her arm dropped to her side. She attempted to appear steadfast, mature, and ready to do this difficult task that had been asked of her. The detective on the phone said they could call Taylor's father, but

Claire knew that would add more time to identify her body, which may allow Dylan to leave without proof of her death.

"I'm ready."

She opened the door. Lucas grabbed the edge, swinging it further open so she could walk inside.

There she saw a woman waiting for her with a kind, but solemn smile.

"Hello," she greeted, "I'm Detective Shelley Dhar. Why don't you follow me?" Detective Dhar wore a black suit that was fitted to her figure perfectly. Her dark brown hair was pinned up into a tight bun. The golden tones of her tan skin brought out the amber in her eyes. She was about the same height as Claire, only a bit taller with her red heels. Claire stared at the heels for a brief moment, pleasantly amused by them and wishing she had a pair before looking back up at the detective. Detective Dhar kept the solemn smile on her lips as she led Claire and Lucas down the hallway.

Lucas's hand rested on the small of her back, encouraging her to move forward. She focused on just taking her steps, nothing else. Right foot, now left. Right foot, again. Now left, again. Right. Left. Right. Left. Don't forget to breathe.

Detective Dhar paused in front of a swinging door. This was it. Claire had to push back the urge to turn around and run out of this place. Lucas urged her forward. She took a step. They let her in. It was time to identify her friend.

Bile rose up her throat as she clutched the porcelain and leaned forward to let it all out. The room had been cold and sterile. She'd only been able to look for a second before the bile began to threaten its escape. She'd rushed out of the room and was pointed toward the bathroom.

"Claire!" Lucas's worried voice said on the other side of the locked door. "Are you alright?"

She wanted to sit and rest her back against the wall, too overwhelmed by the reality that she had just seen her best friend's dead body. Because she'd been in a body of water, she hardly even looked like Taylor.

She stood and walked over to the sink, turning it on to wash her hands. Once they were washed, she splashed some of the water on her face, ignoring the sound of Lucas still knocking on the door.

"Claire! I'm going to knock down this door!"

"No you aren't," she bit.

The knocks stopped.

Her eyes met her own in the mirror. Her chin quivered, but she wouldn't let the tears come. Not here. Not right now. Her focus for now was to make sure Dylan got exactly what he deserved.

She unlocked the bathroom door to find Lucas standing on the other side. His forehead tight.

"I was worried something had happened to you," he said, reaching out to touch her.

She stepped back.

"In the bathroom? I'm fine," she said, though her lower lip betrayed her. "We should go to the station now, speak with the police, and find out what's happening with Zachary."

She began to walk away, but Lucas grasped at her arm, spinning her to face him.

"Take a moment," he said. "You just saw Taylor's body. You should give yourself a moment to process all of this."

"I am well aware what I just saw, Lucas," she said between gritted teeth. "But I cannot take a moment to 'process all of this.' I have to make sure Dylan never sees the outside world again."

She tore her arm away from his touch, walking quickly away from him. Every passing moment made him less tolerable to her and she wondered why she ever let him back into her life. If she wasn't dealing with everything, she'd tell him to just go, but she couldn't. She worried it was the trauma of losing Taylor and all that had happened making her annoyed with him.

James.

She paused. She hadn't called James. She reached for her phone right as Lucas caught up with her.

"I never called James. I don't know if he knows."

"Would you like me to call him?" Lucas offered.

A tear slid down her cheek.

"It should probably be me," she said, "He'll want to hear from me."

"Why don't we go and get in the car first?"

"Yeah," Claire agreed.

She gave Lucas a wobbly smile. These were the moments when she didn't regret keeping Lucas around.

James already knew. He said two words and then hung up the phone. Claire understood. She didn't really want to talk either. The world was not as bright as it used to be, and it never would be again. She struggled to think of the future without Taylor in it.

"You don't have to go in right now," Lucas said. "He's been arrested. Everything else can be sorted out later."

"I do have to go in," Claire said. "I need to know what happens to Zachary."

"Alright."

When they walked into the station, Claire spotted the detective from the morgue. She tried to recall her name. What was it again? Detective...something that started with a D.

"Um...Detective..."

The detective turned, immediately recognizing Claire.

"Detective Dhar," she said. "And you're Claire Donahue. I saw you not too long ago. Would you like to come into my office?"

"Yes."

Claire followed Detective Dhar into her office, only fairly aware of Lucas walking beside her. The detective didn't appear much older than Claire, but Claire never did a good job at guessing someone's age.

Even though Detective Dhar offered her to take a seat, Claire couldn't sit down.

"Where is Zachary?" she asked, placing her fingers against the edge of Detective Dhar's desk.

Detective Dhar glanced down at Claire's hand before glancing up to meet her eyes.

"Who?"

"Taylor's son. Where is he?"

"I'm sure when Dylan was arrested CPS was called unless he had someone there to watch him."

"You don't know where he is?"

"That isn't in my jurisdiction, Ms. Donahue. I do not manage the placement of children in cases such as these."

"He must be so confused. He should be with me. Taylor would want him to be with me."

Claire pressed her finger firmly against her chest. Detective Dhar nodded with sympathy.

"I could go and find out for you."

"Yes, please."

"Alright, take a seat."

This time Claire did sit down. She bounced her knees up and down, trying not to lose it. She knew if she let herself cry, she wouldn't be able to stop.

"He better rot," Claire said to herself. "If he doesn't, I'll kill him myself."

"Claire! Don't joke about something like that, especially not here."

Lucas glanced around the small office.

"Oh, don't be so stuck up," Claire said.

"It's not funny."

Claire rolled her eyes. She wanted to say something more, but the door opened and Detective Dhar stepped back inside her office.

"Yes, he has been put into a temporary placement. I can give you their information so you can try to call. I don't have any control over any of that."

Claire took the paper with the information from her.

"You'll make sure they put him away, won't you? You all failed her before, do not fail her now."

Detective Dhar nodded.

"I have just joined this department. I've been through the files about your friend and Mr. Montgomery. There isn't much I can say about the case, but I can tell you that I do not plan on failing Taylor. She will not be let down again."

"Thank you."

The mask over her face was starting to slip, and she could feel the tears straining to escape. She stood.

"Thank you," she repeated. "Please keep me updated."

"I will."

She spoke with several people from Child Protective Services before they told her she didn't have any rights to Zachary. She would fight for him, but she didn't know where even to begin.

"Hey," Lucas said, entering the back porch with a small muffin and a water.

He placed them down on the table beside Claire.

"I have to start planning her funeral. Lucas, I have to plan a funeral for my best friend. My best friend was murdered by her husband."

The tears came then, overtaking every ounce of her. She fell forward, caught by Lucas, who helped keep her steady. She used her fingers to grasp at him, needing to hold on to something. Lucas lifted her up, holding her, as he turned to sit in the seat. He cradled her in his arms and allowed her to let it all out.

"I don't know how to do this."

"Shh, everything doesn't have to happen today. Today, focus on your grief, focus on getting some rest."

Lucas stood, keeping her in his arms. She brought her own arms around his neck, closing her eyes, as he took her up the stairs. He laid her down before taking off her shoes. He brought the blanket up and over her shoulders, and then pressed a kiss on her cheek. Claire reached out for him, pulling him to her.

"Stay with me," she whispered.

Lucas nodded. He climbed into the bed next to her, spooning her with his body. His cheek pressed against hers.

As his heart beat against her back, it slowly lulled her into a fitful sleep.

Claire only slept for a few hours. When she awoke, she saw there were several messages on her phone from her parents, her siblings, close friends, and coworkers. Now everyone knew Taylor was gone.

She didn't have the energy to reply to any of the messages, though she did appreciate them all. It showed people cared; that Taylor's life had meant something to others.

With a yawn, she slid herself out of bed. She was still wearing the clothes she'd worn in the morgue. Thinking about it had her skin crawl. She tore her clothes off herself and threw them into the laundry bin before going to the bathroom and turning the shower onto its hottest setting.

"Do you want company?" Lucas asked.

"No," she said. "Shouldn't you be at work?"

"I took the day off, remember?"

She didn't. Most of the day was a blur if she were to be honest. She rubbed her forehead with the tips of her fingers as the beginnings of a headache stirred.

"You need to eat," Lucas said. "You haven't eaten all day."

"I'm not hungry."

"But still—"

"I said, I'm not hungry, Lucas. Please, don't treat me like a child."

She stepped inside the shower. Her eyes closed as the hot water sprayed against her skin.

"I'm going to go make something for us to eat."

"Alright."

She was glad for him to leave her alone, but she didn't want him to leave the house. It was like she needed him, but also didn't want to be with him. So many conflicting feelings kept going through her mind.

Once she showered, she grabbed a fresh bathrobe to put on over herself. She didn't feel like getting dressed right now. So she went downstairs to see what Lucas had ended up preparing for them to eat.

When she reached the kitchen, she found him sitting at the island. He stood immediately, walking over toward her.

"I made some comfort food: grilled cheese and tomato soup."

Though she didn't want to eat, her stomach growled, betraying her. She didn't need to say a word, Lucas brought her into the kitchen and sat her down at the island. He then went to pour soup into a bowl and cut a sandwich into four small triangles. He placed the foot in front of her.

"Eat."

Claire dipped her spoon into the red soup, putting just enough to wet her lips and brought it up to eat a small spoon full. It was still hot, but her stomach growled louder, wanting more food. So she got herself a fuller spoonful the next time. Before she knew it, she was dipping the sandwich into the soup to eat more. By the time the sandwich and soup were gone, she still didn't feel satisfied.

"Here, I'll get you more."

She was grateful for Lucas's offer. She ate another sandwich and the rest of the soup, finally full.

"I could get you more."

"No. I'm full now. Thank you."

She checked the time on the oven's clock. It was three in the afternoon. Time moved so differently now. It felt like it was days ago that she identified Taylor's body, but it had only been hours before.

What did she do now? She wanted to curl back up into her bed and cry, but she also wanted to feel like she was doing something to bring her friend justice. Yet neither of those options felt obtainable. Instead, she just sat on the barstool in her kitchen and stared at the time on the clock, watching as each minute ticked by.

CHAPTER 30

Her face filled his dreams. When James slept, all he saw was her and her smile. They'd kiss, like they had the last time he saw her; always chaste, always sweet. But when he woke up, the harsh reality of day would hit him.

He shuffled into the kitchen, reaching for a fresh beer from the refrigerator and not worrying about what time of the day it was. He took a long sip. It wasn't nearly strong enough to knock him out so he could sleep more, but it was something.

Since he and Taylor had become—*them*, he hadn't kept any hard liquor at his place. He only had the few cans of beer left over from when he and his friend watched a football game back in February.

"James!" a voice called from his door. He took another sip of his beer. "James, I know you're in there. Let me in."

He groaned, but he did go unlock his front door. Unsurprisingly, Claire stood looking about as badly as he felt. She glanced at him before passing him and entering his home.

"Well, come on in," he deadpanned.

Claire eyed his place judgmentally.

"Did you forget how to throw things into the trash?"

"It's been a shit week," James said. He grabbed a half empty pizza box off the couch and placed it on the coffee table. "There, have a seat."

Claire didn't sit. Instead, she walked over to his windows and tore aside the curtains, letting the light from outside in. James hissed.

"What, are you a vampire now?"

"No, it's just bright, is all."

"You're depressed. I'm depressed. I get it, truly, I do. But this," she said, pointing around at his disheveled living space, "is not going to get justice for Taylor. Once we put that asshole in prison for life, you can wallow."

"I'm not wallowing in my self-pity," James said with a huff. "She's only just been announced dead. I can have a moment to be sad."

"I never said you were wallowing in your self-pity, James. I only said wallow. And of course you can. I've had my fair share, but we have to focus on the next parts first. We need to make sure Dylan stays in police custody. We need to plan Taylor's funeral. And we need to get Zachary from CPS."

James looked up at that. *Zachary.*

"I actually have something that could possibly help with that. Hold on."

James went into his office, searching for the will he'd done for Taylor. He grabbed it and found the specific piece of paper with Taylor's wishes for her son. Then he took it to Claire and gave it to her.

"Look."

Claire read over the paper. Her eyes instantly glassed over with tears.

"She knew," Claire whispered, tears sliding down her cheeks. "She knew what was going to happen. I wish..." Her head shook. "She really had you draw up papers saying she wanted me to raise Zachary if anything happened to her?"

"Yes," James said. "I had Mom look over them. We can take this to whoever is in charge at CPS. They would have to take it into consideration for his placement. That is, if you want to take him in, Claire. It's a big ask, a big commitment. He would be your sole responsibility. Our parents have said they'd take him in if you didn't want to. But they also want to make sure he's with us."

"Why didn't anyone tell me about this?" Claire asked.

"I should have told you sooner. I'm sorry."

"I do want him. I'm well aware of what it would mean. I want him, James. Taylor would want me to have him."

"She would."

Claire broke then. James was quick to react, taking the paper from her and then pulling his sister into his arms.

"It's not right," she cried.

"No," he agreed, "it's not. It's not at all."

He cried with his sister. He hadn't cried, not since he'd found out. Instead, he'd been trapped—too frozen and too angry to let the tears come. But now he could with his sister in his arms. They were the only two people in the world who both understood how the other was feeling. While others might find Taylor's murder tragic, none would be hit as hard with their grief like they were.

"Zachary," he whispered.

He hadn't thought about the way the grief would take over that little boy. Now at three, he may not understand how his mother would never return, but over time he would learn not only that she wasn't coming back but also that his father killed her.

"Yeah," Claire mumbled, stepping away from him. She turned away, wiping her cheeks. "I don't know what he's been told, or if he's been told anything. And I don't know what I'll tell him."

"He needed Taylor."

"He did." Claire sniffled and nodded. "But now I have to fight for him and plan a funeral. I think if I can focus on those things I can keep from falling deep into my despair. Will you help me?"

"I will."

Funerals were expensive; James began to understand as they were given an itemized sheet of all the elements that went into it. The casket alone could cost up into the thousands. Claire didn't seem to care a bit about any of the prices as she pointed to the things she wanted for Taylor. She had always been a compulsive spender, not paying any attention to the price tags on what she purchased. Though, he would have thought now living on her own that she might care a bit more so these things could fit into her budget.

When the funeral director walked away to grab some different paperwork, James bent over to whisper to his sister.

"How do you plan on paying for all of this? I can help with some of it, but that casket was three thousand dollars. I don't know if we can afford that."

"Mom and Dad told me to spend whatever," Claire said with a shrug. "They said they'll be footing the bill."

"Oh."

"They liked Taylor. They want to help and this is how they can."

James nodded his head.

"Where will she be buried?"

"Next to her daughter," Claire said. "Taylor insisted she would pay for the burial of Mia, so the space isn't large, but there is enough space for her."

James grimaced. So much tragedy in so little time.

CHAPTER 31

Max had two new potential clients coming in today. Usually the high of ending a case had him excited for something new, but there was no high today. Instead of waiting anxiously for the new clients, he dreaded it.

"There's someone here to speak with you," Liliana's voice said through the speaker on his office phone.

They finally updated to a better system than her having to either call down the hallway or walk to his office when she needed to speak with him during the day. It made them appear more 'professional.'

"I don't have any clients until eleven," he said, pushing the button to speak.

"Not a client. Should I send him back?"

"Sure, fine."

A moment later, there was a man in his office. Max stood from his seat to greet him.

"How can I help you?"

"My name is Mitch Westcott," the man said, reaching his hand into his coat pocket to pull out a card before offering it over to Max. "I work for KOTB News. We over at KOTB heard you were the break in the big Taylor Montgomery case, and we'd love to do a feature on you this evening."

"Oh."

Max didn't know what to say. This was what he wanted, to be on the news, have people reach out to *him* about how great a private detective he was. Fame and acknowledgement was always what he'd striven to.

"Alright. I think I can do that. What all does it entail?"

"Just some questions. You'll be interviewed live on air. We can even come here to do it," Westcott said as his eyes looked over his office and he gave a nod. "Yes, I do believe here would be good or outside, weather dependent."

"Do I get to know the questions beforehand?"

"No," Westcott said with a laugh. "It's much better if it's on the spot in this type of interview. That way we get the raw emotions."

"Right," Max replied, rocking uneasily on his heels. "Well, is that all you need from me? Can I know when to expect your crews?"

"Yes, we'll arrive around 5 to set up."

"Okay. I guess I'll see you then."

"Yes."

Westcott gave him a nod before heading out of his office. Max remained standing as the conflicting emotions ran through him. This is what he wanted. This would make him number one on the top 40 under 40s list for next year. Yet, it didn't feel as fulfilling as he had expected it to feel.

"Who was that?" Liliana asked as she entered his office.

"Someone from the local news station. They want to interview me about the Montgomery case."

"And are you going to do it?"

"Of course I'm going to do it. I did solve the case, didn't I?"

"You did. Did it make you sad?"

"To solve the case? No," Max said with a roll of his eyes. "I did what I was hired to do."

"But she's dead, and you saw her body. What was it like seeing a dead body? Was it creepy? Did it make your hair stand on your arms?"

"Liliana, can we please not talk about this?"

"Fine, I was only wondering," Liliana said.

The sound of footsteps coming down the long hall had them both turning around to see who it could possibly be. Max doubted it was Westcott from the news station still here. Plus the steps were lighter.

"Do you spend most of your day chatting about instead of doing work?"

Max couldn't help but smile when he saw it was Claire. She glanced at Liliana then to Max.

"Claire."

His voice was so soft that it even surprised him. He motioned to his sister to leave them alone, and then pointed to the chair for Claire to sit down.

"I'm not here to chat," she said. She held an envelope. "Here. This should be what I owe you. If it's not correct, you can call me and I'll send what else I owe."

Max took the envelope. He ran his fingers over the edge before lifting the flap to look inside. He hadn't taken the time to figure out how many hours he'd worked on this case to know if it was the correct amount or not. He closed the envelope and gave it back.

"I can't take your money, Claire."

"Of course you can," Claire said, not taking the envelope. Max's hand remained outstretched with the envelope held in his fingers. "I'm not some pity case, Evans. Take the money you earned. I hired you to do a job, and you did it."

Max placed the envelope down onto his desk. Then he returned his eyes to Claire. It seemed every time he saw her, she looked more beautiful than the time he had before. He shook away those thoughts. This woman had just lost her best friend in the most traumatic way. It wasn't right for him to feel such a way toward her. And she clearly did not feel the same about him. She bit back at him with hostility at every turn.

"I am sorry, Claire, for what happened to your friend."

Claire's lower lip wobbled, but she quickly got it under control.

"Yes, me too," she whispered. "She was a wonderful person. The world was a much better place with her in it."

"Is there anything I can do to help you?"

Max wanted to find a way to remain in Claire's life. It couldn't be over with this. This could not be his last interaction with her.

"Make sure Dylan Montgomery never sees fresh air again," she said with a humorless laugh. "No, there's nothing you can do. You've already done a lot. Because of you, I know the truth of what happened, and Dylan will be going to prison. So thank you. You really are the best private detective in the area."

Max's mouth curled up, not quite able to pull into a full smile. Her large, brown eyes met his. Max's breath caught within his throat.

"I am," he playfully said, causing a chuckle and roll of the eyes from Claire.

"Good luck with," she began, waving vaguely around the room, "everything."

"You too."

He watched longingly as she moved down the hallway until he could no longer see her as she turned the corner. He then gathered the envelope back up, reopening it to check the amount again. As he grabbed his calculator, he tried to do the math in his head about the hours he worked. He typed it all down. It was the exact right amount. But he couldn't accept it. Sure, he needed the money. He hadn't done any other cases since taking this one on, but this money came with someone's blood on it. It came with Claire's heartbreak on it.

He tore the check into small pieces.

"What are you doing?"

"I can't accept it," he told his sister, wondering why she was even back here in his office.

"We have to pay the rent in *two* days. You have to pay me."

"We can manage," Max said. "And don't worry. You'll get your paycheck at the end of the week, like you always do."

"You really like her, don't you?"

"Like who?" he asked as he played dumb, pulling against his collar.

"Claire Donahue. You think she's pretty." Liliana wore a grin.

"Of course, she is pretty, but I don't know what that has to do with—"

"You should ask her out already. I'm sure she likes you too."

"Alright, enough of all of this. Go on back to your desk where you are supposed to be. Stop coming back here when you are bored. It is not my job to keep you entertained."

Liliana dramatically pouted, and Max placed his hands on her shoulders to turn her away from him, gently forcing her back down the hallway.

Once she had finally left his office, Max went back to his seat. He turned on his computer to have it ready for his next case, whatever it may be. By the computer still sat the picture of Taylor. He lifted it and a lump reformed in his throat. Shaking his head, he placed the picture into the top drawer of his desk. He'd need to get it back to Claire.

He typed in his password to get onto his computer. He marked the Montgomery case as solved and began a new page for his next client. But his thoughts kept going to the picture in his top drawer. The picture of the woman whose life had been unfairly ended.

He pulled the picture from the desk and looked at it again.

"Damnit," he said.

He grabbed the card the man from the news station gave him. He couldn't believe he was about to do this. He typed in the number and brought the phone to his ear.

"Hello?" A woman answered on the other end.

"Hello, this is Max Evans. A Mr. Westcott came by today to ask if I would do a live interview this evening. I can no longer do it."

"Oh, um…" she said, and he heard typing through his phone. "Yes, I see you scheduled here. Could we reschedule for another time? Perhaps." She paused, more typing. "Some time tomorrow or later this week?"

"No, I won't be interviewing about the case. The media has plenty of information on the topic, they don't need any more of it from me. Thank you."

Before Max could change his mind, he hung up the phone. He couldn't believe he just did that. Did he really throw away his opportunity to get his name further out there? That one interview could have opened doors for so much more. But as he looked at the picture of Taylor, all of that faded away. The news stations were already having a field day with her death. Her face would be on the news and in papers for a while until they moved onto other things, completely forgetting about her and her son, until the murder case came up and they could gain ratings from it again. No, Max couldn't be a part of that. He didn't want to be.

He grabbed some tape and taped the picture of Taylor up on the side of his monitor, as a reminder of how fragile life could be and a reminder of the person he wanted to become.

CHAPTER 32

The woman before Claire wore a tight, unrelenting expression on her pale pink face, likely from years of putting up with situations like these in the CPS office. She adjusted her glasses before glancing at the sheet of paper from Claire. Then she put it down, sliding it back over to Claire.

"Sorry about your friend," she said, her voice sincere despite the coldness on her features. "But even with that piece of paper, you cannot get her son. His father, um—" She paused to look at the computer screen on her desk, narrowing her eyes, "Dylan Montgomery has said he's not to go to you."

"What?" Claire asked.

Her fingertips came up to rest above her mouth. *That rat-ass bastard.* She dropped her fingers, working to still her beating heart. It would do her no good to get angry at the woman before her. She didn't get to make these decisions.

"But how can that be? He murdered his wife. Why does he get a say in where Zachary goes?"

"Ms. Donahue, while that may be the case, he hasn't been charged yet. And even if he is, he'll still get to choose. This is something you'll have to take to court."

"Well, I will," Claire said. "My family are all lawyers."

"Good, then," she said.

Claire couldn't tell if she was being kind or condescending. Her tight face gave little way to her real emotions.

"Are you sure there is nothing I can do in the meantime?"

"There is not."

A low sound left Claire as she stood.

"Thank you, anyway."

She turned, her hand resting on the doorknob. Then she paused, a thought passing through her.

"Will they bring him to the funeral? His mother is going to be buried tomorrow."

"I can't answer that," the woman answered.

This time Claire did notice a softness in her eyes, an understanding of the pain of losing someone.

"Thank you," Claire whispered.

She found her emotions were all over the place since Taylor's body had been found. As much as she tried to keep her steady and stoic demeanor, it could easily crack. The smallest amount of kindness would make her eyes well up with tears.

She turned the knob of the door and exited the room, walking through the small building and noticing all of the eyes on her. The old her would have stared at them back, daring them to say something to her and make them flustered. But now she ducked her head and made her way out of the building.

Once she was out, she checked her phone. There was a message from Lucas. Claire bit down on the inside of her lip, feeling overwhelmed by his constant need to contact her if he hadn't spoken to her within the last hour. She placed the phone back into her purse and got into her car. She brought down the visor to block away the insistent sun. Behind her eyelids, tears threatened to escape.

"No," she whispered to herself.

She wasn't about to give in. When she finally did, they always came harshly and with no promise of ending. She couldn't allow that now. Those moments needed to be reserved for when she was at home and either alone or with Lucas. Otherwise, she had to force herself to stay strong.

Her phone rang. She sighed, expecting it to be Lucas. But when she looked down, she saw it was Evans.

"Hello?"

"Um, hi."

He sounded awkward and not quite sure of himself, not like the Evans she'd met in his office not too long ago.

"Do you need something?"

Even though she tried not to snap, it came anyway. She just couldn't understand why he would be calling her now. She'd paid him. Their time knowing one another should be finished now.

"I was wondering if it would be all right for me to attend the funeral tomorrow. Well, Liliana and me, that is."

"Oh," she said as her voice softened.

She fell back deeper into her seat, meeting her own eyes in the rearview mirror.

"I mean—if you would rather we not come, I understand. We just want to pay our respects."

"No," Claire said, "I mean—yes, of course you can come. You were the one who found her, Evans. You should come."

"Are you sure? I—*we* don't want to intrude."

Claire gave a genuine smile.

"I'm sure. I want you to come."

"Alright, we'll come. Should we bring anything?"

"No," Claire said. "Just yourselves. I'll see you then."

"See you then. Goodbye, Claire."

"Bye."

She hung up the phone. A smile crept up her lips, making her grateful for being alone so no one would notice.

She grabbed her phone again, making her way to call Taylor, because it was always Taylor that she called when something like this happened to her. She needed to tell her about the boy that made her blush and discuss how she could feel this way when she had a serious boyfriend.

But then, like a harsh crash of a wave against her skin, she remembered that she couldn't call her best friend. A sob crept its way up her throat, escaping before she had the chance to stifle it. Then the floodgates began, taking over her. She grasped against the steering wheel for support as the tears continued to fall. She didn't try to push them back in, knowing it was pointless. Instead, she resigned herself to a meltdown in the parking lot at the CPS office, not giving a damn if anyone saw.

Flowers filled the room. So. Many. Flowers. Claire kept checking the tags on the flowers, wondering who they were from. Most names she didn't know. James came up behind her, checking them as well.

"Taylor did not know this many people," she said quietly.

The viewing would begin shortly, and she was making sure everything was perfect before the others came in.

"Her story made the news," James said as a reminder.

"Oh god, you think strangers sent these?"

"Why is that bad?"

"Because they don't really care," Claire said with a shake of her head. "They just want to feel better about themselves for doing some random act of kindness."

"I don't believe that," James replied. "Taylor's story touched them. Look at this tag."

He pulled it off the white lilies for Claire.

You gave me the courage to leave. Her hand shook with the weight of those words. Claire read over them once more.

"See, her story means something."

"It means that when a woman tries to leave, the odds are the man will kill her. It's not some inspirational tale," Claire quipped as she tucked the card back where it belonged.

"No," James said in disagreement. "Her story shows how these cases need to be taken more seriously by the police earlier, not waiting until the woman is hurt."

Claire huffed. She had little belief that her friend's death would change anything. All the other deaths of domestic abuse victims didn't. Why would hers be the turning point?

Lucas slid up beside her then. She wondered where he had gone off to. She knew death gave him the *heebie-jeebies* as he called them, so he'd probably gone outside for a little while for a breath of fresh air.

He kissed her, throwing her off guard. She shoved him.

"What was that?" she hissed.

"What? Can I not kiss you?"

"Not here, not right now when..."

Her voice trailed off as she watched Liliana and Evans step inside. Oh, she thought. She rolled her eyes, pushing Lucas further away. She had no time or patience for his jealousy.

She motioned for her brother to join her as she walked over to greet Liliana and Evans. The moment he saw her, Evans brightened, a small smile playing on his lips.

"James," Claire began, "this is Max Evans and his sister, Liliana Evans. Evans and Liliana, this is my older brother, James."

"Nice to meet you," Evans said.

"Thank you for finding Taylor," James said, his eyes glistening.

"Of course."

They stood in an awkward silence for a moment, no one quite knowing what to say. This wasn't like a funeral for an older person who had lived their full life. One couldn't say all the positive things one says at those types of funerals. Taylor's life had been marred by tragedy. She hadn't been allowed to live the life she deserved, and she had been taken much too quickly.

"Cwaire!"

Her heart skipped a beat. She turned to the sound, ignoring Evans and Liliana, who she had just greeted. There he was: Zachary. The little boy rushed to her and she bent down, sweeping him up and into her arms. She kissed his pudgy cheek, still not convinced that he was truly here.

"Hi Zachary, oh how I've missed you!"

"I...I hope it's all right that we brought him," a small woman said, giving Claire a tiny nod.

Behind her stood a taller man, with another child in his arms.

"Yes," Claire said. "I'm Claire. I was Taylor's best friend. I think it's right that he's here. Thank you for bringing him—"

She realized she didn't know their names.

"I'm Stephanie Harland. This is my husband, Eric, and our other foster son, Daniel."

"It's nice to meet you."

Claire tightened her hold of Zachary, so pleased to finally have him back and in her arms. The tears she'd been trying to hold back until the funeral had ended started to come now with Zachary here. She wondered what all he knew, what all he'd been told. Her heart broke for this little boy who had lost his mother to his father's anger and jealousy.

"If it's all right with you, we'd like to get your information. It may help Zachary to have someone he's close to."

"Yes," Claire said, relieved. "I would love that."

She closed her eyes, grateful Zachary was with a good family. She attempted to put him down, but he clung to her neck, not letting go. And she had to admit she really didn't want to let him go either. He was the last thing she had of Taylor.

"Is it okay if he stays with me, just for right now?"

"Oh, sure. We'll be just around here," Stephanie said with a smile.

She walked over with her husband to take a seat in the back of the church.

"Mama?" Zachary then asked, looking up at her with expectant eyes.

"I'm so sorry," she whispered, not able to say anything else and pulling him back into a tight hug.

"Perhaps you should let him sit with them," Lucas said, coming up behind her.

"They said it's fine."

"But you have the funeral to tend to, people to speak with—"

"Are you going to support me in trying to get custody of Zachary?" she cut him off.

Lucas's eyes widened.

"I don't think right now is the best time to discuss this," he quietly said.

Claire nodded, not surprised.

"Yeah," she whispered. "That's what I thought."

They stood there in silence. Claire finally allowed herself to let go of Lucas. She reached out and patted his shoulder.

"We had a good run, you and me."

Lucas stood there for a moment, processing what she said. He opened his mouth to speak before deciding to turn and begin to walk away.

"Where is he going?" James asked her.

Zachary lifted his head at the familiar voice. He reached up, asking for James to hold him. James gave Claire a questioning look if he could take him. She handed him over.

"I think we're over," she said.

"Oh."

And that was all they said about it. They returned their attentions to Zachary, who seemed pleased to see them both for the first time in a while.

When Claire stood up to speak at the funeral, she looked at the sea of people in the pews. Her first thought had been, *I didn't plan for this many people to eat at the wake.* Her second thought had been about all the lives Taylor inadvertently touched. She wondered how things would have been different if Taylor had been able to leave Dylan earlier. Would she still be alive? Or would the outcome been similar?

She blinked, a stray tear making its way down her cheek.

"My best friend, Taylor," she began, her words catching in her throat, "was beautiful. Had she been given the opportunity, Taylor could have changed the world. We were roommates in college. I was the immature one. She kept me in line, even though she was nearly two years younger than me. She wanted to be a teacher, an art teacher in particular. And she did, once she moved in with me. It may have only been once a week, but she adored it. Taylor had such a brightness to her. The one thing in the world she loved more than art was her son, Zachary. Now her son lives without her. Now the world..."

She had to pause. Her eyes fluttered over the crowd before they fell on Evans. He was crying. Not in an obnoxious way, but the silent tears that took over when you were truly touched by what was going on. His eyes met hers. He gave her an encouraging smile.

"Now the world is not as bright without her. We lost a precious soul. Violence took her away from us."

Zachary was back in her arms when the wake began. While Claire had explained to Zachary that his mommy was now in heaven, he didn't seem to completely understand. It broke her heart that she couldn't be the one there for him as he slowly processed he would not see his mother again.

Claire spotted Larry sitting alone at a table in the corner of the dining hall. Claire debated between leaving him alone and going to tell him hello.

In the end, she decided she should walk over to him. She placed Zachary down beside her, leading him over to the table where Larry Smith sat. He glanced up, his eyes watery. He moved his attention to Zachary, giving him a crooked smile.

"He looks so much like she did at this age."

"I'm glad you could make it," Claire said.

"I wasn't a good father," he muttered. "I didn't protect her like I should have."

"It wasn't your fault, Mr. Smith. But you do have Zachary still. Perhaps you could work on getting sober for him? I know Taylor would want you to be a part of his life."

Larry's shaky hands gathered in front of himself as he eyed the little boy before him. He gave a small nod, reaching out slight toward Zachary. Zachary stepped back, hiding behind Claire's legs.

"So, is he staying with you now?"

"Not yet," Claire said. "But I'm working on it. Dylan," she said his name with much animosity, "has said he doesn't want me to keep him. I plan on fighting it."

Larry attempted to look around Claire's legs to get a better view of his grandson, but the little boy hid his face into Claire's knees, nearly making her fall forward so she had to use the chair in front of her for balance.

"He doesn't really know me," Larry said with a frown. "I'd like to help, if I can, with you getting my grandson. My girl would have wanted him living with you."

Claire's eyes burned with the unshed tears that threatened to escape. She gave a small nod.

"I do think she would. I'm glad you came. Will you be around for a few days?"

"No," he said. "I'm going back after we go to where she'll be buried. But I'll come back when the trial comes. I want to see him rot."

"Me too."

She led Zachary back over to the food. He had become overwhelmed with all the people that kept trying to talk to him, so Claire was trying to navigate it all and remind those people that Zachary was not their entertainment.

"Claire," Stephanie said, meeting them at the table. "We're going to have to leave now."

Claire's heart sunk. She looked down at Zachary, not ready to let him go, just yet. While Stephanie and her husband seemed to be good people, they weren't Zachary's family. She was. Zachary belonged with her. She took in a deep breath, steeling herself for the pain before bending down to Zachary's level. With the back of her finger, she stroked his cheek and offered him a smile.

"You're going to leave now," she said, trying not to show him just how upset she was.

It would do no good to get him all upset. She had to do what was best for him. She leaned forward, kissing his cheek. As she did, Zachary brought his arms tightly around her neck.

"No," he said loudly. "Please let me stay!"

It took every ounce of will not to let her tears fall. She touched the back of his head, running her fingers through his hair.

"I'll see you soon," she promised. With her fingers, she untangled his arms around her neck. "Could I walk him outside to the car?"

The foster parents agreed.

Claire buckled him in and gave him his stuffed bear that she had brought with her in hopes she'd see him today. Zachary clung it to his chest, tear stains on his cheeks. Claire's heart broke.

"I love you. I'll see you soon," she promised again.

Then she shut the door. Zachary's cries were so loud that she could hear them with the door closed. She turned away, knowing that she had to walk away from him right now. As she did, the tears came. She couldn't handle it. It hurt, so much.

When she walked back up to the church door, she spotted Max standing there, a somber expression on his face. Claire quickened her steps to him. When she reached him, he opened his arms. She fell forward against him.

"I hate *him*."

"I know."

Max's fingers ran down the length of her spine before resting on the small of her back.

"I know."

CHAPTER 33

Today marked the pretrial date for the case against Dylan Montgomery.

Claire had arrived over an hour early, securing seats for her, James, and Simone. Her heart stammered in her chest knowing that today was only the beginning of what was to come.

She turned her head around, searching for James. He promised to be here early, but he hadn't shown up yet. He was less reliable lately, unable to cope with what happened to Taylor, still shouldering much of the blame.

Her sister, Simone, squeezed her hand as she sat on the other side of her to give her support. Simone never spoke much, instead always taking everything in around her. It was partially what made her a great lawyer. She knew how to listen and pay attention to the details, which in turn helped her to find the holes in peoples' stories. In just a few short months, she would be leaving stay at home motherhood and heading back to the family firm.

The door made a loud creak as it opened, making Claire turn. She hoped to see James finally walking in. But it wasn't James. It was Evans.

There was a fluttering in her chest, so she quickly looked away. However, she was too curious not to see where he decided to sit. She looked around again. He'd slid into the back row, head ducked, as though he wasn't trying to make a show of being there. Part of her wished he'd sat down on the row with her.

"I don't think James is coming," Simone whispered into Claire's ear, drawing her attention back to her. "He texted me that he's had car trouble."

"Car trouble," Claire said tightening her jaw. "I don't think it's car trouble."

"No," Simone muttered. "Poor James."

While she felt sorry for her brother, she was agitated by him, too. Taylor had been her best friend for nearly five years. She'd been her roommate. She was the one who'd tried over and over again to help her escape Dylan. Yet, James got to be one who fell apart because 'he loved her.' She had loved her too. She was the one who understood there was no time to fall apart right now. More had to be done before she could. She had to seek justice for her friend, first and foremost. Why couldn't James understand that?

The judge took his seat and the entire room grew silent. Her chest tightened, causing her to place her hand over it and force herself to breathe. In a moment, Dylan would walk through those doors. In a moment, she'd have to see his face again. She wasn't ready, and yet, she had to be.

The door opened, and he walked out. Claire couldn't focus on what he wore, all she could look at was his face. He wore a smirk and kept whispering to the man who must have been his lawyer. There was an arrogance about him. He really believed he wasn't going to serve time for this.

"What I wouldn't give to spend just five minutes alone with him," Claire muttered.

"Don't allow that pain and anger to consume you," Simone said as a warning. "You are better than that."

Claire's eyes rolled. She certainly was not.

"How do you plead, Mr. Montgomery?" the judge asked.

Claire's attention moved back to what was going on.

"Not guilty, your honor."

"That lying son of a bitch," Claire said between clinched teeth.

"Perhaps we should go outside, get a breath of fresh air," Simone said.

"No, I'm staying. They won't let him go on bail before the trial, will they? Not with all the evidence against him?"

Simone tried to give a shake of her head to calm Claire's worries, but her eyes gave everything away to Claire.

"But he's a murderer!"

"Innocent until proven guilty," Simone said quietly.

She kept her eyes on Dylan, unable to look away. He was unfazed, even as the prosecution gave reasoning for this case to move to trial. That sick bastard really believed he would walk away from this, continue on his path of treating woman horribly, possibly even killing another in the future.

Claire's stomach flipped. She'd never known what true hatred before this moment, but she *hated* Dylan Montgomery.

"Bail is set at 100 thousand dollars."

The trial was over just like that, with bail set. Claire held hope that the bail was high enough that Dylan could not pay it. Though she had no real understanding of Dylan's financial situation.

She stood with her sister, needing to go home and take a long shower. The pretrial made her feel incredibly dirty. She couldn't imagine how the actual trial would actually go.

As they turned to leave the room, Claire remembered Evans had come inside. She looked to see if he was still sitting in the back, but he was already gone. Disappointment consumed her, though she told herself it was ridiculous to be disappointed. Evans was an egotistical know-it-all. She only had a connection to him because he had been the one to find Taylor, and he had been the one to tell her that her friend was dead.

With a shaky breath, she started to walk outside. It was such a still and quiet day, so unlike the chaos in her heart.

"Would you like me to come to your place for a bit?" Simone asked.

Claire shook her head. She did appreciate her sister for being here for her, but she needed this time to sit alone in her thoughts. Having her sister at her house would only make her feel like she had to entertain her or speak with her.

"Go home to your boys," Claire said, bending over to kiss her sister's cheek.

Her hand grasped Simone's, and they locked eyes for a moment.

"Call me if you need me."

"I will."

Claire watched her sister head off in the direction of her car. She'd managed to grab a spot right by the building, not having to park in the garage down the street like her. Once Claire's sister was in the car and had driven off, Claire resigned herself to making the walk to her own car.

There was a coffee shop across the street. She stopped. Coffee sounded amazing right now. She crossed the street and went inside the shop. It appeared Evans had the same idea. He sat toward the back and spotted her almost immediately.

Evans got up from his chair and walked over to her.

"He'll be found guilty," Evans said.

Claire tightened her jaw to keep her chin from wobbling.

"I do hope so."

"Would you like to sit with me?"

It was lunchtime, and the coffee shop was full of people. Most had laptops, working on work during their lunch break with a coffee cake sitting next to their laptops and coffee.

"I guess I should. There's nowhere else to sit."

"Go on and sit. It's been a long morning for you. I'll grab you whatever you'd like from the counter."

Claire opened her mouth to protest, but Evans had already guided her over to the table to sit down. Despite the fact that she'd just been sitting for a while, she found it relaxing to sit down here. She gave Evans her order and a twenty dollar bill before he went off to grab her order.

Even though the coffee shop was packed, the line wasn't long. Evans sat back down next to her just five minutes later. He slid her twenty dollar bill back to her.

"I'm not letting you pay for me," Claire said. She left the money sitting between them. "I know you didn't cash my check."

"It didn't feel right," he said.

"You did the work. You are owed the money. Take it," she insisted.

"Let's not talk about that," Evans said, attempting to shift the subject. "How are you holding up?"

There was the familiar sting in her eyes that came several times a day since Taylor's disappearance. She attempted a smile.

"I'm holding," she said. "I just miss her."

"Of course you do," Evans said.

His fingers brushed against hers. Instinctively, her hand turned to allow his hand to fall into hers, but she gathered her wits and withdrew it just as quickly as it had turned.

The barista called her name for her coffee. She jumped up to receive it.

"I should go," she said, remaining by the counter. She didn't miss the disappointment in Evans' eyes. "Thank you for inviting me to sit with you."

"Of course."

Before she could change her mind, Claire left the coffee shop. She hastened her steps, but glanced inside the window one last time before she turned the corner.

When Claire climbed into bed that night, she received a text from Max.

He made bail.

Those three words sliced at her heart.

How? she asked. *He couldn't afford bail.*

I'm not sure. I could find out, if you'd like me to.

No, that's okay.

Claire dropped her phone down beside her.

Dylan Montgomery would get to continue living life for the next few months with a few restrictions, while her best friend laid beneath the ground. She rolled over to her side, pressed the pillow over her face, and then she screamed.

CHAPTER 34

After taking a long puff, James flicked the cigarette onto the cement ground below him and stamped on it with the toe of his shoe. He hadn't touched a cigarette for years. It was a habit he'd begun at the end of high school.

The nicotine addiction became such a part of his personality that his family stepped in and told him he wasn't allowed in the house unless he showered beforehand. Eventually, he finally cut the habit. But now it was back. It was an easy way to calm his nerves, and it was way less damaging than hiding in a bottle of alcohol.

He walked down the sidewalk toward the cemetery. From the entrance, he could easily make out where Taylor was buried. Flowers and other mementos covered the ground from random people who were impacted by her death. He drew in a deep breath before finally stepping inside and going to the shrine left for Taylor.

Tears pricked behind his eyes. He slowly bent down, his fingers brushing against a teddy bear that had been left.

It was hard to think how Taylor laid beneath all of this while Dylan was still walking around. While on bail, Dylan did have rules he had to follow, such as being within a certain amount of miles from his home and his work. He also was not allowed to have custody of Zachary. From what he found, he got one visit a week with Zachary at a location determined by the courts. None of that seemed like punishment enough for what he did.

"Hi," he whispered.

Words seemed to escape him. There was so much he wanted to say to her, and yet none of the words would come.

"Oh, you're here."

He turned, seeing Claire standing about a yard away from him. She wore wide-rimmed sunglasses over her eyes, making it hard for him to read her expression.

"I come often to visit."

"I haven't seen you here," Claire said as she walked closer to him before her nose curled up. "You smell disgusting. Since when did you pick up smoking again?"

James ignored her question. He picked up a bundle of roses, setting them up closer to where the stone would be placed in a few months.

"Mom and Dad asked me if I knew where you were," Claire continued to speak. "You do have to work, you know."

"Why are you being so cruel?" James asked as he stood, stepping back away from his sister. "Why does everyone just expect me to be alright? You loved her too, you should understand."

He watched as Claire's back stiffened. She seemed to hesitate for a moment as she decided whether or not to speak.

"I do understand," Claire said, her words sharp. "But we have to focus on justice; we have to focus on Zachary. You didn't even come to the pretrial."

"I...I had car trouble."

"Oh, bullshit," Claire spat. "You couldn't handle it. You're not strong enough."

At that, he flinched.

"I tried," he managed to get out. "Maybe I'm not as strong as you, Claire. I just need time."

"There isn't time. He's still out there, likely planning his next victim."

James wiped his brow, it suddenly feeling much hotter outside. He could feel the sun beating down against his forehead and neck, causing sweat to bubble up along his hairline.

"I just miss her."

Claire's lower lip quivered.

"I miss her, so much. I don't know how I'll live in a world without her," Claire murmured. "I don't want us to fight. You're my brother, and you loved her like I loved her. I just...I need you to be present. I need you to fight for her. Isn't that what you promised you would do?"

James swallowed hard before he nodded. He thought of Taylor and what she would want him to do for her, for Zachary.

"Alright, I should go. I do have to work today. I have to wait until the trial is over to fight for Zachary for the best chance of getting him." She paused, thinking over her words. "You do think that's what's best for him, don't you?"

James smiled.

"I do."

"Really?"

"Really."

She patted his arm before walking away, leaving him all alone with Taylor again. He grabbed his packet of cigarettes from his back pocket, hitting the packet against his palm to get out one. As he brought it to his mouth, he decided against it. He couldn't smoke. Not here, not now. Taylor never would have approved.

Deep down, he knew his sister was right. He knew he needed to get out of this funk he was in. But the guilt ate away at him every day from the moment he woke up to the moment he closed his eyes at night and even in his dreams. It plagued at him every second of every day. He should have been able to save her.

CHAPTER 35

Claire still spotted Lucas at work. He avoided her, and she avoided him. After the funeral, she packed up all of his things at her house and placed them on his desk the next day at work. There were no new messages between them. They were over.

Her phone dinged to let her know she had a text message. She glanced over at it to see the text was from Stephanie. She grinned. They'd arranged a playdate for tomorrow around lunchtime at the park. Claire planned on bringing her cupcakes that she knew were Zachary's favorite. She'd been looking forward to it all week.

Claire, I'm sorry, but we will not be able to meet with you at the park tomorrow with Zachary. We've been told we're no longer allowed to let Zachary near you. His father doesn't want you near him, and we must comply or risk having Zachary taken from our care. I'm sorry, truly, I am. If anything changes, I'll let you know.

Claire sat her phone down. *That bastard,* she thought to herself. Dylan wasn't finished hurting her. What he didn't realize, or maybe he did, was that he was also hurting Zachary by keeping the two of them apart.

She took a moment, calming her nerves. This wasn't Stephanie's fault. It wouldn't be fair to blame her. She didn't want Stephanie or her husband to lose care of Zachary. They were kind people. Zachary was safe and loved with them.

I understand. Give Zachary my love.

She left her response simple, locking her phone afterwards and turning off the sound. A message popped up on her computer screen, and she realized she still sat here at work. All of the energy she'd held before seemed to have disappeared with that one message from Stephanie. How was she supposed to stay focused for the rest of the day?

When her day finally ended, Claire drove over an hour to park outside of Dylan's work. She spotted him right away. He stood, leaning over a stack of cartons with a woman across from him. She laughed, enamored by him.

Claire thought she might vomit right there and then. Did that woman know Dylan was on bail and would be on trial soon for murder?

She pulled up a bit closer to get a better view of them both. She doubted this woman was the fiancée. She had turned Dylan in to the police, taking away his alibi. Claire hoped she remained far away from him now. Though Claire doubted she was in trouble, not yet anyway. Dylan was smart enough to put time between his victims. She was sure of that.

The girl that stood across from Dylan looked young, maybe right on the cusp of adulthood. Did her parents know she was out here, speaking to a man nearly 10 years older than her? Her blonde hair was pulled into two messy buns on either side of her head with stray pieces falling over her face. Her fair cheeks had a little too much blush, and her lips were coated in bright red lipstick. She wore a short, cropped top and a mini-skirt. Not really an outfit you'd wear to the mechanic.

Dylan's head turned. Claire panicked. She hadn't really hidden herself. Her car was off, and it would take her too long to turn on her car and drive away. She couldn't very well hide either, so their eyes met. Her demeanor became steely, her eyes cutting right through him. He kept his eyes right on her, a smirk growing on his lips.

She turned on her car then, but she didn't drive far. She moved up the street, parking again and stepping outside. Surely that girl would have to head back home soon; it was getting late. She needed to speak with her, let her know who Dylan Montgomery really was.

Finally, Claire saw the girl walking back down the street. Claire moved quickly to be by the girl's side. The girl looked to Claire before moving even faster.

"Wait," Claire said.

"Why are you following me?" she asked.

"I'm not...I mean, I just needed to talk to you for a moment."

The girl paused her steps, eyeing Claire cautiously.

"Why?"

"That man you were speaking to—Dylan Montgomery, he's a murderer. He killed his wife."

The girl scoffed.

"Oh, and how do you know?" she asked, placing her hands on her hips. "You've watched the news, have you?"

"No," Claire said, quietly. "Taylor was my best friend."

The girl rolled her eyes.

"It's a witch hunt against him. He loved his wife, but she was cheating on him. Did you know that? With some guy named James."

"She didn't—"

"Then she got herself in trouble and killed. While it's sad, it's not Dylan's fault that his wife was a whore."

It took every ounce of will for Claire to not slap this girl right across her cheek.

"I'm only trying to warn you," she said, trying to keep her voice steady. "He's dangerous."

"He's really not. He's sweet. Sorry about your friend," the girl said, insincere.

Claire watched her walk away, disheartened. When she turned to walk back to her car, she saw Dylan standing nearby, right beside the repair shop. He was cleaning off his hands with a rag, keeping his gaze locked on her. Claire growled. Her feet began to propel herself forward until she was nearly a few feet away from him.

"How dare you!" she yelled. He didn't flinch, bringing his arms over his chest. "You don't care about who you hurt, do you? You don't even care about Zachary!"

"I love my son," Dylan said calmly. "Once this trial is over, he and I will get to resume our lives. We'll have to rebuild after what you did to us."

"What I did to you? You really are delusional, aren't you?"

Dylan still remained calm. He took two steps forward so that he now was only an arm length away from Claire. She wanted to draw back, but she wouldn't allow him to know how much he unsettled her.

"Do the right thing for once, Dylan. Let Zachary stay with me. It's what Taylor would have wanted. You're going to go to prison. Don't you want your son where he feels safe?"

"Taylor never should have left," Dylan said, sneering. "I did warn her, you know. Dangerous people out here in the world."

"You. *You* are the dangerous one."

"Well, I guess we'll see, won't we, if the jury agrees?" he questioned as he went back to cleaning his hands. "Don't come back here. I'd hate to call the cops on you for harassment."

He stepped back several more steps before turning to head inside of the shop. Claire needed a moment to steady her breathing. Even if the jury found him guilty, she started to doubt he would receive a life sentence. He'd yet to confess to killing Taylor. People got away with crimes *all the time*. She knew. Her parents spoke about it after some of their cases.

She went to her car, not knowing where she was headed to next. She couldn't go home. Home didn't feel much like home anymore. She needed to speak with someone. She couldn't call James. He was a wreck. She could go to Simone's. Since Taylor's disappearance, Simone had been a wonderful older sister, helping in any way she could. Yet, Simone wasn't who she needed. She needed someone who understood.

Before she knew it, she was parked outside of Evans' PI office. It was late, but light shined through the back window where his office was, letting her know he was still there. She had run through a fast food restaurant and had grabbed some burgers and a couple of sodas. She picked them up, exited her car, and walked up to the front door before she could lose her nerve. Then she knocked.

CHAPTER 36

When Max first heard the faint sound of the knock on the front door of his office building, he thought it was the sound of a branch knocking against something outside. He ignored it, focusing on searching the license plate of the man he'd just been following. This most recent cheating case was more complicated than most. This person knew how to cover his footsteps which made Max wonder if there was more to it than that.

Again, there was a knock. It was louder this time. Then there was a voice. He stood. He quickly made his way to the front door, grabbing the bat he kept against the wall just in case an intruder came by.

He peeked through the window to see Claire walking away. He opened the door.

"Wait! I didn't hear you."

Claire turned.

"Are you hungry?"

She lifted up the sodas she held in one hand and the large bag in the other. He stepped forward to help, taking the drinks first, then the bag.

He pointed for her to come inside. She did, walking into the building and turning on the lights in the front.

"You know, those aren't needed? I do have an electric bill to pay."

Claire gave him a look before turning the lights back off. They both walked down the long hallway into his office. Max realized he had nowhere to set the food or drinks because his desk was a mess. He decided to set them on the very edge and push them back, so that the paperwork would slide with the motion.

"Do you need me to clean off your desk for you? It's quite...messy."

Max chuckled. Now that his hands were free, he was able to gather most of the paperwork and put it into a pile at the corner of his desk. He shrugged.

"This works."

"How on earth do you manage to know what paperwork belongs with what?"

"I just know. I have my own system."

"I guess," she said. She grabbed the bag of food, reaching inside for one of the burgers. "Here. It's just a basic cheeseburger. I forgot to ask for fries."

"That's alright. I'm not much of a fries guy, myself."

"You don't like fries? Huh."

"I didn't say I didn't like them. It's just that they don't make or break my burger meal," he said.

He decided to rest against the edge of his desk, so he could stay closer to Claire. He unwrapped the burger, wanting to have a bite. He was famished. He had planned on grabbing something to eat on his way home, but hadn't expected on staying at work for as long as he had this evening.

"Now," he said, "why are you here? I didn't expect to see you here, especially not this late."

Claire couldn't meet his eyes. Her eyes glistened as her head shook.

"I don't know. I guess I needed someone to talk to. It's just so *hard*."

Max watched as the tears slid down Claire's face. He remembered the first time he met her and how uncomfortable her tears had made him feel then. But now he only wanted to make her feel even the slightest bit better. He moved down to sit next to her on the other chair and brought his arm around her shoulder. Surprising him, it came easily.

"It will take time," he said. "You have to be kind to yourself."

"I just want this trial to be over. I feel like I can't truly mourn until this is past us. It lingers overhead as he lives his life out there. You know, I think he believes he's going to get away with it."

"What?"

"I saw him a little while ago."

"Where? Where did you see him?" Max didn't like the idea of Claire being anywhere near that monster. "Claire, that's not..."

"I'm not scared of him," she interrupted. "He's convinced people around him that he's innocent. Next he'll convince the jury."

"No, he won't," Max said with a shake of his head. "There's real evidence against him. He won't be able to just say he didn't do it. They'll have testimonies from you and others like you that saw the abuse. He has no solid alibi. They won't let him walk. I'm sure of it."

"But are you sure he'll get the harshest punishment?"

"No," Max said regretfully. "I am not sure. I wish I could be sure, but—you never can truly know what will happen in that room."

Claire slowly opened up her burger, taking the tiniest of bites. She then sat it back down, making a face.

"It's cold."

"I could run out and grab us some more? Or you could come to my place, and I could whip us up something to eat."

"You cook?" she said, seeming rather amused at this new knowledge. "Are you any good at it?"

"I am. Liliana says I make the best chicken parm."

"That does sound delicious," Claire agreed as her fingertips came up just mere centimeters from his face as though she might touch him but then she drew them away and stood. "Rain check?"

"Sure."

"You've grown on me, Evans," Claire said. "I think you and I could be friends."

"I think we could," Max replied.

Claire gave him a watery smile.

"You've become a bit less full of yourself. It looks good on you, keep it up."

"Let me walk you to your car."

He was glad when she allowed it. They walked outside. He opened her car door for her, waiting until she sat down to say anything else.

"You can call me at any time, Claire. Day or night. I'll pick up the phone."

"Thank you."

He shut the door and watched as she drove away.

Max's apartment was quiet. He dropped his shoes off beside the door, placing his briefcase onto the table. As he stepped further inside, he grew more uncomfortable with the quiet. For years, he'd complained about the loud upstairs neighbors. But once they moved, his apartment became nearly painfully quiet. His apartment was nestled toward the back, his windows facing rows of trees. The neighbors on either side of him were older and were in bed by dark.

Now when he got home, he turned on his television for noise. His job was lonely enough. He didn't need to feel lonely at home.

As he flipped on the television, he walked into his kitchen for a drink. The burger Claire had brought him hit the spot for dinner. He grabbed a soda from the fridge, knowing he'd regret it when he needed to go to sleep.

"What do you want people to know, Mr. Montgomery?"

Max paused. Certainly, this wasn't a conversation with Dylan Montgomery. What news station would give that murderer the air time? But he found himself drawn to the television to see.

There on the screen was Dylan's face. He wore a distressed frown, letting out a sigh every few seconds. His eyes didn't meet the camera. Instead, he looked at the crowd of people who stood around him outside of the auto shop where he worked.

"I loved my wife. I want justice for her. She was stolen from me, stolen from our son, Zachary. I've been unfairly prosecuted. I did not kill her."

Max had to give Dylan credit. He was a good actor. The mass of people that stood around him all appeared sympathetic to Dylan's pretend plight.

"Liar," Max muttered.

Dylan may have charisma to turn heads out here, but once he was on the stand, it wouldn't be as easy. The evidence would speak for itself. He knew there would be zero doubt from the jurors that Dylan Montgomery grabbed his wife, took her out into the woods, killed her, and then hid the body.

His phone began to ring.

"Hello?" he said before even seeing who had called.

"He's going to get away with it," Claire cried.

Max lifted the remote to turn down the television. He sat down at the edge of the couch.

"He won't," he said strongly.

"But do you see all those people rallying around him?!"

"It's just people, Claire. The jury and the judge will know he did it. The evidence is strong."

Claire let out a harsh hiccup on the other end of the line.

"I wish you could have met her. She was so wonderful," Claire said.

"Me too."

Max rested back in his couch, just keeping his phone against his ear. If this was how he could be here for Claire, this was how he would do it.

"She would draw and paint. And I don't mean just little sketches, either. She was truly talented."

"What sorts of things did she paint?" he asked, turning the channel.

"Well, at first she just painted things she thought we'd like, but she grew with her talents. After she left—*him*—she painted all the time. You know, he wouldn't let her, the asshole. Anyway, her paintings and drawings became darker, but really mature. Just amazing pieces of art. I think she could have been in galleries around the world."

Claire continued to speak about her best friend, her labored breathing becoming steadier.

"What happens if they don't find him guilty?" Claire asked.

"They will."

"But *if they don't?*"

"Then they don't," he said matter-of-factly. "Karma will take care of him then."

Claire let out a humorless laugh.

"Karma? Dylan will happily live his life, not caring for Zachary, if they let him off. I hate him."

"I know," Max said with a frown. "Try not to think too much about it, okay? They won't find him innocent. He will be charged. He will go to prison."

"I guess you're right," Claire said. "I just saw him on the television, and I saw red. Thank you for talking me down."

"No problem."

"Goodnight, Max."

It was the first time she'd called him by his first name.

"Goodnight, Claire."

CHAPTER 37

Two months after her best friend's disappearance, Claire finally gathered up the nerve to enter the room where Taylor kept all her art work. She pushed open the door, her body tense. Everything remained as it had before. There was a half painted picture on the easel.

While she walked further into the room, Claire was apprehensive. It didn't feel right to look at Taylor's private thoughts, her private artwork. But she couldn't leave this room as a shrine for Taylor, either. Something would need to be done with her paintings and drawings. Though, what, Claire wasn't sure.

She walked over to the canvas. As with most of her most recent paintings, there were hands. It was a hand on each side that looked as though it was curved around the frame. Along the hands were lines. Wait, Claire thought. They weren't lines, they were fractures in the glass. The canvas was the glass. The most haunting part of the painting was the outline of the woman's face on the other side of the glass. It wasn't completed, but the distress on her face was profound. It made Claire's heart start to race in her chest. The woman in the picture couldn't escape. She was stuck, just as Taylor had been stuck. She had to turn away.

She closed her eyes, taking a moment to gather herself. Then she moved to the other canvases that sat against the walls. There were several. She was amazed at how detailed and quickly her friend could create such masterpieces.

Her fingers ran over the top of one of them before lifting it up. This one had a similar feel to the other of a woman trapped. The hands on this one were clasped together, almost in a pleading manner, as another hand clasped around the wrist of the arms. There were bruises along the flesh all the way up to the face of the woman whose eyes were full of fear.

Claire placed the canvas back down onto the carpet. Her eyes scanned over the other pictures along this wall. Every single one held the same sense of hopelessness within them. Tears rushed to her eyes; a strangled cry left Claire. Until the very end, Dylan haunted Taylor.

CHAPTER 38

Claire sat at her desk, figuring out the plans for the latest event coming up. There were millions of tiny details this particular client wanted worked out. She saw the table cloths ordered were the wrong color. She groaned.

"Daniella!" she yelled out for the newest assistant.

"Yes, Claire," Daniella sheepishly said, peeking her head around the corner.

The short statured girl gave her an uneasy smile.

"Why did you order the white table cloths for the Dawson event?"

"They—they asked for white."

"No, they asked for eggshell."

"Isn't that the same thing?"

"Maybe to the untrained eye. I can promise you Mrs. Dawson's eyes are not. I need you to call and change this right away."

"Okay."

Daniella skirted away.

"Do you yell at everyone?"

It was James. Claire glanced up, surprised to find her brother here. She stood, making her way over to him and wrapping her arms around his neck. She hadn't seen him in weeks.

"What are you doing here?"

"I thought you might want to celebrate."

"Celebrate?" Claire asked. "What are we celebrating?"

James stepped back, eyeing her carefully.

"You haven't heard the news?"

"What news?"

"Dylan is dead."

Claire could feel her lips immediately curling up into a smile. She trained her face to stop. Then she shook her head.

"How did you know that? And are you sure he's actually dead, that this isn't some trick so he can run off without any sort of repercussions?"

"I heard it on the news," James said. "You haven't heard?"

"No," Claire replied. "I've been avoiding the news lately. How did he die? Painfully, I hope."

"They're saying suicide. They believe his conscious caught up to him. There was a suicide note and everything. He even admitted to killing Taylor."

Claire let out a low chuckle.

"I guess he really did have a heart. Well, I mean, deep *deep* down."

She walked back around to the other side of her desk, taking her seat. Then she pointed at the seat in front of her to him to sit, as well.

"Does this mean I get Zachary now?" Claire asked.

"It should. I'll get started on the paperwork."

For the first time in a very long time, Claire could breathe again.

Now that everything was done, Claire thought she'd feel relief. At times she did. Soon Zachary would be home with her and safe, but she was also overwhelmed by grief. Without having justice to focus on, she fell into her sadness more often.

Right now that sadness seeped in her bones. She rested against the doorframe of the guest room that was now a little boy's room. Zachary's room. She'd chosen an airplane theme, and she hoped he would love it. She'd taken much care setting the room up just right. This would be his home, permanently. She wanted him to feel safe here, loved.

Her hand came up over her lips before a sob could escape.

"Hey," James said, walking in and holding a stack of books in his hands. He placed them on the dresser and pulled Claire into his arms.

"I'm alright," Claire whispered against his chest, gently pushing him away and stepping back. "I'll be fine. I just keep thinking about Taylor, and how we should be getting Zachary's room ready in her new apartment right now."

"Yeah," James murmured. He had helped her pack away Taylor's things and prepare the room for Zachary. Had it not been for him, she didn't know if she'd been able to do it. Almost every item of Taylor's she'd kept and placed in boxes in the attic for Zachary to have when he was older.

"You'll be around, right? To be here for Zachary?"

"Absolutely," James promised. "I'm actually thinking of moving closer."

"Really?" Claire asked, impressed. "But I thought you didn't like the city."

"I don't, but I think it's best if I'm closer to help you with Zachary."

"I agree."

It took two weeks for all of the paperwork to go through, but today, Zachary was coming back home to her. She stood in the doorway, checking the time on her watch every few seconds. Finally, the car came up into the driveway. Her heart skipped a beat. The door opened. The caseworker pulled Zachary out of his seat and then placed him down on the ground.

All the fears Claire had about him forgetting her were unfounded when Zachary ran up to her and accepted her open arms, jumping into them. She kissed his cheek, relieved tears sliding down her cheeks.

"Cwaire!"

"Oh Zachary, you're home."

CHAPTER 39

It took months for Claire to get into a routine. Parenthood had never been in the immediate cards for her, but here she was doing daycare drop off and bedtime stories. She broke down weekly, worried she was not cut out for this life. However, every day when she picked Zachary up from his daycare, she was filled with such love that she knew she could do this for Taylor. She knew she was going to raise Zachary in the values and with the love Taylor would have wanted for him.

"Cwaire?"

Claire glanced up from her computer. Zachary stood before her in his pajamas and with his bear in his arms.

"You're supposed to be in bed," Claire said with a smile. She stood and swooped Zachary up into her arms. He rested his head against her shoulder. "Couldn't sleep?"

She walked him back up the stairs and into his bedroom where she sat with him on his bed. Her hand ran up and down his back as she rocked him back and forth.

"Mama," he murmured. Claire's heart broke.

"I know; you miss her. I miss her too. Why don't I lay down with you until you fall asleep?"

He nodded. She laid him in the bed and pulled the covers up over him before laying down beside him. Her fingers ran over his cheek, and he was out in just a minute. Claire stayed beside him for several more moments before getting up and going back down to her computer.

For weeks, Claire had been debating what to do with Taylor's artwork. Something meaningful; something for Taylor.

Her phone buzzed and she stopped what she was doing. It was a message from Max. Her lips curled into a smile like they did anytime she heard from him. She hadn't seen him since Dylan's suicide was mentioned in the news. Her life had been too busy for them to see one another, but he had messaged her from time to time. Soon they'd have to find the time to meet up.

How's The Taylor Foundation coming together?

Good. I found a location for the first charity event. Her eyes fell to the paintings she'd stacked against the wall in her office. Then they moved up to the picture she'd hung up on the wall. Her eyes watered with tears again. It was the drawing of them eating ice cream.

Oh? Where?

I'll send you a link. Will you be there?

Absolutely.

Claire scrolled through her texts and saw the text she'd sent Larry Smith last week telling him about the foundation she'd created in honor of Taylor to help abuse victims. There was still no response. She'd called him just the day before and no answer. It was disheartening but not surprising. Larry Smith could not be counted on. She couldn't force him to be part of Zachary's life.

"Cwaire?"

Claire shook her head and chuckled. Zachary had his thumb in his mouth. He walked over to her and climbed into her lap.

"Looks like you're going to help me with my project for mommy, huh?"

Zachary nodded. She kissed the top of his head.

"Let's do something to help others. It's what your mommy would want."

Max entered the large hall where the charity event was taking place. It was a beautiful set up with paintings by Taylor hung up all over the walls.

He turned, seeing Zachary running over to Claire's brother James. The little boy tugged him over to where the snacks were.

A voice called for everyone to turn their attention to the stage. Claire stood there, looking as beautiful as ever. Max moved to get as close as he could.

"Thank you everyone for coming here today. Taylor was a beautiful soul. She was a soul that was taken too early, unfairly. Some of her art is up for sale to the highest bidder. Some will be kept at an art studio. All proceeds go to helping women like Taylor leave their abuser. If you are in a situation like she was, we have resources here. And we have resources on the website for The Taylor Foundation. Do not hesitate. We will help you. Thank you."

Max knew Claire was wonderful. He knew she could make a difference. In just a few short months, she'd set up this foundation to help others. He watched as she came down from the stage to speak with other people. He walked over to her.

"Claire," he said.

She turned to face him. Her eyes brightened the moment their eyes met, making his heart swell.

"You came."

"Of course I came. I wanted to see what this is all about. You've done a brilliant job."

"It's important," Claire said. "I may not have been able to save Taylor, but I do hope to help others. Just helping one person will make this all worth it."

"Yes," Max agreed.

"Have any piece in mind you might like?"

"No," Max said. "You know," he then began, lowering his voice, "I've been thinking a lot about Dylan's death lately."

"Why?" Claire asked. "I try not to think of him at all."

"It's just—men like him aren't usually the suicidal type."

"No?"

"No, he was pretty sure he'd get away with it. He wasn't worried about the consequences."

"Maybe he got a conscious," Claire said, starting to walk away.

"Did he?"

"I guess we'll never know for sure."

She patted his shoulder and gave him a wink before walking off.

THE END

ACKNOWLEDGEMENTS

Thank you to my husband, Braden, for always supporting my dream.

To my family and friends, I am forever thankful for your unwavering support and constant encouragement.

To my betas, Emory and Laurel. Thank you for taking the time to read my work and give your unbiased opinion to make my story better.

To my editor, Makenna Albert of On the Same Page. My story would be nothing without you. I know I can trust you with my work and that you'll help me grow as a writer. I am blessed to have you as part of my team. Thank you.

To my sensitivity reader, Kelsea Reeves. I enjoyed working with you and appreciated getting your feedback. Thank you for making me a better writer. I look forward to working with you more in the future.

To my proofreader, Emi Janish. Thank you.

To my cover artist, K.B. Barrett. You took my vision and made it even better. Thank you.

And finally to my readers, I appreciate every single one of you.

ABOUT THE AUTHOR

A.G. Hawkins is an author, mother of two, and a military wife. She is a former teacher, who holds her Doctorate in Education.

Her hobbies include writing, reading, binge-watching television shows, and going to Disney. She loves spending time with her family, especially when they get to travel together. Her passion has always been to tell stories about healing.